MERCENARY'S REVENGE

The helicopters were sweeping down into the square; Frost's men were crumbling in the dust from the heavy machine gun fire. Suddenly Frost screamed, his legs collapsing under him. His legs . . . the pain . . . Frost's breath was coming in short gasps.

Somehow Frost pushed himself up on his elbows and opened fire on the approaching chopper. Miraculously his shots connected and the helicopter burst into a ball of flame. The searing heat from the explosion hammered him backward; he was almost torn apart. But something in his nature told him not to give up, not to die.

Six days later he awoke. "You lost a great deal of blood and your legs were covered with bullet wounds," a nun said. "It was a wonder you survived."

"Do you know why the government killed those men?" he asked.

"I take it you intend to get the people who were responsible for this, but revenge will only—"

Frost cut her off, adding, "Will only be justice. If I survived, it's for a reason—and revenge is all I have . . ."

DISASTER NOVELS

EPIDEMIC! (644, $2.50)
by Larry R. Leichter, M.D.
From coast to coast, beach to beach, the killer virus spread. Diagnosed as a strain of meningitis, it did not respond to treatment—and no one could stop it from becoming the world's most terrifying epidemic!

FIRE MOUNTAIN (646, $2.50)
by Janet Cullen-Tanaka
Everyone refused to listen but hour by hour, yard by yard, the cracks and fissures in Mt. Rainer grew. Within hours the half-million-year-old volcano rose from its sleep, causing one of the most cataclysmic eruptions of all time.

GHOST SUB (655, $2.50)
by Roger E. Herst
The U.S.S. *Amundsen* is on the most dangerous patrol since World War II—it is equipped with deadly weapons . . . and nothing less than a nuclear holocaust hangs in the balance.

AVALANCHE (672, $2.50)
by Max Steele
Disaster strikes at the biggest and newest ski resort in the Rocky Mountains. It is New Year's eve and the glamorous and glittering ski people find themselves trapped between a wall of fire and a mountain of impenetrable snow.

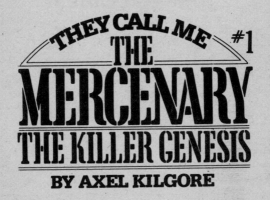

THEY CALL ME #1 THE MERCENARY THE KILLER GENESIS

BY AXEL KILGORE

ZEBRA BOOKS

KENSINGTON PUBLISHING CORP.

ZEBRA BOOKS

are published by

KENSINGTON PUBLISHING CORP.
21 East 40th Street
New York, N.Y. 10016

Printed in the United States of America

To Sharon,
always

Prologue

"Here, take this," Hank Frost rasped, holding out his M-16A1 to Selman. The young corporal, Frost's jeep driver, didn't take it.

"Let me go, Captain—come on, huh?"

"Selman, how many times I gotta tell you—I've done all this crazy business before so I've got less chance of gettin' killed at it. Now take my rifle, Selman. You and Stockton and Montenegro just keep me covered."

"Yeah, but sir, you're gonna need that rifle—"

Frost cut him off. "Look, Selman, I can take care of myself. Your concern touches me, but just shut up, will ya, before those guys up on top of the wall hear you?" And Frost shoved his rifle at Selman, drew his pistol and ran off in a low crouch from the tree cover and over along the adobe and rock wall surrounding the village. The main body of the mercenary force—over 150 strong—was less than fifty yards away waiting at the edge of the rain forest. But before the attack could begin, there were two sentries who had to be knocked out and Frost had been volunteered to Colonel Tarleton for the job by Major Grist, the Battalion Exec. ("Frost is the best man for the job, Colonel. You know his service record—Special Forces in Viet Nam, sniper, worked behind enemy lines sometimes for weeks at a time on special missions. He's fast. He's quiet, good with his hands or a knife . . .") Frost had then been called and had selected Selman and two other men to back him up. If he succeeded in knocking out the two sentries, Frost would radio signalling the start of the attack against the village, the last stronghold of the Communist Terrorist leader Jaimie Felendez. If Frost didn't succeed, after a reasonable amount of time the attack would begin anyway, but with the two sentries in place, many of the mercenary troops under Tarleton's command would be cut down when they gave the alarm.

All this raced through Frost's mind as he squinted his one good eye—the right one—back into the knife-edge of rising sun and climbed the wall.

It wasn't hard going. Though Frost had had to reholster the Browning High Power to keep both hands free there were sufficient chinks in the decades-old structure that with care he was able to scale the wall without mechanical aid, the chinks coupled with the natural vine growth that a good commander would have had cut away made a practical if awkward ladder.

Frost peered over the top of the wall, his camouflage stick-painted face and hands offering, he hoped, no noticeable target. His face was already starting to itch. The sun, though still barely a flash on the horizon, was behind him, which was bad, yet it was unavoidable. Frost ducked his head down as the first of the two sentries became noticeable in the grey half-light walking along the wall toward his position.

As the man walked past him, Frost reached out his right hand, caught the sentry's right ankle and jerked, the sentry toppling forward. Frost was up over the edge of the wall and onto the sentry's back an instant later, Frost's right knee smashing savagely

8

into the downed man's right temple, his knife, in his left fist now, stabbing deep into the arteries in the sentry's neck.

Lying still over his victim Frost listened intently, trying to determine if the few telltale thuds of the sentry falling, his coming over the wall—anything— had alerted the second sentry or the still sleeping Felendez forces on the grounds inside the village. There was nothing Frost could detect.

Stuffing his black beret into the front of his camouflage fatigue blouse, Frost snatched up the camouflaged crusher hat of the fallen sentry and then took the man's AK-47 as well. He rolled the body toward the far outside edge of the wall and pitched it over the side.

There was a heavy thudding sound when the body hit the ground but it had been unavoidable. Frost, the AK-47 slung casually over his right shoulder now continued the dead sentry's rounds. As he walked on, surveying the village inside the wall as he went, he could faintly make out the shape of the second sentry, coming toward him. Frost just kept walking nodding when he was twenty paces or so away from the man and still closing the distance between them. At ten paces, the sentry stopped. Frost had observed the sentries for over an hour and knew full well that the sentries were supposed to cross each other. The surviving sentry stopping now wasn't part of the routine. But the man had still given no alarm so Frost continued walking. Less than a yard away, Frost could just make out the sentry's eyes. They widened, almost imperceptibly, and as the man's mouth started to open to shout and his hand simultaneously tightened on the butt of his rifle, Frost leaped toward him.

Frost dragged the man down, his left hand over

the sentry's mouth trying to stifle any cry, his right arm still caught up momentarily with the sling of the borrowed AK-47. They hit the top of the wall hard, the sentry beneath Frost. Rid now of the too tightly slung rifle on his right shoulder Frost got his right arm around and rammed his right fist into the sentry's Adam's apple, then snaking his right hand back, took hold of the front of the man's hair and with both his hands pulled the sentry's head forward and then smashed it back against the stone surface beneath it. There was an audible cracking sound—the sentry's skull—and Frost hammered the head down onto the hard surface again to be sure of a final death blow. The sentry's eyes rolled open, his tongue lolling from his mouth.

Frost drew himself up to one knee, looking quickly all around him, then snatching the small radio from his belt, he switched it on and pushed to talk. Tossing the borrowed crusher hat away, he rasped into the radio, "Frost to Tarleton—got 'em, over."

It was Tarleton's voice, he recognized it. "Roger, Hank, coming in. Out."

Pocketing the radio, Frost snatched up the borrowed AK-47 he'd taken from the first sentry. Crouching near the interior edge of the wall, the noise of battle not yet begun, he took a rag from his pants pocket, scrubbed away the camouflage stick—the stuff made him itch for some reason—and waited. Frost thought he could hear the team Tarleton had planned to send against the gate, somewhere down there in the compound, but he wasn't sure. Suddenly, there was a starburst flare fired from near the village gate—Frost had expected that—signalling that the guards there had been taken. And from behind him, he heard the shouts of the mercenary battalion, then the first few spasms of gunfire and in seconds the Felendez forces inside the walls were awake and starting to move, men running everywhere, some nearly naked and stumbling into their clothes.

The dawn surprise attack had worked. Behind him, Frost caught a glimpse of the sun finally breaking over the horizon and as he turned back toward the compound, he shouldered the AK-47 and started firing. Already the first elements of the mercenary battalion were inside the wall. When his AK-47 came up empty, Frost discarded it and drew his pistol. Already in the compound below him, some of the fighting had gone hand-to-hand. Frost scanned the wall for a way down, found none, then bracing himself he jumped. A twelve foot drop or so, he landed on his feet and rolled back onto his butt. As Frost started hauling himself up, one of the Felendez men lunged toward him. Rolling out of the way of the attack, Frost made his Browning fire twice, nailing the terrorist in the face. Finally onto his feet, searching now for a working assault rifle or submachine gun, Frost instinctively turned around. Two of the Felendez terrorists were rushing at him.

Frost fired his pistol, missing on the first shot and making a weak hit with the second. The closer of the two terrorists, wounded now, was too close to raise his rifle again and shoot. There was a bayonet mounted at the muzzle of the AK-47 though. As the terrorist lunged with it, Frost sidestepped, lashing out with his right foot in a lethal force savate kick into the terrorist's right kidney. As Frost came out of the kick, he whirled, dropping to his knees and scooping a handful of dirt and hurling it in the face of the second attacker. The man brought his right arm up in front of his face, his rifle forgotten in the momentary reaction. Frost seized the opportunity

11

and used the Browning again, this time with lethal effect, thumping two of the pistol's 115-grain jacketed hollow point 9mms into the man's gut. Frost spun around and drilled the first of the two men twice in the head, right where he lay.

Upping the Browning's safety Frost rammed the pistol into his belt, then snatching up the fallen AK-47 with the fixed bayonet in place, he whirled, another terrorist starting toward him. The terrorist stopped, brought his assault rifle down into a bayonet guard position and edged toward Frost. If this guy wanted to play bayonet drill, Frost rationalized, that didn't mean that he had to. As the terrorist prepared for a lunge, Frost stepped back and flipped the selector on the Ak-47 he held to full auto, flashed its muzzle down on line and let rip. The terrorist just stood there a moment, eyes wide, and then collapsed. As Frost ran past the shot-through terrorist, moving now to join his men, gunfire everywhere about him, the one-eyed mercenary glanced at the fallen terrorist. Frost just shook his head.

Chapter One

The blackish powder stains near the muzzle of the Metalifed SS Chromium-M plated Browning High Power successfully wiped off against the trouser leg of his camouflage fatigue pants, he holstered the customized 9mm, his palms sweaty against the pistol's black rubber Pachmayr grips. Hank Frost leaned down quickly then, taking the handkerchief from his hip pocket and flipping up the faded black patch over his left eye, daubed the sweat away and put the black patch back in place.

"How'd you get that, Captain?"

Frost turned around, a smile creasing his salt-and-pepper stubbled cheeks into deep ridges, the grey-green right eye glinting slightly in the mid-day sunlight. "What, the Browning? Just sent it up to Ron Mahovsky at Metalife one time and he plated it—looked terrific ever since."

"No, sir, not your gun, the eye patch—how'd you get that?"

Frost still smiled—it was the perennial question. "The eyepatch . . ." Frost said thoughtfully. Selman stared at Frost intently, the young corporal's M16A1 assault rifle across his lap as he sat behind the ungainly large-looking steering wheel of the jeep, a black beret cocked crazily back off his perspiration glistening forehead.

"Well, not much of a story on the patch," Frost

said, lighting a cigarette. He flipped the battered Zippo windlighter in his hand a few times and went on, "The first patch was a gift—from my doctor. And after that I just started getting them in large drug stores—always keep about a half dozen or so with me—"

"Yeah, but, Captain," Selman started.

Frost was already ignoring him, pulling himself almost to attention and making a less than formal salute in the direction beyond the jeep. "Colonel Tarleton, Major Grist," Frost said formally.

The tall man with the silver oakleaf clusters returned the salute and said, "Relax, Hank—you too, Selman."

The shorter man, the one with the gold oakleaves, spat a shot of tobacco juice into the ground and said, "You and your element did a terrific job, Frost."

"Thanks, Major," Frost said, going back to his cigarette. He started to lean against the jeep's right front fender but moved away from it, the metal burning hot to his touch.

Tarleton was always out of cigarettes and Frost fished into the pocket of his fatigue blouse and offered the Colonel a Camel. "Thanks, Hank—oh, we got Felendez."

"Then we are done here, aren't we, sir?" Frost asked.

"Yeah," Tarleton said, "I guess we are at that. I radioed to Colonel Chapmann. He's on the way with our money."

"I think Chapmann sleeps with money," Grist muttered.

"Yeah, that Chapmann," Frost said, "he's somethin' else, takes the contracts, hires the people, makes himself the commander then sits on his rear

14

end at some desk fondling the dinero. He's actually coming out into the field—we don't have to go to him this time?"

"You know," Tarleton said, "I don't have a hell of a lot of use for Chapmann either, but he's been good to us. Used to be a hell of a field commander back then in the Congo, but you guys are too young to remember that," and he nodded toward Frost and Corporal Selman.

"Yeah, but my mother told me all about it," Frost remarked, his face creasing again into a grin.

"Bullshit," Tarleton said, laughing. "Why don't you get your people together for later and just have 'em relax—Chapmann should be here in less than an hour."

"What's gonna happen to Felendez?" Frost asked, lighting another cigarette with the stub of the burned out one between his tanned-brown fingers.

"Tried killing himself," Grist said, his voice as matter of fact as if he were reading a supply list. "Got to him before he could though. Guess he wanted to be some sort of martyr to his revolutionary ideals or something. Probably go on trial unless he gets conveniently knocked off; I'd go for that last job for free myself."

"Yeah," Frost murmured, "he was a little butcher, wasn't he? All in the name of land reform and the rights of the people. Funny how jokers like that Felendez talk about the rights of the people and then turn right around and kill the people."

"The hell if I can ever understand it," Tarleton said, stubbing out his borrowed cigarette. "Don't know if I ever will, either."

Tarleton nodded silently and walked away, Grist beside him. Frost turned to Selman, "Well, you always wanted some authority, Selman, I'm making you official rounder-upper—go get 'em. We'll form up in ten minutes on that fountain in the center of the square over there," and Frost pointed toward it. Then, reaching into the back of the jeep he grabbed his own M-16 and hitched the loose web sling over his left shoulder, returned a lazy salute to Selman and walked toward the fountain.

Frost crossed the dusty plaza from the gate where his jeep had been, leaned his rifle against the side of the fountain and plunked down into the dirt beside it. He pulled off his Montgomery style beret and lit another cigarette. Sweat was plastering his thick black hair to his forehead, running down the smile-frown lines on his cheeks, dripping from his drooping black mustache. He unbuttoned his fatigue blouse and pulled it out of his pants and pushed the sleeves up.

He leaned back and closed his good eye against the sun. It had been a rough three weeks, tracking the guerrilla leader Felendez through the subtropical jungles in the middle of summer, fighting the dysentery and the damned flies. And everywhere they'd gone, Felendez had been there, killing in the name of the people—women, children, anybody who'd been handy. Frost thought back to the days he'd read about in history books, when instead of a bunch of mercenaries going out to get a piece of scum like Felendez, the U.S. Government would have gone in to help the friendly government. But those days were gone, he guessed, laughing to himself—saying under his breath, "Or else I wouldn't be working . . ."

Time and the formation came and went. Frost told his men they'd done a good job of work and told them to hang around for Colonel Chapmann and the payroll, and that he guessed they'd all be going home pretty soon. To some of the men that didn't mean much—just unemployment, and Frost was one of these—but to a lot of the men, some Americans, some Englishmen, a few Germans, a couple of black Africans, it meant the wife, the children, the side business that kept them going until they couldn't take all that anymore and looked for real work again. A bunch of empty men with empty guns, Frost thought sometimes. And he was one of these too, or had been until he'd taken up mercenary soldiering as a full-time profession, as full-time as it could be. Sometimes to keep body and soul together that meant the executive protection business, sometimes just acting as a courier and you had to be careful with that so you didn't get in with drug smugglers or something looking for a fall guy.

Frost set his M-16 down again—sometimes you carried one of those, sometimes an FN/FAL or sometimes a subgun, depending on the employer lots of the time, but always the Browning P-35 High Power, always that. As he sat there beside the fountain again in what little shade there was to find, he moved the pistol belt around to get the gun into a more comfortable spot. He wanted Chapmann to come very quickly and go very quickly and be done with it. The Felendez cure had been worse than the illness that tried to rule the country, but not much—and Chapmann was a big part of that illness.

His eye started to close, then he opened it. A voice was shouting from across the square, "Colonel Chapmann's coming, let's fall in." A half dozen orders were shouted and they all devolved to Frost getting his company into ranks and hauling them to attention in the blazing hot sun so Chapmann could tell them they'd done well and give Tarleton the payroll. As Frost got himself to his feet and started buttoning his fatigue blouse, he couldn't help saying to himself, "Big damn deal."

Then Frost started shouting his own orders and in less than a minute his men were fallen in. They didn't look much ready for a parade ground, he thought, but they weren't just parade ground soldiers either.

It was hot to the point of the ridiculous as Frost kept his men at parade rest while Chapmann climbed out of his helicopter and walked toward Tarleton standing far at the front of their ranks. Grist called the battalion to attention and that made the heat seem worse. Frost eyed Chapmann—he wore khakis rather than fatigues, a camouflage scarf at his throat and a black beret just as the rest of them wore. Chapmann's boots were shined to the point that as he moved with Tarleton and Grist beside him toward the front of the formation the sun would catch them and the glint gave almost the appearance of a mirror. Chapmann was unarmed, of course, except for a pistol—this a trademark with him. Like Frost's own handgun, the pistol was a Browning High Power 9mm, but it was highly engraved with ivory scrimshawed grips—a presentation from an African leader years back and something Chapmann always had with him. And, despite the gun's rather pimpy look, Frost recalled, Chapmann was reported to be an excellent shot with it.

As Chapmann, Tarleton and Grist moved closer to the main body of men—discounting the few casualties from the morning's battle there were still nearly 150—Frost watched. He had seen Chapmann only once before, but the man was a living legend in the mercenary business. Frost made the Colonel's age at somewhere in the late fifties or early sixties and the way Chapmann carried himself there was no doubting his fitness.

As Frost watched, Chapmann's shavetail-looking ADC came running from the helicopter and joined the three field grade officers. Chapmann and the ADC spoke, then Chapmann turned to Tarleton and Grist, apparently said something and the two junior officers saluted him. Chapmann returned the salute with strict formality and started off at a jog trot toward the helicopter, his ADC at his side. In a moment, Chapmann was airborne and the helicopter was disappearing toward the horizon.

Grist and Tarleton spoke for a moment, Frost could see, then Grist shouted less than formally for Company officers to put their men at ease and then come forward. Frost looked over his shoulder, not bothering to turn around and shouted, "You heard the man, mill around and look military." Then he stepped off smartly and joined the rest of the line officers in the front of the formation.

Tarleton was already talking—"something urgent at the capitol. But the payroll should be arriving by helicopter in about five minutes. Chapmann said there was no reason to delay the payroll just because he wouldn't be here. When I get everybody in formation again, I'll relay Chapmann's commendations to your men—says you all did a fine job and he looks forward to working with you again."

Frost started to say something, but then everyone turned and looked skyward—a helicopter was coming. The long-awaited payroll, Frost thought. One helicopter, but then Frost saw a second, then a third and still more. Tarleton started to say, "Colonel Chapmann didn't mention anything about a convoy—"

"Hell," Frost said, "I'm getting my men—"

19

Tarleton was shouting at him but Frost didn't care by then—he was already halfway across the impromptu parade ground of the town square, and shouting orders of his own. "Take cover—helicopters—may be a trap!"

As Frost ran, nearing the fountain, his men were already dispersing toward the adobe brick buildings of the deserted village some fifty yards further on. And then Frost heard the first of the guns—the Huey Helicopter Gunships above were sweeping down into the square, their 7.62mm M-60s chattering maddeningly. Frost cursed himself for not having a rifle—he'd left his with Selman. He fumbled his Browning 9mm from the hip holster and thumbed the hammer to full stand, still running. In front of him, he could see his own men scattering, some crumpling to the dust from the machine guns of the helicopters, others making a stand where they were, their M-16 assault rifles blazing skyward.

As Frost kept running, a huge shadow obscured the ground in his path and he craned his neck upward, cursing himself for having only one eye. It was one of the Huey gunships, its machine guns rotating in sweeping motions across the square, the fire from their muzzles like living things, like spitting cobras and just as deadly. Suddenly, Frost screamed, his legs collapsing under him, and he fell facedown in the dirt, some five yards still from the fountain. His legs . . . the pain . . . Frost's breath was coming in short gasps. His legs wouldn't respond to him, so he used his hands, the Browning still clutched in his right fist, dragging himself toward the fountain, defying the fire in the lower part of his body, fighting the cold sweat breaking out on his face, the dizziness.

He had to make the fountain, he told himself,

though somewhere at the back of his mind there was a voice telling him the fountain offered no protection, no cover. Two yards to go and his hands were already starting to bleed as they dragged him—his legs seemed not to be there anymore and he was afraid to look back in case in fact they weren't. His right hand, the pistol still in his fist, touched the edges of the fountain and with his left hand he threw himself forward, then rolled over and propped his back against the natural rocks forming the dish-shaped base of the fountain. He looked down. His legs were still there alright but his camoflauge pants were wet with blood—already, despite the noise of gunfire, flies were buzzing near him.

Using the lip of the fountain as a rest, he started firing his pistol at the nearest helicopter of the six that swarmed like vultures over the square. The chopper made a pass over him and the mortar from the fountain sprayed into his face and hands as the M-60s aboard the Huey disintegrated it. Dusty, muddy water poured from the wrecked fountain's side and washed over him. Frost rubbed his forearm across his eye so he could see again, the helicopter now a dark blur against the burning orb of sunlight. The Browning was empty and Frost snatched a spare thirteen-round magazine from his belt and rammed it up the pistol butt, worked the slide stop and was ready to open fire again.

As the helicopter swept toward him, Frost loosed a two-round burst and somehow—miraculously he thought—connected. The chopper suddenly burst into a ball of flame, searing heat and shockwave from the explosion hammering him back against the remains of the pulverized fountain.

Frost pushed himself up on his elbows and started crawling from the burning wreckage hurtling down on him. Far across the square running toward him he saw Selman. "Captain, I'm coming sir, don't—" but either Frost couldn't hear the rest or the fusilade of machine gun fire from one of the five remaining Huey gunships caught Selman and killed him instantly.

Knowing it was hopeless, Frost tried clawing his way across the ground toward Selman—the little corporal, they'd laughingly called him, like Napoleon; the little corporal though, from a town somewhere in northeastern Georgia. Where the hell was it, Frost thought? Somehow, remembering where Selman came from at that moment seemed more important to him than the five remaining gunships, the dwindling shots coming from the ground, the screams . . .

As Frost crawled cross the square he looked ahead of him. Selman wasn't dead! The little guy—five foot nine if that—was staggering to his feet and hobbling across the square toward him. Frost wanted to shout, "Save yourself!" but the words just wouldn't come out—the dust in his throat, the hard breathing. Selman was still coming, his M-16 clutched by the flash hider in his left hand, using the assault rifle like a cane to help him walk.

One of the Hueys was sweeping toward Selman and Frost aimed his Browning and started firing. And Frost kept firing and firing and Selman kept coming toward him. Then suddenly Selman was standing over him and Frost looked up. "Hey, Captain—" But a Huey gunship's M-60s cut Selman down and he crumpled in a heap of dead flesh and bone on top of Frost. Frost tried to get from under him as the bullets—he could feel them—impacted into Selman's body over him. But Selman's weight, in death, was too much and Frost was starting to get the light-headedness bad again. After a little while Frost couldn't hear anymore gunfire—none at all. And he closed his eyes so he could die if he wasn't that way already.

Frost opened his right eye and the weight of Selman was still over him and there was a sickening smell, so bad that Frost almost choked as the vomit poured uncontrollably from his mouth and nose. There were flies buzzing near him and as he tried to look around him he thought he heard the jungle nightwing sound of bats, but he tried to push that hideous thought from his mind. Down here in the jungle the bats were vampires and carried rabies; and there would be blood aplenty for them this day.

But of course, he realized, the sun almost gone in the sky, that it was nearly night—he'd been unconscious for perhaps seven or eight hours. With strength he didn't realize remained to him, Frost pushed himself from under Selman's body. Frost knew he was burning with fever, and the exertion of movement after the loss of blood was starting to make him feel faint again. At least, he thought ruefully, his legs still had feeling in them—the pain of moving them was excruciating.

He'd been right about the sound of fluttering wings—a bat was sucking at Selman's neck and Frost, the Browning still in his hand after all that had transpired, fumbled a fresh magazine for the pistol from his belt, rammed it home and chambered a round. There was no question that Selman was already dead, he knew, and with his right hand shaking and his left hand shaking when he tried to steady his aim, Frost fired. He missed the bat, but the creature flew off, fluttering sickeningly close to him then disappearing in the shadows.

Frost checked the Omega on his wrist—almost

seven-thirty. From the blood loss, the fact that he realized he couldn't walk, the jungle sounds around him and the creatures the dead victims of Chapmann's slaughter would draw, Frost realized he didn't have much time left. He tried to move his legs, but the pain almost drove him to unconsciousness and the legs would not respond. If his legs had worked, he thought, there would be a chance—he could perhaps find a functioning vehicle and drive himself out. As he lay there, suddenly his eye started brimming with tears and he felt ashamed, not for his plight or his death—both of which he felt were beyond help—but because there would be no one to bury Selman, Colonel Tarleton, Major Grist—any of the others. And with no survivors—he had already begun to discount himself—Chapmann would get away with what he had done, the families of the dead men would never know they had been murdered simply for the money Chapmann wouldn't have to pay them. Frost wondered then about Felendez? Likely, Chapmann's gunships had killed the terrorist leader as well. If Chapmann's men had come along the ground and there had been survivors, like Felendez, they would have been killed.

For a moment, Frost wondered if perhaps others of the men in the dark shadows of the lifeless square had somehow managed to stay alive, then cursed himself that he couldn't move to check among the bodies and perhaps find them. He tried shouting, "Can anyone—" but choked on the last part of his words—he knew the answer.

Frost leaned up on his elbows there, rolled over on his back, the Browning still clenched in his fist. And he stared at the comparatively tiny muzzle. If he didn't pull the trigger, when the animals came, and the bats again, would he still have the strength left?

But there was something in Frost that wouldn't allow common sense and reason to end his life forever. He sat there quietly watching the light fade. He opened his eye, the sound he'd heard awakening him. A glance at the luminous dial Omega Seamaster he wore showed him that he'd been asleep or unconscious for over two hours. But the sound that had awakened him hadn't been any of the sounds sleep had kept him from fearing. It had been an engine sound—a jeep?

Was it Chapmann, back to check his kill, perhaps some of Felendez's rebels—at least in either case, he thought, the kill would be quick and as he thumbed down the safety on the cocked and locked Browning High Power, he rationalized that there was nothing left for him but death and just perhaps he could take some of them with him.

He tried to crane his neck around to see in the direction of the engine sound. It was far to his left and once again that day he cursed the fact that he had only one eye with which to see. He couldn't strain far enough to focus properly. He heard the crunch of boots on the dirt, caught the glare of headlights far to his left and heard the muffled sound of voices. He tried moving and turning himself around, almost losing consciousness as he did from the pain it caused him. The voices stopped then and as he managed to turn, the pistol locked in his fist for one last fight, a flashlight or headlight—he wasn't sure which—caught him, the glare blinding him.

He tried looking away, brandishing the pistol toward the light. Just as he started to twitch his finger against the Browning's trigger, he heard a voice—American. "Hey, hang on, fella—Comprende Ingles?"

"Yeah," Frost managed to shout, then softer said, "I speak English okay. That's about all I do." And as he strained to see in the bright light the darkness from inside him washed over him again and he collapsed.

Sunlight made Frost open his eye and even before he noticed his surroundings, he felt strange. He glanced to his wrist—the watch was gone and, continuing the motion of his left arm he felt at his face—the eyepatch was gone as well. He then noticed his surroundings—a hospital room but somehow not that. There was a table beside the bed and his watch was on it, but the second hand wasn't moving. He reached for it and pain washed over him and he drew his arm back.

He turned his head; a door was opening. There was a woman, wearing a long white dress with a white starched apron covering it, her hair covered with a starched white cowl—she was a nun. Frost didn't recognize the order but had seen nuns dressed that way before—missionary sisters, he thought.

"You're awake, Captain," was all she said.

Frost looked at her a moment. "Do you want the usual questions?" he asked, "or do you want to skip them and just give the usual answers?"

The nun smiled and Frost noticed that she was very pretty. "You're alive, not well, Captain, but you will be in a few weeks."

"You've been here," she went on, "for six days and aside from waking up a few times and calling for some Corporal Selman you haven't said a thing. You lost a great deal of blood, were covered with bullet wounds and insect bites on your legs and for a while we thought you'd been bitten by a bat—but you weren't. You'll have a lot of scars on your legs but once most of the hair grows back you won't notice them too badly. God was really watching out for you, Captain," she added.

"There wasn't anyone else brought in?" Frost asked, his voice low, husky for a moment as the events of Chapmann's massacre washed back to him in a flood of bitterness.

"The men who brought you here were scientists studying the bats, trying to find a way to cut down their population to keep them from having to feed on domestic animals. They checked as best they could there at the village but you seemed to be the only one left alive and then they brought you here. By the next morning, our Father Anselmo drove back there and saw the government forces carting the bodies into a mass grave and realized that for some reason the government wanted you dead, so he said nothing and we've kept your presence here a secret. I hope that's in accordance with your wishes," the sister said, sitting then on a stool by the foot of the bed and taking what he supposed was his chart into her hands.

"Don't you want to know why the government killed those men, sister?" Frost said.

"Yes, I suppose, but it wouldn't affect our taking care of you. God teaches us to welcome both the lion and the lamb, the innocent and the sinners—"

Frost cut her off, his voice sharper than he intended. "Well, I don't know quite what I am sister, but don't tell me in your next breath anything about turning the other cheek."

"I take it you intend to get the men responsible for injuring you, Captain, and perhaps the friend you kept calling for, Corporal Selman, but revenge will only—"

And Frost cut her off again. "Will only be justice, sister. I need a pen and some paper—I've

27

got to copy the names of the men in my outfit while I can still remember them all."

"To tell their families, Captain?" the nun asked.

"Yeah."

"That's a Christian impulse, Captain, here in your sick bed to think of your fallen comrades."

"And a practical one too, sister," Frost said.

"I'd started to say a moment ago, Captain, that revenge will only harden your heart—that's not God's way."

Frost fumbled on the table and got his cigarettes and when he couldn't make the Zippo work the nun took the lighter and worked it for him. He drew the smoke deep into his lungs, then said, "Sister, revenge couldn't harden my heart. That massacre by Chapmann's men at the village six nights ago did that. And if you're right and God kept me alive there's only one purpose I can see for it—and maybe it sounds like phoney dramatics, or it's trite or something, but I don't give a damn—revenge is all I give right now." And Frost turned his face away and stared out the window, the cigarette smoke making his eye tear a little.

Chapter Two

Frost had become very familiar with the garden behind the hospital and the small chapel. He'd spent many hours in the garden each day for the past four weeks and now he sat there for perhaps the last time, smoking through the fresh pack of Camels Sister Genevieve had gotten Father Anselmo to buy for him on the black market—Father Anselmo liked the excuse to smoke American cigarettes too—as he sat there, with his borrowed clothes, a bush jacket and khaki pants and a fresh eyepatch in place, Frost thought of what he now had to do. Chapmann had to be found—for three reasons. Frost wanted the money Chapmann owed, to Frost himself and to the families of his dead comrades. Secondly, once Chapmann realized that he, Frost, was still alive, no place on earth would be safe—Chapmann was well connected everywhere. But the most pressing need for Frost—the one that wrenched his guts each time he considered it—was simple revenge. Chapmann was going to die for the slaughter he'd ordered.

Behind him, Frost heard the short, quick steps of Sister Genevieve, the sounds she made permanently recorded in his brain over these weeks. He stood up, noticing the blueness of her eyes, and almost feeling ashamed of himself as he wondered at the color of her hair beneath the veil she wore.

"You're leaving then, Captain." It was a simple

statement, not a question.

He heard Father Anselmo's jeep honking outside. Frost didn't want to say it, but he said it and wasn't sorry he did. "One question, why did you have to be a—"

"Don't," she said, turning away. Then turning again to face him she said, "Perhaps for the same reason you had to be a mercenary. I remember that afternoon when you told me how you got started in your calling."

"I can't say anymore," Frost whispered, then took her hand and held it a moment. Then, snatching the small suitcase by his feet into his hand, he turned and walked across the courtyard and toward the wrought iron gate. He looked over his shoulder once and saw her wave. . . .

"Here, Mr. Frost," Father Anselmo said, handing Frost a cloth bundle as Frost sat beside him on the front seat of the rocking and bumping open jeep. "I think you might be needing this."

Frost undid the string around the bundle and folded back the layers of cloth—it was his Browning High Power with the chrome finish and Pachmayr grips, the pistol's spare magazines and the Gerber MK I Boot Knife—only the Gerber's holster there. "I'm sorry about your holster, Mr. Frost," the young Latino priest went on, "but it was so saturated with the blood from your leg wounds we had to throw it away along with your clothes."

"That's all right," Frost said, speaking loudly over the jeep's crumbling and noisy exhaust system. "I don't suppose you had any spare ammo around, Father?"

"No," the priest laughed, "but I was in the army myself once so I cleaned the gun for you at least. I counted your bullets—"

"Cartridges, Father," Frost corrected.

"Yes, cartridges then. You have an even dozen in one of the clips."

Frost didn't correct him again—the term was magazines, not clips.

"How do you plan to get out of the country?" Anselmo asked.

"Well, if I told you you'd feel bad—it might be a sin or something," Frost said, fighting the wind to light a cigarette, then lighting one for Father Anselmo and passing it over to him.

"You are probably right, Mr. Frost. Ahh—" and the priest paused awkwardly.

"What is it, Father?"

"I didn't quite know how to say it, but thank you for back there—Sister Genevieve, I accidentally overheard her praying the other evening. I can only imagine what she was talking about—she seemed very concerned for you."

"I am for her, Father. Pardon the crudity, but when the shit finally does hit the fan down here—the revolution—what are you people going to do?"

Anselmo thought a moment and answered. "A provocative question, Mr. Frost—and thank you for changing the subject, among many other things—this too," and he gestured with the cigarette.

Frost had the priest drop him a mile outside of town and they said their goodbyes. Frost was going to say he'd write, but he knew he wouldn't

As the priest vanished down the road back away from town, Frost picked up his suitcase and started walking. He had no intention of actually walking into the town, but instead he planned to walk around it. The town was far removed from the capitol, but Chapmann's men would be there, or if Chapmann

31

had pulled out by now there would still be government troops and Frost had no desire to lock horns with them—he was still walking stiffly from the gunshot wounds from the last time.

Frost's plan was a loose one at best—circle round the seacoast town and steal a powerboat and get the hell away up the coast, he thought, to Columbia where he knew some people and there were some favors owed him. There he could find out if Chapmann had left the country as he thought, and if so where Chapmann had gone. Getting around the outskirts of the town and getting down by the wharf turned out to be unexpectedly simple. Frost walked it out and did his shopping for later that night. Stealing a boat at night would be riskier—a greater chance of someone being on board her, but by the same token a police response would take longer, and that was his greatest fear, having to outrun a patrol boat with a slower craft in unfamiliar waters.

By nine that same evening, having eaten nothing since breakfast, Frost was both starving and impatient. He'd spent the hours until darkness sleeping fitfully in some rocks more than a mile from the town along the coastline, the beach area too rough for navigation and the rocks too forbidding for any casual observers. His clothes wet and smelling vaguely of fish, Frost walked along the beach—hoping if anyone saw him he'd be mistaken for a bum—back toward the wharf, the brightness of the full moon and cloudless sky that night not something he liked but something he was powerless to control. Already, at the mission hospital, there had been soldiers looking for any "yanquis"—the bat researchers who'd saved his life had pulled out several weeks earlier—and the longer Frost stayed in the country the greater the chance of his discovery.

During daylight hours, as he had done when inspecting the wharf area, he could strip away the patch covering his left eye and don sunglasses. Since anyone looking for him specifically would be looking for a piratical-looking one-eyed man, such a simple disguise he'd learned from other times in other lands worked remarkably well. But at night, sunglasses would of course invite curiosity and walking around without the patch would hardly be less cause for attention.

So, patch in place, shoes under his arm and the Browning concealed under his coat with only twelve shots remaining to it, he walked barefoot along the sandy shore, the tide lapping gently at his feet. As the beach arced away from the land, making a reentrant to the sea, the lights of the town—such as they were—began to loom ahead in a bright patch against the horizon. Frost aimed himself vaguely toward them, but always keeping along the beach. The profile of the land began to rise as he neared the outskirts of the town and the wharf area and by that time Frost had finally solidified a plan of action.

The boat he'd selected earlier, he noted, was still there—about a fifteen footer with inboard and outboard capability—likely a smuggler's boat, since it was obviously built for speed and there was an extraordinarily elaborate antenna system aboard as well as a receptacle that seemed designed for radar scanning. If indeed it were a smuggler's craft, then at least its sight would be familiar to police who were probably on the take, yet it might also draw undue attention. But, Frost thought, unless he wanted to move out of the harbor under sail or in a motorized rowboat, it was the best option available.

About fifty yards distant still from the wharf, Frost stripped away his bush jacket and stashed it along with his shoes in the crowded confines of the cloth suitcase Father Anselmo had given him. There was no way to secure the Browning other than by threading the belt he wore through its trigger guard, making the gun for all intents and purposes inaccessible with any degree of speed. The Gerber knife would be his only readily available weapon and Frost verified the firmness of its clip attachment to his belt, the sheath inside his trouser band.

Carefully checking that no one seemed to be observing, Frost waded slowly into the water. He'd expected it to be cold from the temperature of the small waves that had lapped at his feet moments earlier, but perhaps because of his recent injuries, the water seemed far colder to him than he'd thought it would be. By the time he dropped forward when the water was deep enough for swimming, he was shivering. As he moved slowly through the dark waters to conserve his still depleted strength his body began to warm from the exercise, but some of the wounds in his legs began to ache as well and he had to stop twice as he swam toward the power boat to rest and knead at a cramp, treading water as best he could with the suitcase in tow dragged from his left hand on the ends of his shoe laces.

The Omega on his wrist told him that twenty minutes had elapsed since he'd entered the water and as he reached out with his left arm, then his fingers were able to touch the bow of the boat.

As soundlessly as he could, Frost swam the circumference of the craft, perhaps looking for an alarm system or just to familiarize himself with the perimeter of his target. Stopping and holding on for a moment to one of the mooring lines, Frost fished the suitcase up to him and tied it by the sodden shoelaces to the mooring line. The water this close to the wharf tasted brackish against his lips as he pulled his head under the water a moment while he struggled his pistol free of the belt.

Pushing his hair back from his forehead, the Gerber boot knife now clamped between his even white teeth, the Browning clumsily secured in his trouser pocket, Frost swam back toward the bow and tested the coiled anchor chain against his weight, then hauled himself up from the water. Using the anchor itself as a purchase for his feet, glancing across the deck—nothing—Frost heaved himself up and under the railing, then lay perfectly motionless listening for any sound that would indicate anyone's presence aboard, or his own detection.

Putting an ear to the boards of the deck, Frost could hear voices below—at least three, men's voices speaking in Spanish, he thought, but he couldn't make out any of the words clearly.

Frost was committed now. If the men below decks seemed like innocent people, he'd just force them at gunpoint to take him where he wanted to go. On the other hand, if they were smugglers, as he supposed by the cut of the craft, then it would be a fight. For that reason he rested for a few moments there in the silent darkness, flat against the deck to avoid silhouetting himself against the moon. After five minutes, his breathing calmed from the exertion of the long swim, Frost drew himself up to a crouch and edged forward along the railing, the Gerber knife back in his teeth and the Browning pistol now clamped in his right fist, the hammer thumbed back to full cock and the safety up, but his thumb poised over it to bring the 9mm into instant action if needed.

Frost kept low as he passed the wheelhouse—if

that were the right term for a power boat, he wasn't sure. Yellow light from the windows diffused into the darkness of the deck and Frost paused there, listening again to the voices below decks. He still couldn't make much of the conversation, but during periodic lulls between speakers he thought he heard some sort of moaning, but he wasn't sure.

Frost didn't dare look into the wheelhouse, because at that moment if someone were there he would certainly be seen and surprise was his only hope against superior odds. He circled carefully to the door leading into the wheelhouse and poised there, the safety on his Browning now thumbed down.

There was no sound from the lighted wheelhouse. Frost moved quickly then, silhouetting himself for only an instant in the door frame, flattening himself against the wall just inside. The wheelhouse was deserted. Silently, he crept toward the ladder leading below. Now the voices were clearer. Still in Spanish, Frost was more than conversant with the language from his many campaigns south of the border. They were speaking rapidly—or it seemed that way to a non-native speaker at any event—and discussing some girl, her father, and a word that seemed unfamiliar to him kept cropping up, "rescate."

After a few moments, the conversation below continuing, Frost decided it was time to make his move. He took the Gerber from his teeth and clenched it in his left fist, the Browning ready in his right. He made it that there were seven steps to the cabin below and that he could safely get halfway and jump the rest of the way if needed. Disregarding noise now, Frost stormed down the ladder and once his head was clear of the bulkhead above him, he understood the word "rescate"—ransom. The

36

moans he'd heard were from a girl in the far corner of the below decks cabin, her wrists bound in front of her, her ankles bound and a stickball gag in mouth—her eyes wide with fear.

Frost didn't really notice what she looked like other than that she seemed young and gave a vague impression of prettiness—his focus of attention was riveted on what lay between them. There were three men, all in their thirties or forties, one clean-shaven, the others looking as though they hadn't bothered recently. And all three spun toward him as he hit the deck. The closest of the three men started for him and Frost fired the Browning twice. In the confines of the cabin the roar of the 115-grain jacketed hollow point 9mms was deafening. At the close range, both rounds hammered through the man and instead of hurtling his body back against the bulkhead opposite Frost, the man fell forward onto Frost's gun.

As Frost pushed at the man to get his gun clear of him, the second man, the clean-shaven one, pulled a police style revolver—all Frost could make out was that it was some kind of K-frame Smith & Wesson—and made to fire. Frost's Browning was still hung up in the first man's body and he pulled the body in front of him as a shield. Frost could feel the dead man's body lurching as the second man's bullets from the Smith revolver hammered into it. Frost's left hand was free and he hurtled the Gerber knife underhanded across the six feet or so separating them into the clean-shaven man's chest. The revolver went off again as he reeled backward and fell, his body landing across the girl at the opposite corner of the cabin, her moaning screams now harder and faster.

There was still the third man and Frost's gun was

free now but as Frost raised it to fire the third man was on him, hands and feet flailing in a disorganized close-in martial arts attack. Frost couldn't get the gun in his right hand up and on line in the confined space in the narrower forward end of the cabin— and there was no room for a counterattack. Frost simply did the best he could to ward off his attacker's blows with his left arm and at the first opening, went into a wheeling attack of his own, his right knee smashing up and forward toward his attacker's groin, missing the vital area but impacting into the man's abdomen. Frost crashed his left hand downward in a knife-edge blow onto the right side of his opponent's neck then and as the ferocity of his attacker's moves abated, Frost stepped in, his left hand smashing upward, the heel of it hammering into the flesh under the man's chin, then wheeling again Frost rammed his right elbow into the exposed neck, then drove his left knee up and forward into his original target—the groin. As the attacker fell back, Frost made a quarter turn and lashed out with his right foot in a lethal savate kick into the man's nose, smashing the bone and driving it upward into the brain, his attacker dead now before his body bounced onto the starboard side bunk and was still.

"Damn," Frost shouted, rubbing his right thigh. "Oh, dammit . . ." and Frost limped aft toward the girl bound helplessly there in the corner. Thumbing up the Browning's safety, Frost reached down to her with his left hand and loosened the bonds on the gag, then took the ball portion of it from her mouth. "Do you have to curse?" she asked him, almost indignantly in heavily accented but perfectly correct English.

"As a matter of fact, I do," Frost answered. "I

just had more bullets than I could count yanked out of my legs several weeks back and I haven't been exercising that much—you give yourself a charley horse from kickin' some joker in the mouth and see if you don't swear! Try it."

"What is a charley's horse?"

"Never mind," Frost answered, his voice tired. He rammed the gun into his trouser band and spun the girl around roughly—more roughly than he had to—and undid the knots binding her wrists in front of her, then he flopped down beside her on the aft bunk.

"What about my ankles?"

"What do you mean, 'What about my ankles?' Untie them yourself—I'm tired."

"You are not a gentleman," she said.

"Oh," Frost said, "excuse me. Doesn't matter that I just swam over fifty yards, killed three men and gave myself a charley horse—no! But I'm not a gentleman. You're right—I'm just going to sit here a minute and think about how rotten I am," Frost said, then his voice rising in intensity, "while you untie your damn ankles, because you can't help me dump these bodies overboard with your ankles tied."

The girl glared at him and then bent forward to work at the knots binding the ropes to her ankles. Frost watched her. She was dark-haired and her eyes were almost black. There was a small bruise on her left cheek—apparently where some right-handed man had slapped her. Frost's face creased into the heavy smile-frown lines and he stifled a laugh, thinking that he couldn't imagine why anyone would slap a girl like her. She turned to stare at him again, muttering something he couldn't make out in Spanish, then saying, "I broke a nail." Then she looked back to the ropes, then back at him. "Why do you stare at me so?"

Frost looked at her eyes hard, saying, "You're very pretty—and that's reason enough." When she undid the last of the ropes, Frost said, "All right," then stood up, "let's take care of these jokers and get this tub moving."

As she started to stand up, she fell toward him and he caught her in his arms. "My ankles," she said, stammering. "If you kiss me I'll scream."

"You don't have to promise to scream if I kiss you," he said. "You might not get that excited about it." He let her go and started to haul the nearest body toward the ladder.

"You're just going to throw them overboard—now?"

He turned and looked at her. "No, not now—when we're out to sea, but I figured I may as well haul a body with me now just as well as later. Why should you be upset?"

"Well," she started to say.

"Well, what, lady?" Frost asked. "Unless you've got some kinky ways of getting a thrill, those guys had you tied up there because they were holding you for ransom and since they weren't wearing masks or anything they probably planned to kill you. I'm your rescuer—where are my hugs and kisses, how about a little thank you? Hmm?"

And Frost turned back to the body and went about his work. After a moment or so, as he started struggling the body up the ladder ahead of him, he felt a pressure on his arm, then turning saw the girl beside him. "Lo sciento—I'm sorry, Senor—!"

"Frost, Hank Frost." He leaned toward her and smiled, "And what's your name, little girl?" And at that she laughed. The situation, Frost thought, was ridiculous. There was a dead body of a man he didn't know almost pressed between them, the guy's face a mass of blood, his nose crushed into his brain. Frost, he knew, smelled like a combination of fish and garbage from the fifty-yard swim and here he was trying to make time with a girl. "Let's dump the stiff," he said. "We can talk about other things later."

They left the first of the three dead men in the wheelhouse and Frost started to pretend he knew what he was doing when it came to operating a boat after he had fished up his suitcase. He still wasn't sure if he really knew what to call the craft. Finally, as he struggled one of the mooring lines clear, he turned to the girl, who had been watching him. "Hey, I didn't catch your name."

"Anita, Anita Carrero Fernandez Roha Garcia."

"All that name for such a little girl, huh?" Frost said. "You wouldn't happen to be too bashful to tell me you know how to run a boat or whatever this is, would you?"

"Well, since you asked, Senor Frost." As Frost happily discovered, the girl turned out to be quite accomplished with boats—or whatever you called them.

They got under way and left the small harbor area unmolested. Apparently, if anyone had heard the gunshots beyond the confines of the boat, no one was sufficiently interested to call the police. Once they were a few miles out, the girl helped Frost and they shipped the bodies over the side. Frost quickly got the knack of steering and holding a course— with a compass heading she set out and he had verified it wasn't that much different from land navigation, at which he was a past master.

Anita offered to put together some food while

Frost kept the wheel and after about a half hour—it was about midnight then—she brought a tray to him with several steaming hot dishes—rice, some type of stew and some hot bread. Ravenously, Frost took a bite from the bread and shoveled in a mouthful of the stew, burning himself for his effort. In a moment, the girl was back with a tray for herself—only smaller portions—and also a bottle of scotch of an unrecognizable brand and two glasses. She poured a double shot for him and he downed it, realizing he hadn't had a drink in more than two months. "Trying to do me in up here I see," he said smiling.

In the yellow light of the pilot house, just a small bulb burning a hole in the impenetrable darkness of the water around them, the sky now covered with small, scudding clouds moving on the wind and most of the time hiding the full moon, Frost watched her eyes. "You make me laugh," she said.

"Do you like to laugh?" he asked her.

"Yes," she said, then leaned forward and planted a small kiss on his cheek. "I think I owed you one of these," she whispered. Frost took his right hand and entwined his fingers in the hair at the nape of her neck and drew her face to him, then kissed her hard on her pale red lips. "You should eat first," again whispering, "then later, perhaps."

"Good advice," he said. And as they ate, he watched her watching him, awaiting the inevitable question. By the time the food was gone and she'd brought up some fruit and he was working on a third drink, she asked it.

"I feel rude, but I cannot help it—Hank. The eyepatch you wear, was it some sort of accident?"

Frost smiled, feeling as though he should say something like, "No. I just decided one day to gouge my left eye out on purpose." But she was a

42

nice girl, he thought, and since she had volunteered nothing about her kidnapping, she wasn't apparently fully herself yet. He said, "I don't usually talk about it. But you're right—it was some sort of accident."

And she leaned toward him as though he were preparing to confide a secret. Unable to resist the impulse, he gestured with his finger for her to lean close and he put his lips to her ear, then spoke and she drew back. "Senor Frost!" she half screamed, then she began to laugh. And Frost laughed with her. He'd told her that actually it was nothing at all romantic or exciting—he'd been picking his nose, sneezed and his finger had slipped.

They talked for a while longer—his watch reading nearly two A.M. And finally, toward the end of the bottle of scotch, the autopilot slaving away and the radar alarm system operational, she told him about the kidnapping. Her father was a banker and a senator in the Assembly and she hadn't told him earlier, she said, "Because at first I wasn't sure you were a man of good character, Hank." He smiled and told her he wasn't. The three men had been planning to kill her, she had felt that too. They had asked what Frost figured was close to a half-million dollars U.S. for her return. From what she'd heard of their conversation, they were professional smugglers and kidnapping her had just looked like a way to turn a fast buck with less work than smuggling. Frost also learned she was nineteen. Frost didn't volunteer his own age, since, stretching things a bit, he was almost old enough to be her father.

By three, he'd told her about himself, his brush with death, how the sister at the mission hospital who was also a doctor had restored him to health. And Frost remembered those eyes now too as he thought of how much he suddenly wanted this young girl and wondered whether he should. But the problem temporarily resolved itself as they worked their way into a second bottle of scotch. The two of them went below decks, relying perhaps more than they should have for the autopilot and the radar alarm to arouse them. They were out of the shipping lanes and reasoned there should be no danger.

Frost undressed the girl, after she'd first volunteered to undress him. Her breasts were small but pleasant and she was quite thin, but the fragility of her body just made him want her all the more. The two of them crowded into the aft bunk to warm themselves a while and, as Frost and the girl lay in each other's arms, a peculiar thing happened. Frost realized that all the food he'd eaten hadn't compensated for a stomach that had been empty nearly all day, and that the pint or more of straight scotch he'd drunk was doing more than warming his stomach. And the girl whispered into his ear—it was the last thing he remembered—"I never drank liquor before, Hank, does it always make you this—" and she'd yawned— "sleepy?"

Frost remembered, "Yes . . . Yes, it can sometimes," and then falling asleep himself.

His watch read ten A.M. when he awoke, feeling the girl stirring beside him. There were things to do, he knew, but . . . "Hank," she asked, "we didn't do anything last night, did we?"

"No, kid," he said.

"Oh, good," she whispered, "because I wouldn't have wanted to miss that for the—" And she cut herself off.

"The first time?" he asked.

"Si—yes, Hank."

"Well," he started.

"Can we now, I think."

"You sure, kid?" Frost said, suddenly feeling terribly old. She nodded her head. Yep, he said to himself, he guessed she was sure. And, as he caressed her and went very slowly and gently with her he found out that indeed she was sure. . . .

Afterward, having kissed her, petted her and generally tried making her feel happy for having given him her one irretrievable gift, Frost listened to her singing softly, just loud enough to be heard over the running water of the miniscule shower as he washed his hair and his body and tried to rid himself of the fish smell—he thought that oddly it hadn't bothered her. When he left the shower she dried his back and he dressed in clothes he'd hung out over the bow rail the previous night after fishing his suitcase out of the water. The clothes no longer smelled, but he couldn't quite consider them clean either.

They ate lunch, skipping breakfast, and she took the wheel while he cleaned the Browning. The Metalife chrome plating had been unaffected by the salt water bath of the previous night and, though he didn't favor the brand, he'd also found a box and a half of 9mm solids below decks in a locker and at least now the Browning was fully charged and all the magazines filled as well. The remainder of the shells he stowed in the pocket of his bush jacket. He oiled the Gerber and used a rough cloth on the blade to remove any light surface rust that might be forming and left the knife stuck into the desk top by the wheel while the sheath dried some more.

By that night, they would reenter the shipping lanes and then pick up some speed and reach his port in Columbia. Over lunch, they'd discussed what she would tell the police—there had been a storm, her kidnappers had been washed overboard, but before that they'd fought among themselves—oh, it was horrible, the whole routine—and she had managed to free herself and take the helm.

She'd asked Frost if the Columbian police would believe such a silly story and he'd frankly told her probably not but that they wouldn't have much choice, since the boat was known to be used by smugglers quite likely and since her identity established her as beyond repute.

Later, as the sun started dipping into the ocean and the two of them realized there was little time left, without either of them saying anything, Frost and Anita just lay there on the deck. There was no one to watch and they made love a second and last time. Already, Frost thought, she had somehow changed. He could feel her hands kneading at him, guiding him into her, see a young girl who'd somehow been transformed into a woman now. He arched her back up, her hands almost clawing at his chest, her tongue darting into his mouth like some shy thing not knowing what to expect. He found she liked the nipples of her breasts to be touched and apparently touching her there triggered some wildness in her that neither of them had expected. He could feel her moving beneath and around him, her body responding to his hands as though it were a violin and he, Frost, were some sort of concert master. Afterwards, his own cigarettes waterlogged and ruined, he smoked some of the cigarettes he'd found aboard—smuggled American ones, fortunately, Luckies—and sat alone on the deck while she slept with her head in his lap and he watched the sun sink below the water.

Chapter Three

Frost unfolded the list. It had become water-logged, and some of the ink had run, but he could still read the names there, perhaps more in his heart than on the yellow paper. The list of the men in his company, followed by the other men in the battalion, the men who now were dead because of Chapmann. The stewardess brought Frost his drink—he was still on scotch after the time he'd spent on the boat with Anita. Frost thought about her then as he watched the sea of clouds around him now, knowing that below were the blue waters of the Caribbean and that beyond them would be a first landfall at Miami, where he'd change planes for Atlanta. When he and Anita had reached Columbia, he'd taken the dinghy ashore. She had taken the small boat back after a long good-bye and that last parting kiss there on the beach. Things had gone relatively smoothly for him. Though Anita hadn't known, one of his contacts in Columbia had helped to smooth things for her with the police and long before he himself was on his way out of the country she had been packed back home to her father, the banker, even given a superfluous cash reward for having brought in the smugglers' boat and offering proof of their demise—apparently the smugglers had been quite a bit more wanted than either of them had realized.

Frost's contacts in the Columbian military intelligence section that went after the U.S./Columbian drug connection had been able to readily tell him that Chapmann had left Latin America weeks earlier and gone to the small African nation of Nugumbwe, bordering Chapmann's old stamping ground, the Congo. Then Frost's contacts had provided him with some money and secured a passport for him from the U.S. Embassy and given him an airline ticket.

As the jet broke under the cloud cover and he could see Miami off in the distance, Frost reflected that he felt a little naked—his gun and knife of course were stowed aft as luggage and except for his hands he was unarmed. He didn't like flying airplanes these days because of that—he was always waiting for some crazy to hijack the ship to a country where once his own identity were established he'd be quietly killed or imprisoned.

The wait between planes in Miami was short and Frost didn't even bother leaving the security area but did make one phone call. In a half hour he was airborne again with the next stop Hartsfield International Airport in Atlanta. When Hank Frost left the terminal and stepped out into the sweltering near hundred degree heat, a flood of memories came back to him. He'd never actually lived in Atlanta but had passed through it innumerable times, and as he judged from the volume of traffic there, both in the air and on the ground, so did half the rest of the world. He'd read somewhere that Hartsfield was nudging out Chicago's O'Hare Field as the world's busiest airport and standing there trying to hail a taxicab he could well believe that.

Crowds of people made him nervous, even though now the Browning and the Gerber boot knife were

48

back in place—he'd taken them from his suitcase in one of the airport washrooms. Just as Frost felt he'd successfully landed a taxicab, a midnight blue '78 Ford LTD pulled to the curb, cutting off the taxi. The last of the full-size Fords, LTDs seemed to be everywhere you looked in Georgia—perhaps it was a cultural phenomenon, Frost thought. The Ford's door swung open on the curb side and the driver leaned across the front seat, looked up at Frost and said, "You're Hank, right?"

Frost nodded, touched the eyepatch with the tip of his finger and said, "How could you tell?"

"Cut the cracks—hop in." The man was Frost's height, more probably larger, putting him well over six feet, his hair blond and wavy, a neatly trimmed small mustache outlining his upper lip.

Frost, not expecting a ride, stood right where he was, taxicabs honking for the LTD to get out of the way, a black Atlanta cop starting to wend his way through the crowded drive toward them. Frost snatched a look into the LTD's back seat—nobody was there. Then, leaning into the car, tossing his suitcase into the empty back seat, Frost slid in beside the driver and pulled the door closed behind him. No sooner had he entered the vehicle and started closing the door than the driver pulled away from the curb, narrowly missing peeling off the left fender against an airport parking lot bus.

Once they were into the main stream of traffic and moving toward the expressway, the blond-haired man behind the wheel turned to Frost and started to speak, then said, "Hey, what the hell—"

Frost smiled, "I see you noticed my gun—attractive isn't it?" The blond-haired man's eyes were riveted on the muzzle of the Browning Frost held cross-body and leveled at the driver's right lung.

"I'm especially fond of the finish," Frost continued. "Gives it that certain touch—panache. You know what I mean—"

"You son of a—"

Frost cut him off. "I'd watch what I called my mother if I were you—tsk, tsk. Now give me the name, rank and serial number drill—and don't fumble."

"What?" The blond man was barely keeping his eyes on the road. "Major Henson sent me to pick you up—hey, are you Frost?"

"Now that we've established you know who I am, who are you?" Frost said, the muzzle of his Browning High Power never wavering.

"I told you—no, I didn't, I guess. I'm Jed Kominski; I work with Major Henson."

Frost eyed the man a few moments, then said, "Where are you taking us, and how do I know Henson sent you—I didn't ask him to."

The blond man, still dangerously eyeing the gun Frost held rather than the traffic, rattled off Henson's address, the gist of the telephone conversation between Henson and Frost almost two hours earlier while Frost had waited in Miami between planes, then, regaining his lost composure, the blond man said, "Hey, Frost, you wouldn't shoot me; we'd both get killed with nobody driving."

Frost smiled again, his cheeks etched with the smile-frown lines, "Don't be so confident, pal. I used to teach driving for a living. I shoot you, turn the key if necessary, most likely though I just push your body back from the wheel and reach across and steer from here—I can get my foot onto the pedals from here too—just takes some practice. Try it sometime."

The blond man—Kominski—glared at him. Frost

slipped the chromed Browning out of sight under his bush jacket. "Is Henson at home?" Frost asked.

"No, but I'm supposed to take you to him, if that's all right with you," Kominski said, almost hissing the latter remark. Frost just nodded, making something like a gesture of compliance with his left hand and then turning and looking out the window. As they drove and Frost watched the traffic, he reflected that the expressway system in Atlanta was a good one, but the one problem—it was illustrated graphically as one of those foreign-made compact pickup trucks slammed on its brakes beside them following an abortive attempt to get into the slow lane—was the near total absence of acceleration lanes. Any driver entering during a heavy traffic volume period either had to race headlong into the main stream of automobiles and hope for the best or come to a dead stop and hope that the vehicles behind him could do the same. Frost smiled as he wondered how many grey hairs the road system generated each year or how many skipped heartbeats.

After a few more hair breadth escapes from death and another ten minutes of driving, Kominski turned off the expressway and headed toward Stone Mountain along Memorial Drive, but long before even nearing it, turned the car into a parking lot—a pizza restaurant. Kominski, as he turned the key and started to get out of the car, said, "Major Hensen figured you could stand some good food after being in Latin America for so long—and it's a safe place to talk."

As Frost slammed his car door, he nodded acquiescence and followed the blond man inside. The restaurant was semi-dark, and sparsely peopled in the mid-afternoon. Frost saw Henson in a far corner, shot him a wave and went up to the counter, ordered a pitcher of Heineken dark and a glass and after a moment was sliding into the booth across from his old C.O. in Viet Nam.

"Hank, I heard rumors, you know . . . Thank God you're alive." Frost set his glass mug down and he and Hensen shook hands.

As Frost set the pitcher down and leaned into the mug of beer, he nodded, then said, "I'll drink to that in fact. You order anything?"

"No," the older man said, "what do you want—pizza? All they got I think."

"Pizza's fine—want to split a big one?"

Kominski was already standing, Frost realized, because the younger man—the junior officer—knew he'd wind up placing the order. Frost unlimbered a Camel while the three of them settled on sausage with mushroons, and Kominski left.

"You two get along?" Hensen said, his brown eyes squinting into the beginnings of a smile.

Frost grinned back at the older man, the heavily lined face a face Frost knew almost as well as his own, Hensen's hair grayer now, the chin a little less prominent, but the innate toughness still there for all the world to see. "That was a set-up, wasn't it?" Frost asked him, looking down into his beer.

"Yeah—that Kominski's a good kid, tough, fast—but he's cocky sometimes and I guess I figured you'd take him down a peg—that's why I sent him alone." Then Hensen, his whiskey voice cracking, whispered, "He ask you about the eyepatch yet?"

"No," Frost said smiling, "but he will." And the two men laughed. When Kominski returned to the table, the talk began in earnest. "You know why I'm here," Frost said, not bothering to check if he could talk in front of Kominski. If the young blond-haired man weren't to be trusted, Hensen wouldn't have had him there. "I found out Chapmann's in Nugumbwe."

"Wait a minute," Hensen snapped. "Jed, pump some dough into that jukebox and get the loudest songs you can."

The blond man nodded and Frost and Hensen suspended the conversation until the younger man returned. The country music blaring—a song about some sort of super truck driver and the smokeys—the three men leaned together across the table and Frost went on "Chapmann—Marcus Chapmann. He's the one who ordered the whole outfit killed and I'm going to smoke that sucker and enjoy every minute of it. Word is he got himself down to Nugumbwe and he's working for the dictator there—"

Hensen cut off Frost. "That's bad, Hank, real bad."

"Why?" Frost asked, squinting. Before Hensen could answer, a waitress brought over the pizza. Frost glanced up at her. She wore skin-tight faded jeans and a shirt that looked molded across her breasts. As she leaned down to spread the three plates onto the table, Frost commented, "Times like this make me wish I still had two eyes." The girl, brushing her honey colored hair away from her forehead with the back of her hand, looked at him a moment and smiled.

When she left, as Frost reached to grab a piece of pizza, he said, "All right, now why, Hensen?"

"Simple—that little shit dictator in Nugumbwe is a State Department friendly. Corrupt as they come —which I guess explains why he hired Chapmann," Hensen said, his voice ending on a note of finality. "But since he's fighting some Communist guerrillas down there, the Government here is backing the sucker. Seems there's a kind of three-way war down there. The regular army—most of it anyway—has gone over to the right-wing revolution—they seem to be the good guys. The dictator hired a bunch of mercs that didn't care who they worked for and there are still some factions of the Army loyal to him anyway. And then the terrs started to up their activity—so everybody's fightin' everybody over there. That's probably another reason why he hired Chapmann—the world's greatest organizer.''

"And," Frost said, reaching for more pizza, "the bastard doesn't have anything against mass murder either.''

"Yeah, but what the hell's the difference,'' Kominski finally chimed in. "Over there all they got's a bunch of nig—''

And Frost cut him off. "You finish that word, boy, and you're gonna make me get that waitress back over here for another fork.''

"Huh?'' the blond man said.

"I think what he's trying to tell ya,'' Hensen said, "is that Frost here isn't gonna want to use his fork after he jabs it into your throat.''

The blond man started to rise, his hand moving to clear his coat. "The fork's faster, sucker,'' Frost rasped. "I pump this into your carotid artery you're gonna be on the floor and I guarantee you won't see what you're looking at any more once you get there.''

"Sit down—'' Hensen snapped and the younger man obeyed.

"So anyway," Hensen went on, "you got trouble, Hank. Now I understand that the Company has different ideas—supporting the right wing army commander and all, but all on the Q.T!''

"I need some back-up, Steve," Frost said.

"I can't, Hank. I honest to God can't. I can't get out of the country. ATF got State Department to lift my passport—or someone did. Agh—some joker sold me a couple of guns, turned out one of them had been converted—would you believe it—from selective fire to semiautomatic only. Would you believe that? Who the hell converts an automatic weapon to semiautomatic these days? But anyway, you know the drill—I don't have a Class III so they hollered and I'm under indictment. I don't think I'll have a problem once it comes to court, but in the meantime I'm not even supposed to leave the state. But I can get you some guys. I hate to ask," Hensen said, "but you got any dough?"

"I got about seven thousand in the bank," Frost said, "I figure whoever I get to help can take a share of what I recover from Chapmann."

"I know a couple guys who'll buy that I think—after I vouch for your honesty." Hensen wiped his hands on a napkin and lit a cigarette. Frost remembered his old CO had never been much of an eater. Frost, on the other hand, was one of those almost universally hated people who can eat as much as they like and never show an ounce. After he and Kominski—who'd settled down a little—finished a second pizza and split another pitcher of beer, all three men left.

The three men piled into the front seat of the LTD, Frost on the end and Kominski driving again. As they headed northeast out of the city along Interstate 85 toward South Carolina, Frost kept noticing Kominski looking over his shoulder more than he should.

Finally, Frost lit a cigarette and said, "You being followed, Steve?"

Hensen looked over his shoulder then and out the back window. "Probably. Have been for the last few days—thought we'd lost them. This is a borrowed car even."

"Yeah," Kominski said through his ridiculously white teeth, "we're being followed. Son of a—" And he let his voice trail off as he looked intently for a moment at the exit sign they were passing. "But not for long," he swore.

"Who, Steve?" Frost asked, sliding his Browning from under his coat and resting it on the seat under his left thigh. "Feds because of that gun thing?"

"I wish it were, man," Hensen said, reaching under his own coat and extracting a two and one-half-inch barrel Colt Python, swinging out the cylinder and then closing the .357 and sliding it back under his sportcoat. You can always tell armed men, Frost thought. They're the only ones who wear coats in the summer time, or they wear wide flared trousers to cover an ankle holster. But just like pimps, pickpockets, homosexuals and cops, one gunman can always spot another—that way and a variety of other ways.

Hensen and Kominski exchanged glances and just as it looked as though Kominski was going to pass the exit ramp, the young blond man cut the wheel hard to the right and bounced the LTD over the graveled area and onto the exit ramp.

Frost shot a glance over his right shoulder as Kominski slid past the stop sign at the end of the ramp and took a sharp left. Turning around, Frost could see a white GM car of some kind speeding up and apparently pursuing them.

As Kominski lurched their LTD into another high speed left, Frost looked back again. The white car—a Buick he could make out—had taken that last left so fast that one of the hubcaps snapped off and was bouncing across the road. With the windows open, Frost could even hear the thing rattling.

Kominski, Frost thought, was either a fantastic driver or a fool. There were a half dozen safety orange wooden horses blocking the ramp and the LTD simply crashed through them, disintegrating the construction barriers as it rammed ahead. The pavement broke and they were on dirt now, the LTD wheeling in a zig-zag pattern to avoid construction machinery. Over his right shoulder, Frost could still see the white Buick following them. In front of them, the ground was becoming still more broken and uneven. Kominski swerved the LTD to avoid a compressor trailer and apparently misjudged his distance from the embankment to their right. The passenger's side of the car went up—like a movie stunt or something one would see at a dragstrip on a Sunday afternoon. For a moment, Frost was up in the air, that side of the car completely off the ground, the LTD riding on its two left wheels.

And then the car came down—hard, bone shatteringly hard. But it kept on moving. An embankment loomed up ahead of them and for a moment Frost thought Kominski had seen too many movies and was going to jump the thing. Instead he watched Kominski now almost as if it were in slow motion—the blond-haired man wrenched the wheel hard to the left, his left foot stamping down hard on the brake pedal for an instant. The car started spinning into a bootlegger turn as Kominski hammered down on the accelerator with his right. And they started back up on the ramp, wheels in a high-pitched screeching, dirt and gravel spraying behind them. The white Buick now was dead ahead of them and, as Frost craned his neck to see, his Metalifed

57

Browning coming into his hand, from the GM car's passenger side he could see the muzzle of a shotgun. In seconds, Frost realized, he and the shotgunner would pass each other. Through the sea of dust surrounding both vehicles, Frost could barely make out his enemy's face—dark, like his own, but somehow a native darkness that looked less like a suntan than natural coloration.

And then they were opposite each other. The shotgunner started making his move and Frost opened up with his Browning, two shots, then two more. The shotgun discharged and Frost ducked. Then, looking up, the dashboard in front of him was littered with slivers from an eight-inch diameter hole in the windshield. He craned his neck to look at the white car now behind them. And through the swirling dust Frost could see the body of the shotgunner, limp, hanging halfway out the passenger window, the dead man's shotgun lost somewhere in the spreading distance between the two cars.

Kominski was driving hard and they went airborne again but only for a few feet as the LTD bounced back over the lip of pavement and Kominski wrenched the car into a hard right, then accelerated across the overpass, then made a wheel-screeching left into the on-ramp, then flooring it—Frost could see the pedal flush against the floorboards—accelerated down the ramp and onto the highway. The white car was now nowhere to be seen.

Frost shifted the Browning to his weaker hand—the left—and slowly lowered the hammer with his right thumb and first two fingers, then slipped the gun back in his trouser waistband.

Turning to Hensen, Frost's face creased into a

grin. "Looks like you were right—they were following you."

"No kiddin'," Hensen said in mock exclamation. Then suddenly, Kominski started laughing and laughing until he let out an ear-piercing rebel yell.

Frost said, "You know, I hate to mention this, but either we slow down, ditch this car altogether or cover the windshield—I'm getting blown to bits here, not to mention the glass." But all of that became unnecessary. Kominski pulled off at the next exit and after a few minutes of driving at about forty—most of the glass already blown away by now anyway—Kominski turned up a rutted red clay road, here driving still more slowly and twice having to drop into a lower gear. After about ten or more minutes, Kominski turned up a gravel driveway and stopped. Almost sighting through the hole in the windshield, Frost could see a massive white frame house, much in need of a paint job. The house, partly because of its size, looked somehow out of place, but also because the only other signs of human habitation Frost had seen had been single and double-walled trailers. Gingerly, Frost climbed from the front seat, carefully brushing the glass from his clothes and hair. Frost was more careful with the operation than most men would have been—with just one eye left to lose or damage it was only natural that he should be.

The house itself seemed deserted as did the grounds. As Hensen started walking toward it, his feet crunching the gravel audibly in the stillness, Frost touched a hand to Hensen's arm and said, "Wait a minute. The LTD is this guy's car, right? Means that probably anybody who made you driving the LTD also made this guy—we could have a houseload in there. Now who was following you—who are these guys?''

Edgy, constantly eyeing the house as he spoke, Hensen turned to Frost, saying, ''All right, Hank, you got a right. It's a bunch of Cubans. They run one of the big drug operations headquartered out of Miami. Hired me about three months ago to bring in some cocaine for them and some maryjane out of Columbia. So anyway—''

Frost interrupted, ''But you weren't about to do that, so you took their money and then set it up with the cops and turned the guys in. Right?''

Hensen smiled nervously, ''Well—yeah. I figured they couldn't squeal to the cops, just be incriminatin' themselves more. You know.''

''And they want to kill you,'' Frost said. ''Okay, Right. Let's check the house—Jed, stay by the car with the motor running.''

''I don't take orders from you, Frost,'' Kominski said.

''Tell him to stay by the car with the motor running,'' Frost said to Hensen.

''Stay by—''

''Oh, hell!'' Kominski said. Then, turning to Frost. ''Hey, I been meaning to ask—how come the eyepatch?''

Hensen just groaned. Frost, getting the Browning in his hand—he'd fired four and carried one in the chamber so that made ten rounds to go—turned to Kominski, smiled and said, ''Vanity—that's why I wear the patch. Just vanity. See—my right eye is a kind of grayish-green color. But now my left eye is a kind of greenish-gray color. And just between us fellas, I couldn't make it with the women that way—too busy staring at my eyes. No kidding.'' Frost broadened his grin at Kominski and winked his eye.

Hensen was laughing as Frost clapped his old CO on the shoulder and the two men started toward the house.

As Special Forces personnel who regularly changed from green berets to CIA civies, both men had become just as familiar with entering a suspect house as a couple of inner city cops would be. "Hey, you want the door?" Hensen said.

"Yeah," Frost shrugged. The one-eyed man stepped onto the side of the porch and flipped the railing, flattening himself against the house wall abutting the porch as Hensen took the front steps two at a time and flattened himself flanking the half-glass door on the opposite side. Frost passed under the window ledge toward the door, dropping to all fours for a moment, then straightening himself as he took the flank of the door on the doorknob side.

Frost reached out with his gunhand and knocked briskly on the door. Both men waited but there was no answer. "What's the guy's name?" Frost rasped to Hensen.

"Bobby Coleman."

"Hey, Bobby—Bobby Coleman!" Frost shouted, rapping on the door again. But there was nothing. Frost gestured to Hensen that it was time to go into their number. The older man stepped back and lined up on the doorway, the snubby Python clamped in his gnarled fist. Hensen half wheeled and lashed out with his right foot, dead on at the lock and the door sprang inward. As Hensen stepped away to flank it again, Frost charged through the door and dove to the floor just inside and to his right. He crawled a foot or so and got behind a large overstuffed couch—still nothing.

"Hey, Bobby Coleman! Anybody home?" Frost shouted.

Nothing. Then Frost shouted, "Hensen" and Hensen was through the door and opposite Frost, both men commanding the hallway and living room with their pistols. "Up or down?" Frost rasped.

"Ah, what the hell—you're younger. I'll take down."

"Right," Frost said, then was up and running toward the staircase at the far end of the hall. From the corner of his eye, Frost could see Hensen moving in the direction of the dining room. When Frost reached the head of the stairs he dropped to a crouch. There was still no sound beyond those Hensen was making downstairs, going through doorways, searching rooms. Frost began his check upstairs. There was a nursery at the head of the stairs, still under construction, a half-assembled crib in the corner and a crib mattress beside it, still wrapped in plastic. There were rolls of wallpaper on the floor, only one of them opened—as if the woman of the house, Frost imagined, had bought them and wanted to hold one of the rolls against the wall to check the pattern or something.

There was a pretty much normal master bedroom that looked like it needed a paint job and another two bedrooms, one empty but spotlessly clean, the second apparently used as a storeroom. There was a riot shotgun there, a Remington 870 with a folding stock, some backpacking stuff and a crude reloading bench for shotshells. From the apparent age of the house—around the turn of the century Frost guessed—there likely wasn't a basement.

"Frost!" He heard Hensen call his name and he raced back toward the staircase and started down two at a time. He reached the base of the steps and turned, seeing Hensen leaning half through a kitchen doorway opposite him. "Anything upstairs, Hank?"

"Not really. How about down here?"

"Same deal," Hensen said. "A bunch of food out like somebody was gettin' ready to make dinner, and some of the kitchen knives were on the floor. Back door was open. There's a kind of barn out back—I'm gettin' bad vibes on that. Let's take a look."

Frost just nodded, then followed Hensen.

The backyard had a well-cared-for flower bed, a half-wrecked pickup truck and a beat up, half-assembled swing set. From the house and now the swing set, Frost guessed Bobby Coleman and his wife were expecting their first child. At the entrance to the barn, Hensen said, "You wait here, Hank—I'll shout if I need you."

Frost just looked at him, then nodded. Hensen slipped between the half-opened double doors and disappeared, the Colt revolver in his hand. By his watch, Frost noted Hensen had been in there for three minutes and as Frost was just starting in after him, Hensen came back through the doors. "Don't go in."

"Why not, Steve?"

"Just don't go in, Hank—huh?"

"You know I gotta," Frost said and he slipped through the doorway past Hensen. It took a moment for Frost's eye to become accustomed to the semidarkness and then he saw why Hensen had tried to keep him outside. A man about his own age—early thirties—was hanging by his heels half dragged out from a support beam, the top half of his body on the ground, the skin on his legs peeled away in patches, burn marks all over his chest and his testicles, his face half beaten to a pulp. His bloodied wrists were tied in front of him with what looked like barbed wire and there was a barbed wire garrote around his neck. Then Frost saw the woman and he turned around and vomited. The smell he noticed a few seconds earlier as he's entered the barn had apparently been from when Henson had done the same thing. Frost dropped to one knee on the ground there and looked back at the woman. Her face was black from a noose around her neck that swung her from one of the rafters a foot or so off the ground and her hands were tied over her head, as though she'd been suspended from the rafters by her wrists first and after a while the noose had been used to strangle her rather than hang her. Her feet were bare and burned black.

There was a still smoldering fire beneath her. And the part that was the worst to see, Frost didn't even want to think about—her swollen, pregnant belly had been sliced open. He couldn't leave her hanging there. He vomited again and wasn't ashamed for it, then wiped his hand across his mouth and found a step ladder, brought it over and climbed it and put his left arm around under the dead woman's armpits and held her awkwardly as he cut the rope on her neck and the rope on her wrists with his knife. He got her down as gently as he could, found an old tarpaulin and used his knife to cut the thing in half, then covered both the dead husband and the wife.

Frost walked outside, slumped down to his haunches by the barn door and lit a cigarette, his hands trembling. Hensen looked back inside, then turned to Frost and said, "Jesus—I couldn't—Thank you," and then the older man walked away. Frost was too drained to do anything but sit there and stare at the swing set.

They'd ditched the LTD a few miles away from the house, wiping the car as clean as they could of prints, having done the same thing at the house itself, then hiked in five miles to the nearest town. From there Hensen placed a call and an hour later a young black man showed up and gave them a lift into Atlanta. If any of them had been in the mental shape to think straight they could have called the guy before they'd ditched Coleman's LTD and saved the five-mile walk, but the physical strain of that had almost been good for Frost, Hensen and Kominski. At least Frost felt that way. After finding the bodies, neither of the three of them had said much of anything, perhaps because nothing hardens a normal human being—no matter how much he may have killed in combat or what-have-you—to something like they had found back there in the barn.

Finally, as they entered Hensen's suburban Atlanta apartment, Kominski, checking the place ahead of them, said to Hensen, "You know they're going to be here tonight—they've got our movements pegged."

"Yeah," Hensen groaned, "I know." And that was all he said. While Kominski fixed some drinks—none of the three of them felt like eating—Hensen walked into his bedroom and came back out with two folding stock Remington riot shotguns and a pair of Government model .45s. He went into the bedroom again and returned with ammunition.

Kominski brought the drinks then and quietly he and Hensen set to loading the guns on the table, then all three men checked their personal weapons. "You know, we could call the cops," Frost said after a while. "Drug Enforcement people would love to have those goons."

"Yeah, we could," Hensen said, almost bitterly. "But we might not be able to make the killing stick on them and they'd just get a big fine and maybe a couple of months in jail and they'd still be alive."

"I know what you mean," Frost said.

Kominski then said the first words he'd uttered since they had left the Colemen house and he'd insisted on looking in the barn, just as Frost had done. Reaching under his coat and producing a Walther PPK/S .380 to add to his bright-chromed .45 Colt Government already on the table, he said, "How could anyone do that?"

Frost put his right hand on the younger man's shoulder. "Never mind, Jed, just thank God you can still ask that question and don't already know the answer like we do."

As the night wore on, they smoked, drank a little, put away coffee to keep themselves sober and awake and eventually tried eating, though still no one had the stomach for it and most of the food just sat there on the table with the guns and the spare ammo.

Though they had been expecting the attack all night, when the apartment door crumpled inward at two forty-eight A.M.—Frost had just glanced at the digital clock on top of the TV set—they were still taken by surprise. There were six men, all Latino looking, all heavily armed—three with submachine guns. The first man through the doorway had one of these. Kominski, sitting closest to the door, was the first on his feet with both his pistols in his hands and as the subgunner fired into him, Kominski started emptying both pistols, still firing as he crumpled to his knees, the guns falling limply from his hands as he slumped forward. The first subgunner, though, was hit. Frost pumped two 9mms from his Browning into the same man and the guy went down. From his left, Frost heard the roar of a riot shotgun—Hensen pumping and triggering the Remington's seven-round extension magazine until it was empty, taking out two more of the men as they came through the doorway and then injuring a third. Frost stepped toward that man and fired his pistol point-blank into the man's face and then turned away. There were still two men left, one with a subgun. Frost caught a glance at the SMG as the man who held it wheeled toward him—it was a British Sterling with a silencer. As the subgunner opened fire, the weapon's muzzle sweeping toward him, Frost fired twice and dove toward the gunner's feet to get under the level of his fire and bring him down. Then Frost heard the bark of Hensen's second riot shotgun and before Frost reached the subgunner, the man slammed back hard against the wall by the shattered door with a load of double "O" Buck in him, his subgun still firing as he sank to his knees. Frost shot a glance to Hensen and saw his old CO's body lurch, spin around then start to fall to the floor, the riot shotgun going off one more time into the coffee table and making it almost explode. Frost rolled and scrambled to his feet. There was still one man left and as the Cuban wheeled toward him, a licorice-black automatic pistol in his left fist, Frost lashed out with his right foot, catching the pistol against his heel and knocking it from the Cuban's hand. As Frost brought his own gun on line to fire, the Cuban dove toward him and they both went down. Frost's pistol skittering across the floor as he fell, he brought his knee up, catching the drug-runner in the gut and rolling him away. His pistol halfway across the room, Frost got up into a crouch, his boot knife in his hand. As he got to his feet, the Cuban rolled and flashed the biggest Arkansas Toothpick Frost had ever seen. It had to have been shoulder carried, Frost thought—the blade was at least twelve inches long. What he could see of the hilt was very ornate. Frost edged a step back.

"I'll carve you up just like I did that woman and her stupid husband. Neither one of them would tell us where we could find Hensen so we decided to have some fun anyway. Now you get to have some fun!" And the man laughed. Frost glanced down to the comparatively puny Gerber in his hand, but in his mind's eye he saw it more like an avenging sword. Frost feinted a rush toward the drug smuggler and the man sidestepped just the way Frost had thought he would. Then Frost lashed out with a savate kick and caught the man hard in the gut. Frost broke the cardinal rule of knife fighting and threw his blade, underhanding it toward the drug smuggler's center of mass as he staggered back, and knife catching in the guy's left side.

Then Frost dove toward him, falling over the outstretched knife arm and bringing it up as he smashed forward with his left knee. He connected with his target, the Cuban's elbow, and snapped it. Then Frost grabbed his own knife from the man's side, wrenched it out and hammered his double-edged blade down hard into the torture slayer's heart.

Frost staggered up to his feet. Already in the distance he could hear police sirens wailing. Expecting that, in the event of a fight he'd been careful to touch nothing except his glass and his coffee cup and he poured their contents out on the floor and pocketed them. Frost had long ago developed the habit of loading his pistol magazines while wearing a glove, so he was positive there would be no latent print on a cartridge case. He looked to Kominski—the kid was dead from multiple wounds. Frost clambered over the smashed coffee table and bent down to Henson, lying there on the rug on his face in a spreading pool of blood. Frost started to roll him over. "Don't move me, Hank."

Frost dropped to one knee beside his dying friend. "Can I do anything?"

"No . . ." Hensen groaned. "I'm almost glad—I've seen too much, you know?"

Frost muttered that he knew. "I can help you though, Hank, I thought of something I forgot to tell you." Frost could barely hear Hensen now and put his ear close to Hensen's lips. "Chapmann—something about old Marcus. Seems—seems that Chapmann has a big Swiss account, deal with some banker in Zurich was all I got. If you can't nail him in Nugumbwe because you can't get any help or anything, wait for him there. I wish I could do bet—" There was a kind of gurgling sound and a hiss of breath and Frost stood up. The sirens sounded less than a block away. It would be corny, trite, he thought, to give a last salute to the man who'd been his CO in Viet Nam, his friend for better than the last decade. Trite, corny—but Frost did it anyway, self-consciously and quickly and then he ran as though somehow the apartment walls were watching him.

Chapter Four

Henry Stimson Frost had done remarkably well in school—he'd had to since it had been his entire life back then. His parents had gotten divorced a few years after he was born and the courts had given his father custody of him. That meant military schools, since his father was a career military man and rarely in one place long enough to establish a household or do anything that didn't pertain to his job. There'd been Korea, which had forced the divorce between his parents because his father had been up for early retirement when that came along—he was already a major having worked up in the ranks from a World War Two draftee in the army, and was almost borderline by the Korean War period because of his age. But Kenneth Henry Frost had gone and distinguished himself, returning with a full colonel's silver bird and just shy one wife, his son in "the best school" they could find. Early on—as early as third grade—Hank Frost had started doing his level best to do away with the name Henry, despite the fact that he liked what he'd heard about his grandfather, whose name it had been originally.

His grandfather had been a newspaper editor in Arizona prior to World War I, worked in a civilian capacity for the government and then stuck with that until he'd married late in life and settled down to teaching school in the Midwest.

In school, Hank Frost had excelled at sports and English literature. His terrible abilities with math not only had sabotaged his entrance exam for West Point but had also kept him from getting into European History—a subject he thoroughly enjoyed. But he couldn't remember dates to save his life.

Brigadier General Kenneth H. Frost had died of a sudden stroke just after Hank had graduated from high school and the younger Frost had always partially blamed his failure with the West Point exam for that. Hank Frost at that point decided to switch careers, went to a civilian college and didn't even take ROTC. By then he'd decided he didn't want a life that was a carbon copy of his father's. Instead, thinking perhaps more of his grandfather, he aimed at English and journalism. Viet Nam was a going thing then and by the time he had graduated with a bachelor's degree in English literature and the standard routine of noxious education courses under his belt, he had resigned himself to the inevitable and enlisted. The logical thing to do seemed to be signing up for Airborne and he did that, then switched into Special Forces and went overseas. In Viet Nam, he'd eventually risen to the rank of captain, rejecting a promotion to major because he hadn't wanted to be taken out of the field and didn't like the way the war was being run anyway and hadn't wanted a hand in administering it however slightly. Two things happened in Viet Nam—neither of which Frost ever seriously talked about. He had killed innumerable men in an operation similiar to but less publicized than the Phoenix Project and he had lost an eye and got sent home—but the specifics of either he never mentioned.

Frost had tried to remind himself of the old saying, "In the country of the blind the one-eyed man is king." But when he came home, he wasn't a king, just a guy with a disability looking for a job like thousands of other guys. He remembered that after World War II, his father a military hero then, Kenneth Frost had been offered an empty desk and a vice-presidency with a medium sized corporation in the aircraft industry. Hank Frost, on the other hand, had to drive a taxicab while the summer passed and he finally got his teaching certificate verified and eventually landed a job as a high school teacher in an inner city school in the Midwest. Teaching English there had been more difficult than teaching English to the foreign born, he'd often thought—at least that way he would have been starting from scratch. Most of the kids he'd worked with had been decent enough, black kids who sort of wanted to learn but were rarely given the opportunity and couldn't read to save their lives. And that was when he'd started trying to make jokes about his eyepatch too. The kids would always ask and he had no wish to tell the real story so he'd started up a repertoire of bad gags about it.

But the teaching thing didn't last long. There'd been a woman teacher, Viola something, just out of school herself—one of the new generation of dedicated and young black teachers who looked at working in the ghetto as a sort of mission—Frost hadn't ever been able to determine for himself if that was the right way to look at it or not. But one day, the woman hadn't shown up at lunch where Frost and some of the other teachers sat each day to commiserate, and another woman, her best friend, had said she'd looked in the women teachers' lounge but hadn't seen Viola either. The principal had sent out a note to her and Frost had volunteered then to check the classroom she'd used the last period. As

Frost had turned from the staircase into the nearly deserted fourth-floor hallway, he started hearing some shouting, then screams. He started running, He's nearly fallen on the slick stone floors as he rounded the next corner. And then he'd stopped. About a dozen kids were standing by the open door of Viola's classroom, not moving, not talking, some perhaps petrified with fear, others morbidly curious. Frost walked over to them and pushed his way through the crowd, hearing, then, another scream coming from inside the room.

Frost stood in the doorway for a minute—the woman teacher was huddled in the far corner of her classroom, her dress torn half away, her face bleeding and there were two boys—each one substantially bigger than Frost—standing over her. As the one reached down and started to grab her, she screamed again.

"What's the matter with you people?" Frost had said incredulously to the kids in the doorway—some black and some white, some male and a few female. "You just going to stand here?"

But Frost didn't. He started across the room, calling the two boys by name as they started wrestling the woman teacher onto her back there on the floor. Frost grabbed the one closest to him and spun the kid around, just hauling his right fist back and landing a haymaker on the boy's jaw and knocking him against the chalkboard and down. The second kid—bigger than the first—started for Frost with a knife and Frost just reacted. Frost wasn't in a classroom anymore, fighting a student who wasn't yet eighteen (despite the fact the boy outweighed him by a good fifty pounds). Frost went into a standard martial arts knife defense routine, disarmed the boy and crushed his windpipe to the point where the boy nearly died as a result. And Frost lost his job in exchange for criminal charges against him being dropped.

That's when Frost started drinking a little. He decided to go after a job driving a truck. While he waited for a license he worked as a behind-the-wheel driving instructor, which afterward he concluded had been the most dangerous thing he'd ever done in his life. Once he'd finally hit the road, though, truck driving didn't look so good to him. He worked for a big outfit but balked at hassling the independents and eventually balked his way right out of his job. Any money he'd had was long run out and so he took a job for a while as an unarmed security guard, then had gotten a Private Investigator's license. He still had that license, renewing it periodically; but it wasn't like the movies he soon learned. Transom peeping—the alternative to being a fancy night-watchman in civies or getting the goods on a paperclip thief—was having a degenerative influence on him. If his own parents and their divorce hadn't soured him against marriage, the divorce cases he handled of wives and husbands cheating on each other finished the job nicely.

And then one morning Frost woke up, more hung over than usual and try as he might he couldn't remember anything that had happened after four o'clock the previous afternoon. As he started to pour a morning pick-me-up for himself, he put the bottle down and suddenly realized he was becoming an alcholic, going down the drain. Trying to get his mind on something else he grabbed at a stack of unopened mail. Bills, more bills and a letter from an old buddy in Viet Nam—the guy was in the Rhodesian "police" now, the paramilitary group that "policed" by hunting down terrorists in the bush and was essentially a ranger type outfit made up of mercenaries but called a police force since in most of the western countries, if you joined the Rhodesian Army you automatically forfeited your citizenship. But these guys, like his pal, weren't in an army— they were "police."

Frost thought a great deal about his friend's letter over the next few days while he worked himself relentlessly in the neighborhood gym to help himself dry out. No sane man liked killing, he'd thought, but he had been good at it. And, killing the right people didn't bother him either, like it had bothered some of his buddies. It didn't give him nightmares. He'd been trained really for only one marketable skill ever since he had been a little boy in military school—to stalk the enemy and kill the enemy. He never would and never could go back to teaching. And, Frost had a natural dislike for dictators and Communists, whether one-in-the-same or called something else. Why not, he thought?

Frost made some contacts, found out what his prior rank and service record would get him and took the standard two-year package. He spent a few more days ironing out his personal affairs and left.

Since those first days, Frost had been everything from a "ranch guard" in Rhodesia—he'd often thought the country should have adopted as its motto, "The land of euphemisms"—to a combatant in several brush fire wars in Africa and Latin America. He'd worked executive protection teams and added a few other experiences to the list of subjects from his past he would never discuss.

The life as a mercenary had proved to be what Frost had been looking for. After the Angola thing had blown all to hell and mercenaries started making big news, like a lot of people Frost had needed money. When one of the big European magazines had asked to interview him and offered the equivalent of five thousand American dollars just for him to pose for their cameras in his cammies and black beret and answer some questions he'd jumped at the chance.

"What made you become a mercenary, then, Monsieur Frost—or should I say Captain?" The slightly effeminate-looking man in the seersucker suit had leaned back then, catching a glance at the cassette in his recorder presumably to verify that everything was running well.

Frost lit a cigarette. "I told you already, but if you mean why do I stay in the business, I can tell you that."

"Oui—please tell me that, then, Monsieur Frost."

Sighing audibly, Frost looked past the interviewer and across the hotel balcony to the sweltering street below them. "It's not a nine-to-five job, for openers. You're the same way I am, that's why you're a journalist. Would you really want to be chained down to some goddamned desk or some assembly line, writing the same reports or putting the same tab A into slot B everyday, day after day until by the time you can retire and do something you're too old to enjoy it? Probably until you couldn't even remember what it was that you had wanted to do in the first place? I don't think you would.

"Well, neither do I," Frost said. "The press, the paperback writers, everybody all of a sudden has discovered mercenaries, just like we weren't around all these years. Hell, the Greeks and the Romans used mercenaries, and there were mercs before then too. You guys seem to want to put us all in a goldfish bowl and check out what makes us tick, then just watch a kid sometime climbing over a back yard fence to see what's so good out there in the alley that his parents don't want him near it. What's intriguing to any man about a woman he's just met? How does it feel when you drive a sports car—like that Porsche you tooled up here in—for the first time, or the first time you get it flat out on the highway?"

"How do you say it in English—I do not get behind you? No—I don't follow you."

"You do," Frost said. "Everyday when I wake up I'm doing something different. Now maybe I'm wearing the same clothes and boots I was wearing the previous day, or the day before that even. Maybe I've got ants or something worse all over me from sleeping on the ground, and maybe some joker's going to try and kill me, but I know every moment I'm alive that I am alive.

"See, the average mercenary or any kind of adventurer doesn't get into what he does because he wants to kill people; and the last thing he wants is to get killed himself. Don't believe that occupational hazard thing—that's something you tell women to impress them. You become an adventurer or whatever because there's always something new to see, to do. You can see the world, the whole world, not just the inside of a tour bus.

"You see," Frost went on, "the guys the rest of the world calls mercenaries are really the only ones who aren't mercenaries. We do what we want, we get paid for it, but you and I both know you don't get rich fighting somebody's war. And mercenaries don't do it for the money—they do it for the adventure, for the action, because they believe in the cause they're fighting for. Most mercenaries today are anti-Communists. But the guys who work that nine-to-five job for a few hundred a week or less—now they are the mercenaries. They're usually doing something they don't like just for one reason—money, dollar signs or Franc signs, or whatever the hell you'd call them.

"When I was a teacher, I was a mercenary—I liked the kids but hated every minute of the stupid drivel that passes for education these days. But I did it for a paycheck. When I was a security man and watching somebody's goddamned factory or chasing somebody's husband who was cheating, then I was a mercenary."

"You are not a mercenary then?" The young journalist asked.

"If you mean somebody who fights wars the so called 'big governments' of the world are too chicken to get involved with, yeah. If you mean somebody who'll fight under any flag so long as it is anti-Communist and isn't anti-American, then yeah. They call me the mercenary, but the people who will read this and then go back to working at jobs they hate, supporting political programs they don't believe in and dying of boredom are the ones." Frost stubbed out his cigarette. His voice rising, he asked, "And they called me the mercenary?"

Frost had gotten a polite note and half the five thousand dollars as a kill fee—the interview hadn't been quite what the magazine had been looking for.

And, as he sat aboard the jet as it began to drop altitude toward his first landfall in Africa, Frost realized that some of the things since the Chapmann massacre were going onto that list, too. He hadn't been back in Africa since he'd done a few things as a contract employee for the Company during the Angolan Civil War.

Frost caught his connecting flight, checking that

his weapons were transferred safely. Before leaving the states, he had gotten the best deal he could on a well used .460 Weatherby Magnum bolt action with a 3-9x variable scope on it. He had no intention of using the gun because he had no intention of going after a rhino—it was part of his cover as a would-be hunter and a legal rationale to transport his Browning as a back-up pistol. What happened to the Weatherby after his landing in the Congo and meeting with the white hunter friend who was covering for him was of no concern to him. His pal in the Congo would supply the weapons Frost really needed.

And the man was ready to do just that when they rendezvoused at the airport in Kinshasa. They drove for a while and as they did Frost and Derek Kingston caught up on their friendship. They'd met years back when Frost had worked in Rhodesia and then again when he'd been in Angola. Kingston, though he didn't openly mix in politics, was a sympathetic anti-Communist and some said that he was the British Secret Intelligence Service resident agent for the Congo. But it would have been senseless for Frost to ever ask Kingston about that because regardless of whether or not it were true the answer would certainly be the same. Frost and Kingston decided to stop for a drink before beginning the long ride to Kingston's station, an hour's drive from Kinshasa itself. They picked a sidewalk cafe, almost Parisian in its look, with its colorful Cinzano umbrellas protecting the scattered tables from the strong afternoon sun.

Frost ordered a gin and tonic and Derek Kingston the same. Frost watched as Kingston took a cigarette from his tarnished silver case, offered one to Frost who refused and then lit up. Kingston was probably just barely thirty, and perhaps the youngest professional hunter on the African continent. His skill with a rifle was almost legendary and he was a better-than-average man with a pistol as well. Perhaps the fascinating thing about Kingston was that he played his part so perfectly—the slightly rumpled but terribly expensive white suit, the slight but still perceptible bulge under his left armpit from a shoulder holster, even the handgun he carried, a hammerless Browning .380 automatic. Blond-haired with a stagey-looking handlebar mustache, the vintage Jaguar convertible he drove was the perfect finishing touch.

"I say, Hank, is my tie on backward or something?" Kingston's voice and accent sounded almost "stagey" British as well—and he knew it.

"Well, old boy," Frost laughed, "not really—just sitting here thinking you look like a refugee from a British spy movie or something—no offense."

"None taken, dear fellow. I got hold of your kit, by the way—just what you usually use—surmised that would be what you wanted." Frost lit his own cigarette as Kingston began rattling off the list. "One of the big Gerber fighting knives, an H-K assault rifle with the retractable metal stock, a bunch of .308 FMJ stuff and eight extra magazines, no scope. I surmised you'd bring your own pistol, but if you didn't I can loan one I think."

"What's the rifle?" Frost asked. "an H-K 32A2 selective? Or no, that's an A3, isn't it when it's got the collapsible stock?"

"Right you are—I just keep thinking of the thing as a German G-3—stuck to the thirty-round magazines for you. Thought those big forty-rounders might get a little heavy for you. Also got you a guide—you're a damned loon for going in alone to start so I figured I could at least send a man along to look out for you—my best chap. I'd trust him with my wife, if I had one." Their drinks came the Kingston stopped talking until the waiter left.

"Do you hear anything on Chapmann?" Frost asked.

"Nasty business, I'm afraid. Chapmann seems to control most of the country. What he doesn't run with an iron hand is a sort of no-man's land that the right wing army dissidents and the Communist terrorists are fighting to control—not spilling over much into our country here though—at least they seem neat about it except for an occasional raid along the highway. You're getting yourself into it this time, Hank."

"I heard a rumor," Frost said, "back when I was down in Columbia, that although State Department supports Dr. Kubinda's government in Nugumbwe, the Company is supporting General Endibwe and the right wing army rebels—know anything about that, Derek?"

"I'm just a hunter, old boy. How would I hear anything like that? Could be just speculation," Kingston said, lighting another cigarette and playing with his Dunhill lighter a moment.

Frost leaned a bit closer to Kingston across the table. "Could be, pal?"

"Yes, Hank—indeed it could be, and in fact," Kingston flashed a cautious glance around the cafe then lowered his voice. "It is true—chap named Curtis. I think you've met him before. At least that's what I hear," Kingston said, smiling conspiratorially.

"Thanks, my friend," Frost said and the two men finished their drinks in relative silence.

They drove then, as the sun was already starting

to set, on toward Kingston's comparatively palatial house an hour distant from the city. Dinner was superb, prepared not by a houseman as it had been the last time Frost had visited Kingston, but by an exquisite young black woman whom Kingston indicated was his mistress. And Frost discovered why Kingston would trust his "wife if I had one" to the black guide who would be accompanying him before first light the next day—the guide was the young woman's brother. Frost retired to his room early that evening, bidding farewell, he thought, to Kingston's girl, needing to check his weapons before he slept. But the next morning, at four-thirty, she had been up already for half an hour, he discovered, and prepared a breakfast that had Frost been called upon to describe it, he would have labeled as deliciously memorable. Kingston just sat quietly drinking coffee. Frost, as he downed his last coffee and he and Joe-Joe Kitabe prepared to set out, realized sadly that the young woman's peerless culinary skills were totally wasted on Kingston, who ate like a bird and seemed to have little preference at all in his diet. They bid their farewells, the young mistress to Kingston, kissing her brother and shaking Frost's hand and telling him, "God Bless you both and bring you a safe return." Frost said his thanks and mounted the Land Rover beside Joe-Joe and as the sun flashed over the horizon behind them they set off.

After the first ten miles or so Frost and his companion settled in with each other. "Kingston tells me you his friend a long time, Captain Frost."

"I guess that's true," Frost said, trying to light a cigarette in the wind. The Rover was open on the sides but mercifully had a hard top to protect at least a little from the sun they'd encounter toward midday and throughout the afternoon.

"Me, I don't like to ask, but you were injured in the war maybe, Captain?"

"What?" Frost said, "The eyepatch?"

"Yeah—if Captain don't mind tellin' me."

"Well," Frost said, starting to smile, "it's really not an interesting story—you see, although it's a little known fact, I happen to be one of the relatively few people who shares a genetic commonality with the president of the United States. And, though it didn't make the papers, there was a tragic accident not long ago. Military records were searched and what-not and they discovered my organ compatibility with the president. Well, the rest is history really—just doing my patriotic duty." And then Frost tried to look even more serious. "I'm sure a chap like yourself would have no quarrel with that."

Joe-Joe, looking quite serious himself, fell silent for the longest time after that, then about five minutes later he started laughing almost uncontrollably, to the point where he almost lost control of the Land Rover when they hit a good-sized pothole. "Kingston—Captain, he said you one funny guy—" and Joe-Joe kept chuckling for miles and miles.

Toward midday, after they had rested for a while and snatched a hasty meal—sandwiches Joe-Joe's sister had made and put in a cooler (it was the first time Frost had eaten a sandwich of minced lobster and the sauce she'd used should have elevated her to sainthood), they resumed their journey toward the border and into Nugumbwe.

About twenty minutes along the track, Frost spotted a plume of dust about three miles or so back along the crude road. "What could that be, Joe-Joe?" Frost asked.

The black man looked back over his shoulder. He shrugged, then said, "Could be animals, but I don't think it 'tis—been there last ten minutes, maybe. Look to me like somebody be followin' us. Could be, Captain?"

Frost nodded and Joe-Joe looked back to the road. "Might by my friend Chapmann's boys— maybe somebody else. This road used much?"

Joe-Joe glanced at Frost a moment then said, "Mostly by terrorists, maybe. Ha!"

Frost liked Joe-Joe but thought at the moment that he wasn't much taken with the man's sense of humor. Frost looked into the gun rack for the reassurance of the H-K assault rifle and Joe-Joe's Remington 700 BDL bolt action, then looked back along the track behind them again and studied the constant plume of dust for several more minutes.

By twilight, Frost felt ready to pack it in, knowing they couldn't cross into Nugumbwe at night because there were no roads where they were going and it would at best be slow going, partly through rain forest. And that would be suicide with a vehicle at night, if not exactly for the occupants then definitely for the Rover.

They kept driving for another half hour, Joe-Joe knowing a good spot he said for the evening camp, a little off the savannah and in a stand of trees, providing them some shelter and a less exposed position, as well as wood for a fire. Frost noticed a small stream not far from where they stopped and when one listened hard, it sounded like the proverbial babbling brook, Frost fantasized. Perhaps because the land was comparatively flat and there was virtually nothing of human habitation where they were, the sunset seemed to drag on endlessly into the night, but then suddenly there was darkness and a new set of sensations filled the night. Animal noises, real and some probably imagined, were always just outside the perimeter of the camp. Frost and Joe-Joe decided to light no fire, though it would have been a wise defense perhaps against animals. But it would have been an open invitation too—an invitation to the Communist terrorists from Nugumbwe who had incursed that far into the Congo before, they knew. As Frost and his comrade Joe-Joe sat quietly in their campsite, their only hedge against the darkness a sheltered Coleman lamp, eating their cold meal from the stores prepared for them early that morning by Kingston's mistress, Frost watched the torchlike thing that was a beacon in the darkness perhaps a mile behind them.

A campfire—nothing more than that, but a roaring blaze that would have kept you warm in December in the northwoods, he thought, and either a fire lit by persons who had nothing to fear from the Communist terrorists or by persons so stupid as not to know the terrorists should be feared. Frost couldn't tell and wasn't about to risk his neck to find out.

But then, suddenly, that changed, for above the animal sounds of the night, Frost and Joe-Joe heard the unmistakable spasms of automatic weapons fire coming from the mysterious campsite.

Chapter Five

Frost jumped to his feet, his H-K almost springing into his left hand. "Terrorists?" He asked Joe-Joe superfluously. The black man had already tossed his bush jacket over the Coleman lantern to hide its light and was reaching down to dowse it.

"Fools back there," Joe-Joe said. "Lighting the fire—fools."

"I'm going to take a look, Joe-Joe. Listen for a warning from the perimeter defense wires and keep your gun handy—maybe stay near the Land Rover but not in it." Frost started into the darkness.

Behind him, he heard Joe-Joe saying, "Don't do some foolish thing, Captain."

Frost turned. In the velvety darkness he could no longer even see Joe-Joe. The man was a professional hunter, used to the African night, used to moving soundlessly. And the dark skin of his birth was a decided advantage in that context. Frost said, "Don't you do some foolish thing either, my friend," and he left.

Only a tyro would have called the area Frost traversed a jungle—it was simply a rain forest, despite the fact that it was in near spitting distance of the equator. But because of its comparatively moderate density, even despite the animal sounds and the other night noises and the cushiony layer of decaying plant life on the ground beneath his feet,

Frost still had to move slowly to avoid detection. And, each step he took could have been his last. As his right eye grew more accustomed to the darkness—trees a hundred feet tall created a canopy effect that shut out the moon and stars almost completely—he became more and more aware of the life teeming around him. He could hear the belching thunder of the Rana Goliath, a frog large enough to swallow a field mouse whole. For all his caution though, Frost covered the mile to the campsite and its roaring bonfire quickly, then stayed back, hidden in the shadows.

He crouched in the humus forest floor behind an isolated but dense clump of bushes.

The scene unfolding before him, Frost thought, was almost a classic in the long bloody annals of ineptitude. There was a Land Rover, much like the one he and Joe-Joe had ridden that long day, only with the top down, and he could see three white men and one white woman near it. By the almost daylight brightness of the fire, he could see but one bolt action rifle in the camp.

There were seven other men, unmistakably terrorists, their disgustingly ubiquitous AK-47s in hand for the most part or on the brightly lit ground near them. Some of the terrorists were rifling aluminum or steel-looking cases which under normal circumstances Frost would have thought best used for transporting firearms, but what the Terrs were strewing about the camp were cameras, 35mms, movie cameras, stripping rolls and reels of film and winding them about the Land Rover like pretty ribbons on a Christmas tree. The girl had long blonde hair, and as her wrists were twisted behind her and her hands tied together one of the terrorists grabbed her by the hair, pulled her neck back and laughingly tied the hair itself to her wrists so her head was locked back at a bizarre angle, her neck drawn awkwardly and, Frost guessed, painfully. Another Terr pushed the girl down to her knees with his rifle butt and left her there, her face perpetually tilted upward from the tension of her hair being tied back, her mouth open to scream but all that was audible was a kind of rasping, choking sound.

But there were other screams to be heard—one of the three white men was smashing his head with a rock, evidently trying to kill himself or drive himself insensate. Frost could understand the man's reasoning. His lips had been cut off and the lower portion of his face was a mass of blood. Finally, one of the terrorists took his rifle butt and swatted the lipless man in the back of the head and then the man's screams were suddenly silenced.

The second of the three white men was getting what was a standard terrorist routine, Frost knew. The man had been staked down to the ground by his wrists and ankles and the Terrs were systematically axing away his fingers, then a foot, then his left forearm, seeming to delight in the man's screams and slapping his face to revive him each time he started to pass out. Shock would kill him before loss of blood did, Frost knew.

The third man was faring no better. As Frost assessed the situation, trying to determine how best to intervene if in fact he could, the third man's hands were being lashed tightly behind him, then a long tether line strung from his bound hands and tied to the bumper of the Land Rover. Then the man's feet were staked to a large tree trunk at the perimeter of the camp and he was put up into an awkward sitting position. Frost had to act quickly, he guessed. As one of the terrorists started up the

Rover, Frost stepped from behind the covering brush and opened fire, his H-K on full auto, spitting short, three-round bursts as the gun was designed to do. But as Frost systematically executed the terrorists—starting with the armed men first and working his way towards the ones still going for their guns—he realized, on the edge of his consciousness, that he was acting just a little too late.

Frost tried hard, exposing himself to danger by diverting fire toward the terrorist starting to move the Land Rover, and his shots connected, but even in death the terrorist driver had his victory. As the Terr slumped over the wheel, his foot apparently gave sufficient impulse to the accelerator for the Rover to lurch awkwardly forward.

At the edge of his field of vision, almost in slow motion Frost could see the white man's arms coming up behind his back, then bending at unnatural angles and then ripping from their sockets as the poor devil started a scream that died in his throat. Too late, the Rover smashed into a tree trunk some ten yards from where it had started.

Bullets were whizzing toward Frost's position now. He dropped to one knee and continued firing. There were two of the terrorists left. Frost caught one of them with the last rounds out of the H-K. The second man, rather than coming after Frost, was already beside the girl, the bloody axe used to hack one of the three now dead white men to pieces clenched in his fists, the dark skin of his hands visibly glistening with the blood of his victims in the hell-like firelight.

As the terrorist started his axeswing toward the exposed throat of the blonde-haired girl on her knees before him, an almost blood-curdling scream finally issuing from her, Frost snaked his right hand toward his left shoulder, the empty H-K launching from his right hand now and sailing into his left. His right hand caught at the Pachmayr gripped Browning 9mm and ripped the gun from the Safariland 100 shoulder rig he used, that whole split second like something taking place in slow motion, a poetry of death scene from a Japanese Kabuki play. As his pistol cleared the leather, his mind was computing the surest target area so that even in death the terrorist couldn't complete his lethal axeswing. The distance was perhaps fifteen feet. Frost's pistol was on line, the terrorist's axe halfway to the girl's throat. And Frost did the only thing he could. His first rounds from the Browning impacted into the junction of the Terr's right wrist and forearm, the only possible slim but anatomically sound target that could stop the swing. The rounds slammed home, blood gushing from the Terr's right wrist. Frost was clamping the pistol in both hands now as he kept up sustained firing, the 115-grain JHP 9mms hammering now into the terrorist's head and throat and chest, the swing finally stopped, the terrorist just sinking to the ground in a dead heap.

Frost reached the girl a second later, her breath coming in gasps now. She was choking hysterically, he knew. There wasn't time to untie her, to free her hair so that her neck could be released and she'd stop gagging. Frost whipped the big Gerber MK II from his belt and carefully guided the blade between the small of her back and her hair where it was bound to her wrists and then sliced. She started to heave forward and he caught her in his right arm and held her there, already her breathing starting to even and the coughing subsiding.

After a few seconds, Frost bent the woman forward, used the knife again to cut her wrists free, noticing now he'd lopped away perhaps five inches of her hair a moment earlier.

You'll be all right now,'' Frost said, trying to sound as though he believed that himself. He knew, instead, that the odds were heavy against them. The gunshots might well bring more terrorists at any second. He propped her trembling body against his knee, rammed a fresh magazine into the Browning and left the gun cocked and locked for more instant use—though he disliked the carry system intensely—and holstered it in the Safariland rig under his left arm beneath the olive drab bush jacket. He helped her unsteadily to her feet and left her wobbling there a moment, snatching up his H-K and feeding it another thirty-round magazine.

Frost left the selector on full auto, his right trigger finger just outside the guard. At the back of his mind, he was hoping that Joe-Joe had stayed with their own Land Rover, despite the heavy gunfire and the screaming. Mechanically, Frost checked the bodies of the terrorists killing the engine and lights on the Rover, then came at last to the body of the man who'd been bludgeoned by one of them, the man's lips cut off. To his surprise, Frost discovered the man was still alive.

At the instant that he discovered the man was breathing, Frost wished desperately that he had a silencer. Nothing Frost could do for the man would stop the massive bleeding sufficiently to prevent death from shock, and were Frost somehow able to prevent even that, the rusty fighting knife on the ground a few feet from the man, the obvious tool used in the torture, would have by now started the man on the road toward tetanus and God only knew what other diseases. On closer examination, Frost could see that the back of the man's skull had been caved in by the blow from the terrorist's rifle butt. Frost had seen enough death to know that for this man death was the only, inevitable result of the wounds, but he had no way of knowing if the man, seeming to be semiconscious, was still experiencing pain. And what if the man became clear-headed for a few moments before his death?

Frost knew they couldn't save him and they couldn't bring the man with them to let him die later. What if the man had a sudden moment of clarity before death and found himself deserted, alone? Frost didn't wish that on any man. He glanced over his shoulder, flicked the selector on the H-K to safety and set the rifle down. Frost drew his pistol again from the shoulder rig. The girl wasn't watching. He downed the safety catch and pressed the pistol to the dead man's chest. He would fire once. The concussion from the shot would send pain vibrating up Frost's right wrist and forearm, he knew. Then, Frost noticed the throb of pulse at the man's neck had stopped. As he upped the safety lever again, he checked that the girl's attention was still diverted, then listened for a heartbeat, felt for other vital signs. Had Frost been forced to make the mercy killing, firing into the chest like that, the chest itself would have served as a resonating chamber—a sort of self-silencer.

As he holstered his pistol, then looked up at the darkness surrounding the camp, he stood. Frost shot a last glance to the dead man, thankful shooting him had been unnecessary. Would it have been right, he asked himself? He didn't know, but he knew that to have let the man go on in his pain perhaps, or to awaken alone just prior to death, would have been worse.

Frost reached down to the girl, offering his left

hand. "There's nothing more for you here, not now. Come with me—" and when she looked at him, her eyes glassy in the firelight, her face a mask of confusion, terror and incomprehension, he leaned down to her "—I'll take care of you. You'll be fine, you'll see. Now please—"

As he started to take her from camp, he thought of all the things his professionalism dictated that he do—sabotage the AK-47s he was leaving behind and any other weapons, instead of that perhaps, take them all with him. But there was time nor method for either, though leaving guns behind you for the enemy to use later was amateurish and potentially suicidal. But now, while he prodded the girl as gently as possible to make their way through the rain forest and back, back along the route he had just come, toward Joe-Joe and their means of escape, time was his most important consideration, so important it outweighed anything else. He shifted the packweight on his back when the girl stumbled and they stopped for a minute to rest. And then he got her to her feet and they walked on—she like a Zombie, lifeless, automatonlike, one foot shuffling before the other only by the force of his—Frost's —will.

After more time had passed than Frost cared to think about, they neared his camp. A man with less experience, a man perhaps less self-possessed might have walked right in. Frost instead took the girl with him and circled the camp, as quietly as possible. When he reached the spot on the perimeter where they'd started he sat down on his heels a moment and ran his right hand across his face in a gesture of exhaustion and disgust. Even in the poor light, and though the camp area was just barely visible, one thing had been clear—the terrorists had been there and gone and though he hadn't seen Joe-Joe, Frost sensed somehow their ephemeral friendship had come to an end—a violent one.

Chapter Six

Frost, even in the darkness, could see the crude booby trap device on Joe-Joe's body there in the Land Rover, but though it was crude he knew of no way to disarm the device. Had there been the time to bury Joe-Joe, there would have been no way to retrieve his body for the purpose—without detonating the device. Crude but effective—an appropriate epitaph for any Communist terrorist and the cause of the epitaphs of too many good men, he reflected. The wires to the perimeter defense lines were still up—that meant Joe-Joe had been long-distanced by a sniper probably, then the terrorists had just walked right in, Frost's guide and hunter already dead. And, as Frost and the girl huddled in the shadows near the Rover, Joe-Joe's deathly presence less than a yard from them, Frost realized that the sniper could still be out there.

With everything inside him, Frost wanted to wait out the sniper, to get the man, Joe-Joe's killer, but he knew that was only tempting death for himself and the girl he'd acquired as dependent on him now for her own survival. The longer he waited there Frost knew, the greater the chance of more terrorists arriving and the poorer his odds for escape.

Gesturing to the girl to be perfectly silent, they started out. At the back of his mind Frost was calculating the odds on the sniper nailing them. The weapon would be silenced, probably set with some sort of lock to keep it in a single-shot mode to avoid mechanical noise of the action opening and closing after each shot. The silencer's cone of effectiveness could easily encompass the entire camp area and the only noise perhaps would be the supersonic whistling sound of the bullets as they cracked through the air around them. Specially loaded subsonic rounds, since the silenced rifle's action would no longer be cycled by gas pressure and hence dependent upon a certain level, could be used as well. And then there would be no sound at all. Bitterly, he realized the sniper could in fact be shooting at them now. With the soft ground from the eons of decaying leaf matter and the sparsely placed tree trunks it might even be impossible to detect impact noise. As they moved soundlessly through the campsite toward the trees, a fly zipped past Frost's left ear. Was it a fly he wondered then, or was it a rifle bullet? He tried to shake the thought—the last thing he needed, Frost realized, was fear of something that for now was beyond his control.

As they crossed the perimeter alert wires, Frost realized they were leaving behind all the supplies, the medical kit—everything that was not in his pack or on his belt—and he silently was thankful that he hadn't left the pack behind when he'd left the camp earlier, or else that too would be gone. He had seven loaded magazines left for the H-K assault rifle he carried and perhaps a hundred rounds of additional ammo, enough for a modest stand against small odds. He smiled bitterly there in the darkness, the all but insensate girl beside him who had yet to speak a word—a modest stand against small odds! Frost had come there with one purpose, to get

Chapmann and to take on Chapmann's entire army, if necessary, to do it.

His only chance—and that was where he was headed—was the Land Rover by the girl's camp, if it too by now hadn't been booby-trapped, if the crash against the tree trunk hadn't cracked the radiator or disabled it. And, perhaps there too, he could acquire what was still useable from her supplies.

As they backtracked through the darkness, though, Frost started having second thoughts about the sniper—a leaf next to his head split from the sapling it had been attached to a microsecond earlier. Frost dragged the blonde-haired girl to the ground. There was no sound. Running his hand up along the sapling he thought he felt an impact indentation from ahead of him. Precious little to go on, it was his only possibility. Keeping his voice as low as possible, he rasped in the woman's ear, "I've got to try to get that sniper. I'll come back for you." Even in the almost total darkness, though she said nothing, Frost could faintly see something in her eyes. It was the same look he'd seen in the eyes of men going on suicide missions, animals that were about to be killed to be put out of their misery. "Look," he said, squeezing her hand in his own, "I will be back—that sucker out there isn't going to get me—I'll be back—promise." And Frost left her there, dropping flat and bellying his way as silently as possible at a right angle to the sniper. Moving the girl to a different location would have been pointless and simply given the sniper better opportunity to get them—and more time. The forest loam ground cover was to Frost's advantage now, its softness helping to muffle any telltale noises he made himself. Frost had done duty as a sniper on several

97

occasions and had already formed the opinion that the man he was up against wasn't as good as he should have been. Granted, Frost thought, as he made his way between the massive trees, stopping every few moments to listen more intently for any sounds that seemed out of tune with the environment, that the rain forest darkness was more intense than a sniper might normally expect to encounter. The scope the man used was probably some sort of starlight system, Frost speculated, a vision intensification type device, basically intensifying the available light that was all about you but not sufficiently great for the human eye to use unaided. Hence, if the available diffused light were drastically lower, as it was here in the blackness under the treetop canopy far overhead, the starlight scope would be proportionately less effective—why, Frost thought, the sniper wasn't killing him at this very instant.

Knowing something about the likely characteristics of the weapon the sniper used and knowing a good deal about silencer effectiveness, Frost had a relatively firm idea where the man had to be—a rough square yardage area that Frost would have to penetrate as stealthily as possible. Twenty minutes perhaps had now elapsed and Frost was at last behind the approximate position of the sniper. Now it was a matter of waiting for the man to trigger a shot. Frost got himself into a comfortable position where he could see his wristwatch and then just didn't move. He was gambling—if the sniper had changed position or had him located, he was a goner. Thirty-five more minutes elapsed—insects were becoming a major problem and to his right, Frost thought he made out the shape of a snake coming toward him. He edged his hand down to the big Gerber knife at his belt.

Frost's muscles ached, his joints were stiff, but he didn't yet dare to move. Then he heard it—perhaps nothing more than the primer detonation for it sounded like just a child's cap pistol discharging. There was no time for stealth now. Frost hauled himself to his feet and started running toward the sound—a fool play he thought, but his only chance alone and pressed for time. Frost wanted the sniper to see him and be forced to abandon the rifle momentarily and its hopelessly clumsy scope for such short range and use a pistol or standard assault rifle. As Frost closed the distance to where he'd heard the telltale sound, there was a blast of light and sound—a heavy caliber handgun going off. Frost dropped to his knees and, his H-K on full auto, sprayed the area surrounding the shot. He hauled himself up again and ran toward the target.

The second pistol shot went off almost in his face and he dove to the ground and rolled, firing toward his suspected target. There was a groan. Frost still couldn't see the man. The H-K in an assault position at his hip, Frost moved cautiously forward. He couldn't see the body of the dead terrorist sniper until he tripped over it. The dead man had worn some sort of dark cammie-pattern coverall, his face and hands smudged to kill any glare, despite his black skin. The rifle too was barely visible, camouflaged like the man's clothes. The scope, Frost discovered, had not been as elaborate as he had estimated—just a telescopic sight, wide-angled but not a night vision device. How the hapless sniper had been able to use it all in the darkness was a mystery to Frost.

Frost then perfunctorily checked the body,

verified death, searched the man for any documents and found nothing but a few packs of chewing gun and some other personal items. Frost put the dead man's hat over his face and left him there abandoning the weapon again. Frost walked openly—if the sniper had not been alone something would have happened already. He bypassed the girl and went back to his and Joe-Joe's campsite, took aim with his H.K and fired, triggering the booby trap. The explosion roared into a fireball lighting the night around him for a moment. Another dumb play on his part, Frost thought, but at least it would keep Joe-Joe's body from the insects and birds—any large animal would have triggered the device. Frost felt he'd owed the guy that much out of friendship.

After five minutes or so, Frost found the blonde-haired girl, still huddled by the tree trunk where he had left her more than an hour earlier. As he guided her along the rough track through the rain forest toward the abandoned campsite and her Land Rover, Frost surmised that the girl seemed so much in shock that she likely didn't even have any awareness he'd returned, simply was walking now because something or someone was prodding her. He wondered vaguely if it would be a condition she would come out of naturally, or if the psychological trauma she'd suffered would be something that would require professional help in order to be remedied; if indeed it could be remedied at all.

When they reached her abandoned campsite, the sounds of small animals near the dead bodies unmistakable to him, Frost simply sat her down by a tree trunk and told her he would be in sight. He went to the Land Rover, pushed the body of the dead terrorist from it and found a flashlight on the seat. Using it, he inspected the Rover for damage from the crash against the tree trunk. The front bumper was crushed and the right front fender had taken some of the impact, but the radiator seemed intact and, when Frost tried to crank the car, it started. Both headlights worked, although the right one was hopelessly out of alignment. He left the vehicle running, and moved around the campsite, gathering up some of the weapons and what food and medical supplies there were that were not damaged beyond use. He found one of the camera bags and what looked like some of the girl's clothing too, this latter in a suitcase. These he loaded into the Land Rover as well.

Then Frost fetched the girl, put her aboard in the front passenger seat and took the safety belt and buckled her in. Backing the Rover away from the tree trunk, he wrestled the wheel to straighten the vehicle as he cut it around the trees and bounced the vehicle up toward the road. Once clear of the trees, he killed the headlights. It seemed almost as bright as day back along the dirt road by comparison to the rain forest behind them as he started cutting through the savannah. There would be perhaps fifty miles of road ahead and then the rain forest again as they entered the country of Nugumbwe. Each mile that they drove took them farther from the horror the girl had endured behind them and closer to what other horrors Frost could only guess at, for each mile brought him that much closer to Colonel Marcus Chapmann.

Frost reached across to the girl and tried to hold her hand. Her fingers didn't respond, nor did they recoil—it was as if she were dead but somehow still breathing. Frost took his hand away, a chill in his spine.

Chapter Seven

Sweat was beading on Frost's face as he lay spread-eagled face down under the blazing early morning sunlight—and Frost knew the heat would get far worse. The girl, still unbroken in her silence, lay beside him—she followed him like a puppy and seemed to be, if anything, more withdrawn than on the night of the slayings two days ago. Before them lay the last major village between them and the Nugumbwean capitol of Buwandi, and the only road went right through it. To circle round it would have taken another day or more, since the ground was flat and Chapmann's men were everywhere in the countryside nearby. Frost was almost tempted to take the girl back to where they had hidden the Land Rover, but she might somehow give them away if he did. But the scene unfolding below couldn't be too good for her mental state, he thought.

There was a slaughter going on, a summary execution of the right wing army revolutionaries who had been the village defenders—and Chapmann's men were the slaughterers.

When they'd crossed the border perhaps thirty-six hours earlier, the going had been slow. Terrs were likely everywhere, Frost had thought, and then there were Chapmann's troops to worry about and just because Frost's own sympathies lay with the right wing army didn't mean there would be any hesitation on their part to kill him. Frost and the girl had traveled slowly, using the headlights only when absolutely necessary, for the most time squinting into the darkness with but the aid of the parking lights.

Around four-thirty in the morning, just as they had been leaving the rain forest and heading toward the road again, they had flatted one of the tires and Frost had changed it—meaning too that the next flat would leave the vehicle undrivable.

By six A.M., they had been nearly out of gas, but there was a village up ahead—he and Joe-Joe, when discussing the journey, had determined to stop there since it was reported to have stores of gasoline which Chapmann's Army used. The question which he and Joe-Joe hadn't quite settled, which now confronted Frost and the girl, was just how to go about stealing some of the gasoline without getting caught or killed.

They'd left the Land Rover hidden then too and come on foot. It was an ordinary enough village, thatched roof huts, some feeble masonry structures, but at one side of the village a barbed wire enclosure wound around several prefabricated metal buildings. There were signs indicating that the buildings' contents were flammable and Frost assumed that the gasoline was stored there in cans and drums. He wanted to steal sufficient gasoline to fill the Rover's tank and gasoline enough for their emergency cans, which were already depleted.

As Frost and the girl watched the fenced compound, he intently, the girl in her seeming trance, he had almost decided that the job couldn't be done, at least not in daylight. But watching the compound, he noticed a Land Rover, almost identical to their own but with Nugumbwean government markings and serialization, come down the road, stop before the gate, honk three times and be admitted, after showing some identification papers that were looked at very quickly if at all—at least as far as Frost could detect. The lines in Frost's face furrowed into a smile. They watched for twenty minutes as three more Land Rovers came and went, apparently taking their fill of the gasoline.

Under his breath, Frost said, "I wonder if they give trading stamps?" The girl registered nothing. Frost hated it when his attempts at humor didn't even elicit a negative response. Shrugging, he grabbed the girl by the hand and they crept off and back toward their Rover. Only they didn't stop there. Cutting through some scrub brush they half ran, half fell down the sloping hillside toward the dirt road below them. The Bushnell armored binoculars he'd taken with him for observation of the village showed a lone Rover speeding toward them down the dirt road from the village, the driver a white man dressed in camie fatigues, as had been the other of Chapmann's men who had gone into the fenced-in area for gasoline.

Wishing again that he had a silencer, Frost told the girl to stay put, ran back up to their Land Rover and returned in a moment with two cans of beer. He dropped to his haunches, pulled the pop-top tabs, emptied the cans and used the can opener on his folding knife to broaden the holes to approximate the muzzle opening on the H-K, sliding the first can down over the assault rifle's flash hider. The Frost lined up the second can's opening with the muzzle and using the wide first aid adhesive tape from his pack fixed the cans together on line. Frost slung the "silenced" H-K over his right shoulder and took the girl's hand and led her down into the road.

Checking again with the binoculars, he could see the targeted Rover just coming down along the bend of the road and about to turn toward them, still some two hundred yards distant. Frost took the girl into the middle of the road and turned her around—she was still in the trance-like state. He shrugged his shoulders and as gently as possible clipped his left fist across her chin, caught her unconscious form in his arms and posed her in the middle of the road—artistically he thought—so the Land Rover's driver would either have to stop to avoid hitting her or run right over her. And Frost hoped it wouldn't be the latter.

He ran back then to the side of the road and in the shelter of some brush unlimbered the H-K with its homemade beer can suppressor—good only for one shot he knew. He moved the selector switch off safe and to semiauto, fixed the .308 comfortably to his shoulder and waited.

Already, Frost could see the outline of the Chapmann Land Rover and the dust cloud behind it. As the Rover came down the road, its fuel tanks virtually gushing over and three jerri-cans mounted in the rear seat, the driver evidently saw the girl. She was blonde, she was pretty—even at a distance—and he should have stopped.

"Damn!" Frost rasped aloud. "That twirp isn't gonna stop!" Instead of slowing, the driver just began to speed up, perhaps expecting a terrorist or rebel army trap. Frost couldn't afford a miss. He stood to his full height, reshouldered his weapon and fired. He'd purposely gotten high enough to shoot down so his slug wouldn't have to penetrate windshield glass—that would have resulted in a miss.

As Frost heard the muffled shot of his H-K, the homemade silencer falling to pieces, its work done, the driver grabbed his face with both hands and slumped back in his seat, the Rover swerving and going over a small embankment, missing the girl but not coming to a stop. "Damn!" Frost said again, then slinging the H-K he took off at a run in an attempt to catch up with the now driverless Rover. The vehicle, on the far side of the road from him now, was moving in comparatively slow, concentric circles, but ever widening ones. The dead driver's foot must have somehow been wedged against the accelerator pedal, Frost guessed. It took about a good three or four minutes of running himself breathless and feeling like an idiot, but he was finally able to get alongside the Rover and heave himself aboard, pushing the dead man out from behind the wheel and screeching the Rover to a halt.

Frost sat there a moment and caught his breath, then lit a cigarette as he climbed down from the vehicle to walk back and check the dead man's pockets, finding little but identity papers which he carefully saved. He found a wallet too, inside it a few pieces of folded money and a picture. The inscription on the photo read, "To snookums, from Poopoo." Frost turned it over and studied the woman's picture. He had never been one to make light of the dead, and certainly a man's taste in women was something highly personal. But, Frost felt, the girl in the photo was possibly the ugliest woman he could ever recall having seen. Then he looked down at the dead Chapmann merc at his feet, saying, "Snookums?" Frost dragged on his cigarette, replaced the photo in the wallet and put the wallet beside the dead man. "Snookums?" Frost shook his head, threw the dead man's pistol—a junky one—into the brush and climbed back into the liberated Land Rover. He stopped the vehicle in the road, retrieved the girl, who was just starting to come around, and helped her shakily into the front passenger seat. Frost couldn't afford to be caught with one of Chapmann's vehicles, so he drove it up the hillside, parked it beside their own vehicle and siphoned the gas between the tanks. It took longer than he liked, but there was nothing else to do. Then, the filled jerri-cans transferred, Frost turned the stolen Rover around, aimed it toward the edge of the hill and stopped it just before the slope. Getting out, he released the emergency brake and popped the clutch and the Rover careened down into the road.

There was no explosion—just a small fire since there was almost no gas in the thing. Frost rounded up the girl again and they hit the road.

They drove almost continuously throughout the balance of that day, making camp for the night in the best spot he could find, the ruins of a Christian mission. The thought crossed his mind that perhaps he could get the girl to cook for him at least, but one look at her glassy eyes convinced him that was impossible. So, he sat her down and used the small Coleman stove to heat some cans of food. The girl hadn't eaten since he'd found her and made no sign of any interest in food when he offered it to her, so he moved over beside her and between mouthfuls for himself spoon-fed some of the canned stew to her, the whole thing reminding him sadly of a family he'd known a few years earlier who'd had an autistic child. It was the same way with this girl. Frost was beginning to wonder if he'd done her that big of a favor by saving her life.

The sun was setting and darkness was beginning

to engulf the campsite. He wished for a fire but knew he couldn't risk one. He was still deep in enemy territory and compounding the normal risk was the fact that there were for all intents and purposes still three enemies.

Frost and the girl sat side-by-side. It dawned on him suddenly that he didn't even know her name. As the hours ticked by and he downed more coffee, watching the girl just staring off into the darkness, he tried formulating a plan of action to undertake once he actually reached the capitol of Buwandi. That should be by the next evening or the following morning, he gauged, if his luck held and he didn't run out of gas again.

He was almost surprised, too, that some of Chapmann's people hadn't picked up their trail after he had iced one of Chapmann's officers to steal his gas that morning. Frost assumed that the only way to go once he was in Buwandi would be to make contact with the CIA man, Curtis, seeing if he and Curtis could pool resources and that could somehow help him to get Chapmann where he wanted him.

Frost yawned, checking the luminous face of the Omega on his wrist. His hand, as he'd moved his left cuff to read the watch, had brushed against the girl's left breast as they sat there beside one another. He turned and looked at her—it was as if he weren't there.

Suddenly—he really didn't know why—Frost took the girl's face in his hands and raised her lips to his. As he bent down to kiss her, he stopped. "Hell," he said to himself, because by now he was convinced the girl couldn't hear him. He let her go, turned around and climbed into his sleeping bag, setting the Browning pistol under the bunched up jacket he used as a pillow. After several minutes he rolled over. The girl was still just sitting there. He sat up, helped her to lie down and then lay back again beside her. Frost was tired, slightly bored and terribly disgusted—and he wasn't able to fall asleep for at least another hour.

In the morning, the girl was just the same and he had no way of knowing if she had even slept at all or just lain staring all night into the darkness. He fixed them some breakfast and as he ate the beans and chewed at a chunk of bread, his beard scratching, his body feeling as though it had been two weeks instead of two days between showers, once again he spoon-fed her. As soon as it was fully light, they took the Rover down from the wooded area and back onto the road.

Twice the previous day he'd seen dust rising from columns of Chapmann's men and twice pulled off the road ahead of their seeing him, waited them out, then driven on. There had been no observation planes either—meaning Chapmann was on a low budget, getting careless, or there was something big afoot in another part of the small country. The latter idea was the one Frost most favored, especially since both troop columns had been coming from behind him and heading toward Buwandi or at least in that direction.

And, by the time they'd reached that knoll where they now lay watching the executions, the sun even at nine-thirty in the morning hot enough to fry eggs, Frost knew where the two troop columns had gone. He realized that within hours of he and the girl arriving there, there had been a major battle, perhaps several hundred people killed—not only combatants, but women and children as well.

And still Frost and the girl were trapped, unable to go either through the village or around it. So they waited. By ten-thirty or so, more of Chapmann's forces had entered the village, then joining with the bulk of Chapmann's forces already there, moved out in a direction taking them somewhere south of the capitol city of Buwandi. A dozen of Chapmann's mercenaries were left behind, though, as a holding force perhaps, along with two dozen black African troops, these among the loyalist forces.

By noon, most of the mercenaries had drawn off among themselves and most of the native troops were rounding up the women and children still left in the village and assembling them in the village square.

Frost, hidden on the knoll beside the perennially silent girl, said, "Hey," then edging closer, "come on, kid—you're not gonna want to watch this."

It was the first time he'd had a reaction out of her. She looked at him, still saying nothing, and shook his hand away from her arm. Perhaps, he thought, he'd been thinking more of himself than the girl, because he knew what was about to happen and had no desire to see it. But he turned back to face the developing scene anyway.

The native troops were going through the two dozen or so women, pushing the older ones out of the line and herding the younger ones together. Most of the women were in one state or another of semiundress, some still holding babies in their arms, some nursing. Whatever doubts Frost might have had as to what was going to happen, this separating of the women perfectly eradicated. There would be a communal group rape scene while the drunkenness continued, then afterward someone would get too drunk or one of the braver women would try to stab or shoot one of the native troops, but however it came about, the inevitable would happen—more slaughter. Frost realized, on quite a practical level, that Chapmann could not leave witnesses around to testify to the executions of the rebel army troops that had already taken place. And, though Chapmann himself wasn't even there, the operation had that certain Chapmann flair all over it.

And then the raping began. One of the soldiers, an officer apparently, grabbed one of the youngest-seeming women and tore her dress away, leaving her standing there naked in the square. Then the officer started hitting her, slapping her face and her breasts, then after a little of that he took the woman by the wrist and dragged her half walking, half stumbling across the square and into one of the few still standing huts. After a moment, there was a scream. And as the other women were one by one attacked, some of the native troops just bringing the women down into the dirt in the middle of the square and jumping on them, a few fights starting because there were more troopers than pretty women. Frost turned to get the girl beside him away. But she was no longer beside him, already walking purposefully back toward where they'd concealed the Land Rover. Frost looked around him quickly to determine if she could have been seen, but he didn't think so. Keeping to a crouch for the first few yards until he was away from the brow of the hill, he ran after her. By the time he reached her, one of the liberated Chi-Com AK-47s the terrorists had used against her companions was locked in her hands.

He stood in front of her, blocking her way. She still said nothing, but her eyes were somehow different. For the first time, more animated now than since he'd met her, he noticed that she was a truly beautiful girl, despite the stringiness now of her hair, the smudge marks on her face and arms, the tattered jeans and blouse.

"What the hell do you think you're doing?" he snapped.

She looked at him, said nothing, then in an instant he was down on his knees at her feet and she was walking past him.

"You—" he started, but the pain was too intense and his breath was coming in short gasps—she'd snapped the butt of the AK-47 hard into his crotch and the pain was still so bad he couldn't stand. He wanted to shout at her, but that wouldn't do any good, he reasoned—maybe she still couldn't even hear him. But he knew what she was planning to do.

Still unable to straighten up fully, he got to his feet, snatched up his rifle and loped after her in a kind of awkward crouch, dropping to his knees again by the brow of the hill. She was already half down the hillside, and still no one had noticed her. He doubted she even knew enough to take the assault rifle off safe before she tried firing it.

At the midway point, the girl stopped. Frost wanted to shout for her to come back, but then he looked beyond her. The women holding the babies were now the targets of the native troops and their orgy of rape—babies were being ripped from their arms and hurtled mindlessly to the ground as their mothers were systematically assaulted. Suddenly, Frost heard the blond-haired girl screaming, the first sound he'd heard from her since the moment he'd saved her.

"You goddamned bloody bastards," she shouted. Perhaps because of a too genteel upbringing, he thought later looking back on it, she apparently had nothing else to say, but just kept screaming the same thing at the top of her lungs, the AK-47 in her hands starting to fire.

Frost had two choices, one sensible, one stupid—he decided on the stupid one of helping her rather than the sensible one of getting in the Land Rover and driving like hell in the opposite direction.

He could stand erect now if he didn't breath too hard, and running as best he could he reached the Land Rover in less than thirty seconds, climbed painfully aboard and gunned the engine to life, then took off toward the brow of the hill and down, firing his H-K ahead of him around the side of the windscreen, shouting at the top of his lungs, trying to make the soldiers down in the village think they were under attack by more than just two fools.

Thirty-six men, he thought. And even though virtually all of them were half inside a bottle, that didn't mean there wasn't any fight left in them. There was no hope of defeating such a superior force, Frost assessed, but he could achieve the same effect—get their attention long enough for the surviving women and children to escape them—by getting them to come after him.

Frost floored the Rover down the hill, the girl already to the hill's base, and gunfire from scattered mercenaries and fewer still of the native African troops starting to spray toward her. As he reached where the girl was standing and firing, Frost skidded the Rover to a halt, shouted to the girl to hop aboard and opened fire with his H-K to cover ther. The girl hesitated and stood her ground. Frost shouted, "Come on, dammit—if you really want to do something for those women and kids, come here—otherwise just stand there and commit suicide and don't help anyone!"

"Yes," she said, quietly, so quietly he could barely hear her, the din of the gunfire intense now. And then she started running toward him in the Land Rover. And as she reached it he cut out the emergency brake and let out the clutch and skipped first gear entirely as the Rover gradually picked up speed then got a sudden burst of momentum when he downshifted for the RPMs and then upshifted again as he hit the flat straightaway of the village square.

Already most of the Chapmann forces were on their feet, guns in hand and firing at them. The girl beside him was firing back from the Rover's passenger seat, then stood up and fired over the front windshield. Frost, his H-K empty now, unlimbered the Browining into his left hand and fired haphazardly along the side of the windscreen.

There was no telling how many of the enemy forces Frost and the girl accounted for as they raced through the village square, but bodies fell and some guns stilled and behind them, as they cleared the square and headed out of the village, already two Land Rovers full of Chapmann's men were hot on their tracks. Frost could see the women with their children running, walking, in some cases one women almost carrying another, escaping from the village and the confusion.

As Frost pushed the Land Rover to its limits racing along the road leading out of the village, he spotted a dust cloud in the distance in front of them. "Hang on," he shouted to the girl, then Frost wrenched the Rover's steering wheel and headed the vehicle off the road and across a broad expanse of high grass to their left. The two Chapmann vehicles from the village still followed them and, after another minute, the cause of the dust cloud Frost and the girl had seen became visible—a U.S. M48 four-man medium tank. The girl beside him whispered, just audibly over the wind, the gunfire and the engine noises, "My God!"

Frost had one option left and no choice but to take it. "When I say so," he rasped, "get ready to grab the wheel. I'm going to jump clear of this thing and try and get aboard that tank, then I can turn the gun around and mop up these men chasing us."

Frost didn't wait for an answer. As they humped over a small rise and down again, Frost shouted, "Now!" then sprang clear of the Rover, his H-K in his right hand. He hit the ground hard and rolled, pulled himself up into a crouch and dove into the high grass. From his vantage point, Frost could already see the girl sliding into the driver's seat and getting the Rover under control. And, not twenty-five yards in the opposite direction behind her and coming up fast was the 1950's vintage tank.

Frost rammed a fresh thirty round magazine into his H-K, then reloaded his Browning pistol as well. As the tank followed after the Land Rover, in the wake of the Rovers carrying Chapmann's mercs and the native African troops, Frost got to his feet and ran up alongside the tank and dropped behind it, then pulled himself aboard, the turret rotated away from him. The H-K slung over his shoulder, the pistol rammed into his trouser band, Frost clambered precariously over the top of the metal monster and toward the hatch. It was bolted shut; he tried opening it from the inside. For an instant, Frost wished it had been like it always was in the movies—the tank commander standing up half out of the hatch. Then, just simply blow the guy away and drop a grenade inside—but a dummy grenade—and all the guys inside would come piling out in a panic and the good guy would jump into the tank and take control. Someday, Frost promised himself, he'd write his own war movie. This tank was buttoned tighter than a drum and he didn't have any inert grenades with him—darn, Frost thought.

But as the M48 tank started closing the gap on the Land Rovers—over this kind of terrain it could actually move faster and maneuver better—the tank commander did the accommodating thing. Frost thought that his faith in Hollywood movies was almost restored. The hatch opened and the commander or somebody stuck his head up.

Frost, concealed on the man's flank behind the turret, pulled himself up to his knees and reached his left hand out, grabbed the tank commander by the throat and shoved his Browning in the guy's face and pulled the trigger. As the tank commander's body collapsed, back into the bowels of the tank, Frost jumped in after him feet first. What happened inside the tank was incredibly fast and, even to Frost, incredibly brutal. There were three men, all working various controls, none with individual weapons to hand.

At point-blank range, using two-round bursts, Frost simply shot each of the three men in the head, without their having even the slightest chance to resist.

Stepping over two of the bodies, then a third, he pushed the driver out of the way and got behind the controls of the 810 horsepower air-cooled engine himself. Grinding the vehicle to a halt, Frost went aft and locked the hatch, buttoning up against anyone doing the same war movie number he had done.

Then Frost got the big tank moving again, his plan a simple one—he would position the vehicle to interpose himself between the girl and the Chapmann troops. It took less than three minutes to get up beside the Land Rovers carrying Chapmann's men, and in another two minutes he was well past them and grinding the tank to a halt again. He left the controls and moved to the big 90mm gun. After a few seconds of puzzlement, he fumbled one of the huge shells into the breech, closed the breech and pressed the firing mechanism, the gun roughly sighted for the first of the two enemy Rovers. The target vehicle disappeared in a ball of fire. Frost, smiling, said to himself, "Pretty damned good!" Then chuckling as he sidestepped the spent shell casing, Frost rammed a second shell home. Again he lined up the sights, leading the second Land Rover a bit since it was already driving in the opposite direction and trying to get away. "Eat lead, suckers!" he rasped and pressed the firing mechanism. The second Rover, like the first, went up in a gush of flame, this time pieces of the vehicle sailing high into the air from the force of the explosion.

Frost climbed out of the gunner's slot and went back and unbuttoned the hatch. The girl had stopped her Land Rover and was looking in his direction. He waved toward her and after a second, while recognition apparently dawned on her, she started driving toward him. The Land Rover stopped two or three yards from the tank. Frost, lighting a cigarette with his battered Zippo, said, "Pretty fair shootin', huh?"

The girl said nothing for a moment, then standing up and leaning across the Rover's windshield, said, "I don't even know your name for sure—are you Hank Frost?"

"Uh-huh—that's me," Frost said through a cloud of cigarette smoke. "And who might you be, since we're exchanging confidences here?"

"I'm Bess Stallman; I'm a reporter with the INB Telecommunications service—you saved my life, didn't you?"

"Yeah," Frost said, then smiling, "But shucks ma'am, twern't nothin'," and as he said it for the first time since he'd seen the girl she actually smiled. Admittedly, he felt, he didn't have her rolling over in uncontrollable fits of laughter, but at least she had smiled.

"Why do I have a haircut, Mr. Frost?"

"Long story, honey—tell you later. How come you know my name, if you can't remember anything else—in fact I don't think I ever mentioned it to you?"

"I was following you, Captain, wanted a story on mercenaries. That is what I should call you?" The girl seemed totally different, bright, aggressive—and Frost liked her.

"Yeah, that's what they call me," Frost said. "Mercenary. I guess it's as good a term as any—I looked ii up once in a thesaurus. You could call me a mermadon, which means about the same thing, but then nobody'd have a snowball's idea in hell what you were talkin' about. Hey," Frost said, snapping his cigarette away, "what do you say we continue this conversation a little later? Right now, why don't we take this little machine here and give it back to the nice people who own it—at least a few pieces of it? I think that some of Chapmann's men are still back in the village."

"Just a minute," she said. "Colonel Marcus Chapmann's men did that back there, executed those soldiers, raped those women, tried to kill us?"

"Yep," Frost said. "Busy little suckers, aren't they?"

"But that can't be," she said, incredulously.

"You're a mercenary. I thought you were going to join Chapmann—you worked for him before, I know that."

"Yeah," Frost said. "You're right there, all right, and Chapmann is why I'm here."

"But if you're not going to join him—"

"Hell, lady," Frost said, lighting another cigarette. "I'm here to kill the bastard."

Frost got the girl to help him clear the tank of the dead crewmen, then had her follow in their Land Rover a good distance behind while he rolled the tank back to the village. Apparently thinking the tank was still in friendly hands, Chapmann's remaining forces, about a dozen men, assembled in the village square right in front of it when he stopped.

Frost had salvaged one of the cammie fatigue uniforms used by Chapmann's people and one of the black berets. Wearing the Chapmann uniform blouse, Frost unbuttoned the tank and stuck his black-bereted head out, the twelve men standing neatly arranged in front of him. In his right hand, just inside the turret and out of sight, was a .45 caliber greasegun he'd found in the tank.

"Who's in charge?" Frost said. He wanted to get all the Chapmann men at once and couldn't risk just using the tank to destroy the village in the event that any women or children were still there and had been unable to escape.

A tall man, blond-haired man, his beret in his right hand, walked from one of the far huts. He was obviously the man in charge—there were captain's bars on his fatigue blouse. Frost repeated his question. "Who's in charge here?"

"I am. Did you get the man and the woman?"

"Taken care of, Captain," Frost snapped back.

"What's the problem, what about those explosions?"

"Oh, the explosions," Frost said. "Well, you see—Oh, you are the man in charge of all the troops who were here?"

"Yes, what do you mean 'were here'—hey, that eye patch."

"Yeah," Frost rasped, bringing the greasegun out and opening up with it, his first three-round burst knocking the captain—the man in charge of the mass murder and the rapes—flat down dead. Then Frost sprayed into the men nearer to him. It was totally unexpected and most of the men were unarmed. Frost gunned them all down without a shot being returned.

He reloaded the greasegun, then stood there, still in the hatch, looking for any telltale signs of life. A moment later, the girl pulled up in the Land Rover, got out and walked among the dead bodies. After a long silence she looked up at him. "You just killed thirteen men, Frost."

"No," Frost said, lighting a cigarette. "I just avenged that execution scene earlier and all those women who were brutalized. And I got myself thirteen bodies closer to Marcus Chapmann, lady—that's all."

Chapter Eight

"You were very gentle to me, that's all I can remember," the blonde-haired girl named Bess Stallman said.

They sat close together in the darkness still some twenty-five miles outside the Nugumbwean capitol city, in a campsite in a cave behind a waterfall. It was damp and cold, but the water cascade over most of the opening provided sufficient cover that Frost risked a medium-sized fire. They'd talked about the violent events several nights back, and the deaths of her friends, though Frost had spared her some of the more graphic details. She'd said she didn't know what had happened to her, but the intervening time from the beginning of the terrorist attack until she'd suddenly found herself running down a road screaming obscenities and holding a rifle in her hands had been a near-total blank. All she could even faintly recall was Frost's presence and his being "gentle to me."

"Why were you guys following me, then?" Frost asked, lighting a cigarette, offering one to her—which she refused—and stripping away his pistol belt with the canteen and the big Gerber knife strung from it.

"You are well known in your trade, so when we were here for a story on the Nugumbwean Civil War, already knew Colonel Chapmann, the famous

121

mercenary leader, was involved in it, and saw you, we decided the best thing for us was to tail you.''

"Haven't you guys ever heard the old saying, "Better safe than sorry?" Frost asked.

"You mean the big fire—we didn't know."

"I mean the fire, just one gun between the four of you—"

"That was mine," she said, cutting him off. "The cameraman, the soundman, my producer—none of them liked guns. My father used to hunt a lot when I was a kid and I got used to having a gun around when I was out in the woods. So, I figured it would be smart to bring one here—but it didn't do us any good, though," she concluded, her voice trailing off with a note Frost felt sounded like bitterness.

"Well, no offense, but even though your heart was in the right place, your brains weren't. Most of the legitimate hunters won't even go near any of the terrorist areas. I think most of the missionaries have guns around. Back in Rhodesia, a woman couldn't even drive to town for groceries without a shotgun or an FN-FAL. I used to see rifles in guy's bags on the golf course. Why no guide?"

"Well," she said, "we figured that following you we wouldn't need one and we didn't know who we could trust. I guess it never occurred to us we'd get in trouble, or that we'd lose you. God, Frost, I feel bad enough—"

And she got up and walked toward the mouth of the cave and stood there behind the wall of the waterfall just staring, her back toward him.

"Dames," Frost said under his breath, shaking his head. He hauled himself to his feet and snapped the cigarette butt from his fingers into the fire. "Can you cook?" he shouted over to her, "Or are you too liberated for that?"

She turned and faced him, hands on her hips. "First question 'yes' and second question 'no.' What've you got that's cookable?"

Frost pointed her in the direction of his pack and a small cardboard box taken from the Rover after he'd stashed it a half mile away out of sight and camouflaged. It was risky leaving the vehicle out of their control overnight, but they'd needed a campsite and if worst came to worst and the Rover were stolen, they were close enough to the capitol to steal transportation that could get them there.

While the girl busied herself with making them dinner, Frost went over to his pack and fished out a map of Buwandi, then sat by the light of the campfire smoking his way into a fresh pack of Camels while he mentally took apart the capitol city map and tried to fix the layout in his mind for future reference. He lost track of time, then heard Bess calling to him, "Okay, Frost—chow down before I throw the crap out."

As Frost walked over toward the fire and sat down, he said to the girl, "You know, one of the things I've come to love about you in these few hours we've spent together—is that you're such a perfect lady, so genteel."

She handed him a plate and he looked at the contents, then made a show of grimacing and turning his face away.

"The hell with you, Frost," she said, then sat down and started eating. "This isn't bad," she said through a mouthful of the unidentifiable mixture of beans and meat.

Frost took a bite. "Oh, hell no—most delicious thing I ever ate in this cave," he said.

"You ever been in this cave before?" she asked.

"You wouldn't want me to tell ya'," Frost

answered, then returned to his food.

"Why'd I get the haircut, Frost—those guys try scalping me or something?"

"Close," he said, then told her about the impromptu haircut to keep her from choking to death.

She nodded, grunted a "thanks" when he was through, then clearing her throat and washing down the last of her food with some coffee—Frost hadn't screwed up the nerve to try it yet—said, "You know, for a rough, tough guy with one eye—you gotta tell me about that in a minute—you're pretty decent, even though you do kill people like you expected to run out of corpses or somethin' and had to fill a quota. You didn't do anything to me, did you, I mean while I was like that? Did you?"

"What is that, the world's most popular female question?" he stormed. His thoughts flashed back to Anita and her question that first morning on the boat, what seemed like light years ago. "Of course I didn't—but I've got no objections now."

"Yeah, I sort of figured you wouldn't, Frost. But one thing first. How'd you get that eyepatch? I know it's none of my business, but I figured I'd ask anyway."

The lines in Frost's face creased into a smile. "No big deal, really," he said. "I don't usually talk about it," he went on, "but if you promise to keep it confidential . . . Kind of silly, really. You see, when I was a kid, I got this part-time job once, working in a Chinese restaurant—you know, just helping out, moving boxes of Wonton soup mix, counting the fortune cookies at the end of the evening, stuff like that. Well, as luck would have it, I got in early this one night and old Foo Young, the guy who ran the place, asked me to bring a fresh pair of chopsticks to table fifteen.

Guy there'd dropped his. So—to make a long story short—I took the chopsticks in my left hand and started to walk over to the table. For some reason—I'll always puzzle over it—I was carrying them kind of close to my face. I'd always heard Mrs. Foo Young telling her kids, 'Don't run with chopsticks in your hands,' but you know, you don't heed advice like that until it's too late. But anyway, the guy at table fifteen had a big egg noodle hanging out of his lips and signaled for me to run over there with the chopsticks. Well, you can probably guess the rest," Frost said, looking down into his hands. Then, his voice cracking a bit, Frost went on. "I slipped on a litchi nut someone had dropped, fell forward—I just don't want to talk about it anymore . . ." At that Frost stood up and walked away from the fire, lit a cigarette with all the dramatic flare he could muster and waited.

"Oh, hell Frost—make love to me," he heard Bess say, and he turned around and as he walked over to her and helped her to her feet he held her there in his arms and heard her laughing . . .

Frost found Bess to be a great deal of bravado and smart-talk on the outside, but making love to her showed him a different side. She was very tender, more concerned for what he wanted than any woman he'd had in a long time, and responsive too. They lay together near enough to the flickering fire for added warmth, naked inside Frost's zipped open sleeping bag, a couple of blankets over them. Holding her against him, he could feel the heat radiating from her breasts against his chest. He held her neck in the crook of his left elbow, his lips touching her throat, her face, her eyes—then kissing her. He could feel her left hand gently prodding at his testicles. Once, she pulled hard on the hair there and he pushed her hand away and slapped her rear end none too gently. "You're a kind of guy I never met before, Frost," she whispered in his ear as he bent to kiss her neck.

"Is that good or bad?" he asked, his lips to her ear.

And as he kissed her and lifted his face away, she answered, her eyes closed, her arms tight around him. "That's good, Frost—very good." He arched her back and pressed her abdomen up against him, felt her hands gently rubbing at his crotch.

"You'd make a lousy explorer," he whispered, saying. "Here," then brushing her hands away a moment and guiding his penis inside her. The tips of his fingers felt the moisture at the furry triangle there, the warm wetness. And, for a while, he kept his hand there, massaging her gently. Then he brought his hand away, tracing an imaginary line across her abdomen with his fingertips, stopping at her left breast and holding her. She opened her eyes a moment and looked at his hands on her breasts. "You know, your fingernails are dirty, Frost."

He kissed her moist, pale lips, then looked down at her, saying, "You always say romantic stuff like that?"

"No," she gasped, her body moving under him, trembling slightly. "I just . . . never . . . had a man . . . make, make love to me before when he hadn't washed his hands first."

"Can you learn to live with it?" he whispered in her ear. She was shuddering now, and he was starting to as well.

"I already have learned to live with it," she moaned, her lips to his ear, her arms clamped tightly around his neck, her body arched up against his like a happy cat ready to purr. Her breathing beside his ear was faster. He grabbed her hair at the nape of the neck, pulled her mouth up to him and kissed her savagely. Frost felt her erratic shuddering at his groin growing in intensity, felt her pelvis pushing up hard against him. He moved his right hand down to her rear end and pushed her crotch up harder against him and felt her fingers stiffen against his back, felt her nails dig into him, her body twisting. Her breath let out in a long gasp and then her trembling body collapsed into his arms.

"I like dirty hands," she whispered, and ever so gently she bit his ear . . .

"You know," she said, bending over the morning fire to get the coffee, "there's one big problem with this romantic stuff out here in the boonies." She was just wearing a shirt—one of his—over a pair of her panties.

"And what's the problem?" Frost said, smiling as he watched her nicely rounded rear end.

"Well, though my finer sensibilities prohibit me from being specific, fish and company aren't the only things that stink with the passage of time," and she turned her face away in mock bashfulness.

"The shower awaits," he said, gesturing toward the waterfall in front of the cave.

"We got the time—it's safe?" she said, her voice undisguised in its eagerness.

"Yeah," Frost said, "and as a matter of fact, once you clean up, keep an eye peeled and I'll do the same. Here," and he fished a bar of soap out of his pack and tossed it to her.

After they'd both showered, she borrowed the scissors he used to trim his mustache whenever he remembered and while he shaved—he felt foolish, why shave?—she trimmed her hair to even it out in back. "How do you like my hair bobbed?" she asked.

"Terrific, kid," Frost grunted, then went back to his shaving. They finished the coffee and packed things away. It was nearly six A.M. and past the time Frost had wanted to get started. Picking their way carefully along the wet rocks at the edge of the waterfall, both Frost and Bess left the cave behind them with a little feeling of sadness. Frost guided them back to the vicinity of where he had cached the Rover overnight, carefully approached the spot checking his traps for any signs of tampering, scouting the area for any signs of enemy activity. Once he felt certain he was unobserved, he checked the Land Rover itself for any signs of booby traps, then cranked the engine—he was almost out of gas again—and drove the short distance to where he'd left Bess.

Once she was safely aboard, Frost kept off the main road as much as possible and by not long after sunrise, they were well within five miles of the city. Entering the city itself promised to be more challenging than Frost would have liked. As the capitol, under indirect siege by the Communist inspired terrorists and the right wing coalition based upon the rebel army, it was the most closely guarded objective in Chapmann's responsibility—it was the seat of power, the office of the dictator and most importantly to Chapmann, Frost felt, where the official checkbook was kept. But yet, Buwandi was a market town, like most capitols having become prominent because of the trade there and the growth of government around the trade to administer it—and tax it.

And that would also make it Chapmann's biggest headache—there were market baskets, carts, trucks, everything conceivable relevant to trade to be checked at the city's multiple gates. The old city, in reality, was all that was still walled with real rock or masonry—but the modern city was just as walled as its original counterpart, now the kernel of the urban area, for as Frost and the girl approached the rise still more than a mile distant from the city and alternated on Frost's armored binoculars observing it, its most obvious feature was a high barbed wire fence surrounding the entire town. There were four guard gates he could make out at the distance and sentry towers interspersed at intervals roughly two city blocks apart. Not all of the towers were occupied, as far as Frost could ascertain, but some of them appeared to be. Apparently, Chapmann's forces were not on alert. Thank God for small favors, Frost thought.

"Well, how do we get in, hotshot?" There was a faint smile starting at the corners of her eyes, and for the first time Frost took a good look at her—he'd seen her almost constantly now for almost four days, but never really stopped to actually look at her. Her eyes were brown, her face almost the sunken-cheeked model look, but the cheekbones were a little too prominent for that. Her straw-colored hair—more than just blonde in the sun—not only looked appealing, but started him thinking.

"Well, how do we get in there? What—you suddenly go strong silent on me?" she chided.

"No—" he said absently. "Shh, just a minute—" Frost wondered if it would work, guessed that it might not. But he couldn't think of a better way into the city and wasn't eager to try going under the wire fence after nightfall since that would just heighten the chances of them being spotted as they waited through the day. In itself, getting past the fence might be next to impossible. Why not, he thought? The area behind the barbed wire fence was probably mined anyway.

"Can you do a German accent?" Frost asked Bess.

"What? German accent—Why?"

"Well, Chapmann's got a daughter by his first wife—I don't have any idea if you look like her, but your hair is the right color and his first wife was German and I think the daughter was raised in West Germany."

"Oh . . . Frost," she said. "You want me to—"

He cut her off. "You can think of a better idea? Then shut up. Come on, we gotta steal another Land Rover." And he grabbed her by the hand and they went back to their vehicle, coasted it down the hillside opposite the town and brought the engine to life when he hit the road. They drove back about five miles along the main highway, fortunately not encountering any Chapmann forces. The Rover's gas gauge indicator needle was already on "E" and sinking fast.

After they'd hidden the vehicle, they found a spot of high ground and sat there until well past noon, waiting for a target—Frost's eye almost aching from the continued use of the binoculars, waiting for a Land Rover with a Chapmann officer to come in sight.

After a while, after saying she was hungry for about the tenth time, Bess said, "Hey, Frost, can I ask a dumb question?"

"I don't see why now should be any different," he said. "Go ahead."

"Now, I don't want any eyepatch jokes—just give me a straight answer."

"What, about the patch?" he said.

"No—don't start going into some damned grisly joke—but why does a one-eyed man use binoculars instead of just a telescope?"

Frost put the Bushnell armored binoculars down on the rock in front of him for a moment and stared at them, then looked at her and said, "Gee—I don't know! You're right, you know—I never thought of that! Look at all the money I could have been saving all these years. I was just so used to using binoculars all my life that I just kept right on using them. Well," he said exaggeratedly, "I'll be—"

"Oh, shut up, Frost—you realize how damned silly you look squinting down the road with a pair of binoculars with one of the lens caps still on? Now be serious—what, you get them for a Christmas present or something?"

Frost just looked at her a moment, lit a cigarette, then said, "If you actually want to know the truth, I always use binoculars—if one lens were to become damaged, all I have to do is use the other one—okay? Make sense?"

"Okay," she said, then fell silent. As Frost went back to looking up the road—and he finally spotted a Land Rover with two uniformed men riding in it—he realized embarrassedly for the first time since he'd lost his eye that it was pretty stupid for a one-eyed man to use binoculars. He made a mental note to buy a monocular, first chance he got.

Frost and the girl had already arranged what to

do. She'd lie in the road again, acting as though she were unconscious—she hadn't remembered the last time and wasn't particularly happy when he'd told her she'd almost been run over. He gave her his pistol and showed her how it worked. This time, though, as the vehicle approached she'd start to stir, in order to convince them that she was still alive. Frost drove their Land Rover into position on the road, drove it right up into the largest tree trunk he could find, so the old damage would show—the gnarled bumper, and out-of-shape fender, etc. Then he even propped the hood. To add to the effect, he took a large rock and threw it through the windshield from the inside in front of the steering wheel to heighten the appearance of an accident. Frost helped the girl to get down and positioned himself by the side of the road. There was a chance, he knew, that this close in, the men in the Land Rover might hit the radio and just bypass Bess and call into the capitol for an ambulance, but it was a chance he couldn't avoid.

As the Rover approached, clearly Frost could see a black native trooper driving and a white Chapmann officer beside him. For a moment, Frost thought it was going to be a repeat of the previous dodge and they were going to run her over. But at last, after what appeared to be a hasty conversation between the Chapmann officer and the driver, the Rover started to slow, then as Bess started moving—"writhe in agony," Frost had advised her—the Rover stopped and both men got out.

A smile creased Frost's face. The men were well-trained, approaching the woman lying on the ground cautiously, evidently suspecting some sort of trap but not listening to that sixth sense that could have saved them. Instead, they were doing the good guy number and rescuing the damsel in distress.

After both men had scanned the area surrounding the damaged Land Rover and the injured girl, then turned their backs to Frost's position as they leaned down to assist the girl, Frost stepped into the open, the H-K in his hands on full auto. He shouted, "Freeze—one move and we cut you down," his intent to imply that there were more guns trained on the men than just his own.

As the men turned, the girl rolled over and got to her feet, Frost's Metalifed Browning in her hands. As he'd warned her, she got out of reach of the two men quickly, stepping back almost to the damaged Land Rover to help Frost cover them.

The men didn't make the move they could have. They surrendered the initiative and Frost knew he had them. Frost was already wearing the Chapmann uniform he'd taken when they'd had the episode with the tank the day before—the cammie fatigues, the black beret and his own captain's bars.

"You a spy?" the white officer said.

Frost answered, "No, actually this is a surprise security inspection and you guys just failed—only thing is Colonel Chapmann doesn't know about it either. Now, drop your pistol belts and step a pace back from them—move!"

In short order, Frost had the men disarmed, then faced them back to back and using a length of rope from their vehicle tied them together, then moved them awkwardly back to the tree trunk against which Frost's Rover was parked. He secured both men to the tree.

"You aren't going to—" Bess said, hesitantly.

The officer and noncom driver seemed to have the

same question in mind. Frost turned to them, saying, "And, as a reward for your good deed of stopping to help this fair young lady, you shall both be spared—and once you get out of those ropes, help yourself to the Land Rover—all I need from it is this," and Frost reached under the open hood and snatched away the distributor cap.

The black driver was more Frost's build, so Frost took his pistol belt and put it on, completing the Chapmann uniform. Checking the officer's papers, Frost found that he and the girl were really in luck—the officer was from a post a hundred miles away and it was possible that none of the guards at the gate would recognize the man on sight. Possible, but not definite, Frost reminded himself.

His own pistol tucked safely away under the uniform blouse, he stowed the captured Chapmann men's weapons under the back seat of their Rover. The vehicle he was borrowing had all the appropriate Chapmann unit insignia and the Nugumbwean flag. Frost and the girl got aboard, the rest of their belongings already transferred and stowed.

Once they'd started down the road, the girl turned to Frost and said, "Why didn't you kill those two men?"

Frost just shrugged, lit a Camel for himself as he held the wheel steady with his right knee, and answered, "I don't know—guess because they didn't try to run you over. I couldn't just sour them on having a sense of decency, could I?" His face creased into a smile.

The girl said to him, "I don't think I'll ever understand you, Frost—yesterday you killed so many men I lost count, today you decide to play Mr. nice guy."

"So," Frost said, "you found me out—and here I

was trying to impress you."

They continued toward Buwandi in comparative silence, nearing the funnel of roads into the main gate just a little after one in the afternoon. "Now remember," he reminded her, "just act imperious, let me do the talking most of the time and when you do talk try to sound German. Remember, that sucker Chapmann thinks of himself as some sort of little tin God and you'd know about it and probably act accordingly."

"Oh, Frost," she said, complaining, but Frost guessed she'd give it a good try. And as they stopped in line behind a live chicken truck which smelled badly and emitted feathers each time the wind blew, Frost figured that in a moment or so he'd know just how good a try the girl could make. He'd already ditched his eyepatch and wore dark, aviator-style sunglasses.

Guards ahead checked the poultry truck and its driver, made the man exit the truck cab and submit to a physical search. Frost memorized the routine. And he also scanned the strength. There were six men by the guard post, two doing the actual inspection, four others as back up and keeping the traffic ahead moving once the inspection was complete. These guards also handled the rare foot travellers. Frost thought that if he had set up the guard fence there would have been a separate lane for official traffic, but that didn't make the chicken truck in front of him get out of the way any faster.

At last, the truck moved on and Frost pulled the stolen Rover up to the guard post. As the guard—a corporal—approached the vehicle and saluted, Frost snapped, "Captain Havenshire, Second Brigade— this is Colonel Chapmann's daughter—probably seen her picture on his desk."

Frost liked that last line, since it both made sense, showed his own intimacy with Chapmann and made the corporal want to agree to inflate his own sense of importance. "Yes, sir—pleasure to meet you ma'am," the young corporal said to Bess. Frost glanced at her out of the corner of his eye, then heard her say, in what sounded like German, something about how happy she was to be on her way to see her father.

The corporal, obviously uncomprehending, took a pace back and saluted as did the PFC beside him. Frost returned their salute smartly and stepped on the gas. Once they were past the guard post and inside the city, Frost turned to the girl, saying, "I wouldn't have guessed you spoke German."

"I don't," she said, laughing, "but my grandmother always spoke Yiddish around the house and I figured in a pinch it would be close enough."

Frost laughed, then said, cautioning her, "Don't try that again, though—a good number of Chapmann's men are German, some of the senior officers ex-SS men from the war."

"Oh, they'd love me," she groaned. "I'm Jewish."

"Well, I'd say that could prove quite interesting where we're going," Frost said enigmatically.

Frost had been in Buwandi years before on several occasions and knew the city well enough, after refamiliarization with the map, that he was able to find their destination easily. He parked the Land Rover with the government insignia in front of a store and then he and the girl surreptitiously traveled the back alleys for perhaps a quarter mile until they finally stopped at the back door of a relatively modern-looking shop. Frost hammered on the door with his fist for a few minutes until, cautiously, the heavy gauge windowless metal door opened a crack and a feminine voice asked, "Yes, who is it please?"

"Is this still the shop of Achmed Benzahdi, the gems merchant?" Frost asked.

"A moment, please," the woman's voice said. And, in a moment, the door opened on a chain and Frost saw the mustachioed held-moon face of Benzahdi.

"Yes, sir. Please, may I help you—our front door is open."

Frost took off his sunglasses, half his left hand over the left eye and said, "Remember me?"

"Hank, Hank Frost? Allah be praised, I'd heard you were dead—come in my boy!" Frost guided the girl in ahead of him. The back of the shop was dark, small and the walls lined with cardboard boxes of various sizes and shapes. Frost and the girl followed the merchant's path between the walls of boxes and instead of going all the way forward toward the shop area itself, followed the portly little man up a narrow flight of steps and to a dark stained wooden doorway.

The Moslem carefully took a brass key from the right hand watch pocket of his vest and slowly inserted it into the deadbolt lock. Frost followed the man inside, the girl Bess walking behind him.

Inside was a living quarters, the polished hardwood floors dotted with oriental rugs, brocaded cushions and several small teak tables. On the walls, paintings from both Eastern and Western artists were hung. There were several women's voices faintly heard from another room and after Benzahdi directed Frost and the girl to sit down on a low settee, the little man, still standing, clapped his hands and two chadar-clad women entered the room. They almost floated like little dark-cloaked ghosts across the floor, the head to toe veils with tiny delicately laced openings their only windows on the world. Benzahdi said something in Arabic and the women disappeared, returning after a moment with wine for his Western guests and fruit, then leaving again, all without speaking a word.

"How is your wife, these days, my friend, and your daughters?" Frost asked politely.

"They are extremely well, Hank—you have not introduced your young lady friend."

"Ahh," Frost said, smiling, his eyepatch put back in place right after they'd entered the room, "this is Miss Bess Stallman—she's a journalist. Her friends were murdered by terrorists a few days ago and we've been traveling together ever since."

"How were you able to enter the city—I know you are not working for Chapmann after what I heard." And his eyes glanced downward at the uniform Frost wore.

Frost laughed, lit a cigarette, and as he looked around for an ashtray one of the chadar-clad women—from her slimness, one of Benzahdi's two daughters—whisked into the room, ashtray in hand, set it on the table beside him and then vanished. "We got into the city easily enough. What, has Chapmann been bragging about what he did to my unit?"

"Colonel Chapmann is not bragging, Hank," the Arab said, "but not keeping it a secret either—just rumors, but from the right quarters that they seemed correct—were they?"

"I'm the last survivor, my friend."

"Then, why are you here—to take whose life? It was madness to come. And to endanger the life of a woman thusly—I gather you had no other choice."

Frost, as he sipped at his wine—thankful the girl was keeping quiet, apparently realizing she should—filled Benzahdi in on most of the details, including why Bess had started out for Nugumbwe to begin with. When Frost was through, the Arab said, "And so you wish to kill Chapmann and if possible recover your money—how do you intend to do that?"

"Well, as a matter of fact, the only way I think that I can is to make contact with Peter Curtis—he's with the company here. You should know that."

The older man laughed. "I must say, my young friend, you are certainly quite—what is the expression—to the point, aren't you?"

"You mean," Frost said, "because I've always assumed you made more money selling information than selling gems, and so logically you'd know who the CIA man was?"

"You people are lucky I'm pro American—especially being a Moslem, these days. I could have pointed the finger of guilt at Mr. Curtis three months ago—Chapmann would pay a fortune to know who the CIA resident agent is and where he is."

"You know that too?" Frost asked.

"Yes," he said, almost sounding tired, "or at least where he was and how you can find him from there."

"Then you'll help me?" Frost asked.

"How could I not, my friend—because of you my youngest daughter was returned to me alive and unharmed, her life and her virtue preserved. What is it that you wish?"

"To know," Frost answered, "where to find Curtis, get as much information from you as you have regarding Chapmann's operational procedures and one other thing."

"This latter?"

"The girl—I'll be honest, she's a Jew. I can't withhold that from you, although I was thinking about doing that earlier—" Frost was intentionally making a gesture of good faith with the man. He knew from past dealings that like many Moslems, Benzahdi wasn't overly fond of the Jewish people, but he also knew Benzahdi was not overly interested in harming them either. "Can you keep her here in your house, safely, while I got make contact with Curtis."

"Hey," Bess started. "I go where you go—,"

"Silence," the Arab said. Bess looked daggers at him but for some reason fell still.

"Can you," Frost said, "keep her here?"

"I don't suppose there is any reason why not. She is that important to you?" Frost nodded. "Then we must disguise her, as a Moslem woman, because soon, when Chapmann's 'daughter' does not arrive at the palace, there will be a search to find the mysterious woman and the officer who brought her. The blonde hair would be what you Americans call a murdered giveback—"

"Dead giveaway," Frost said, trying not to smile.

"Yes—Dead giveaway," Benzahdi said thoughtfully. "But we can hide her. I will send one of my daughters to stay with my cousin who lives here in the city also, not far, and then your Miss Stallman can assume my daughter's identity—as long as she keeps to the chadar it will be possible to carry on the masquerade for a short time."

"Wait a minute," Bess started. "You want me to run around like—no offense, Mr. Benzahdi and I appreciate your trying to help—but I'm not going to wear one of—"

140

"Honey," Frost said, turning to look at her. "Do you want Chapmann to give you as a present to some of his men? Do you want them to start whittling on you until you tell them the story of your life? Do you want to be dead? Or can you put up with a head-to-toe veil for a few days?"

"And doing as a Moslem woman—conducting yourself as do my wife and daughters whenever there is any possibility you could be watched," Benzahdi added.

The girl threw up her hands. "Where do I change?" she asked, lighting one of Frost's cigarettes.

"I thought you didn't smoke," Frost said.

"I gave it up two years ago."

A half hour later, Frost was walking back toward where he had parked the Rover, no intention of driving it through town unless there were absolutely no indications it had been staked out. He wanted the H-K assault rifle locked in the Rover's tool compartment, but could live without it. He smiled as he thought of how awkward Bess had looked in Moslem dress in comparison to Benzahdi's daughters. Whereas they had seemed to float across the floor under their veils, Bess had sort of bumped.

Wearing his sunglasses again to alter his appearance, Frost found a spot where he could observe the Rover without himself being observed. After about ten minutes, assuming safely that there was nothing amiss, he stepped from the alley doorway, walked up to his vehicle, got in and turned on the engine. As Frost started to pull into the street, three of the Chapmann mercenary soldiers started across toward him from the opposite corner—one of them a major.

"Just a minute, Captain!" the major shouted and

141

the three men ducked out of the way of a passing fuel truck and jogged across to him.

"Yes, Major," Frost said.

"You new here? I haven't seen you around before?"

"I'm Captain Havenshire, sir—Second Brigade—just running an errand." Frost eyed the three men carefully, then taking a gamble, asked, "Which way are you gentlemen going, sir—maybe I can give you a lift?"

The major looked at the two noncoms with him, then said, "Well, it's only a couple of blocks—not more than a mile, but yeah—why not? Thanks, Captain—?"

"Havenshire, sir. Morris W. Havenshire."

"Well," the major said, smiling, obviously feeling awkward at the borrowed name Frost had given him, "Well, Morris—yes, than you—hop in men."

Frost kept a straight face as they shot small talk back and forth while he drove them through the erratic traffic, then halted the Land Rover in front of a seedy-looking inn—Frost had a fair idea what sort of place the three were going to. As the Chapmann men got out, the major turned to Frost and said, "Hey, look, Havenshire. If you've got the time, the girls here are, ahh—well, anyway if you got the time."

"Wish I did, sir, but I'm running late already—had a breakdown on the way in that got me off schedule. But how about a raincheck—I should be getting back here sometime soon?"

"Yeah, fine," the major said—"Look me up. The name is Perlbach—P-E-R-L and then like the musician—Bach."

"Right you are, Major," Frost said, then with a salute, turned his Rover back out into the traffic

142

and drove a circuitous route toward the import house where he would either find Curtis in hiding or find information on his whereabouts.

Once at the import office, after Frost identified himself as a friend of Benzahdi and convinced the proprietor he was also a friend of Curtis, he found that the CIA man had left the city three days earlier and was using a base camp some fifty miles from the city, in the hills. Verifying the approximate location on his map, Frost thanked his informant with the equivalent of forty dollars, returned to his Rover, started out, having checked the gas gauge—he still had more than a quarter of a tank and two cans in the back.

Frost left the city by a different gate to avoid being recognized by the guards who had admitted him—with the Chapmann uniform and the official vehicle, leaving Buwandi at least just meant getting a salute and a wave past the rest of the traffic. Frost noted the greater efficiency of the detail running this gate and chuckled to himself that he should write a letter of commendation to Chapmann about them.

Once outside the city, Frost felt comparatively safe sticking to the main road, especially since he was heading away from the city and in the opposite direction from the Chapmann men who had loaned him the Land Rover in the first place.

Frost had driven for nearly an hour by the time he reached the edge of the hill country and then took the Rover—four-wheel drive all the way now—on up the rutted trail, in spots washed out from apparently recent rains. After fifteen more minutes of driving like this, the dubious road became impassable and Frost pulled his vehicle off to the side, got his pack and his assault rifle, and started walking. He removed the sunglasses he'd worn, reinstalled his eyepatch and stuffed the Chapmann insignia black beret inside his uniform. He stripped away the Nugumbwean forces armband insignia from his sleeve.

As he clambered up the muddy wash, slipping once in the ice-slick clay, Frost thought he sensed an ambush. He stopped still, things starting to go pretty much as he had expected. He took the H-K from his shoulder and held it in the air. He was gambling—instead of the Curtis people from the right wing army faction they could have been terrorists or even some of Chapmann's men. "My name is Hank Frost—I'm a friend of Peter Curtis," Frost shouted.

Feeling something akin to a nineteenth-century cavalry scout trying to enter an Apache stronghold, Frost shouted again, "Hey—I'll stay right here. I don't want any trouble. Understand?" Frost had no way of knowing if indeed they did understand English, but he had no recourse. He spoke Spanish reasonably well, could hobble along a little in French and German and could even make it on his own with Portuguese, but he knew nothing of any of the African tongues.

After a moment, four men cautiously broke from the bushes surrounding the road on two sides, all four black Africans and wearing the insignia of the right wing army. Though he had no guarantee they wouldn't shoot him anyway, Frost still breathed a sigh of relief.

"You guys understand English?" Frost asked, smiling hopefully. "I hate Chapmann, I—" But apparently they didn't understand English, but did understand the word Chapmann. The four men charged at him, apparently thinking it wouldn't be necessary to waste the bullets. As one of the two

144

closest came at him, Frost knocked aside the leading edge of a bayonet-mounted M16 mounted with the extended stock of his H-K. "Look, fellas," Frost said, still forcing a smile. "Friend—Peter Curtis—friend." A second man came at him and again Frost knocked away the bayonet. Now all four were on line against him and Frost's back was to a steep embankment. Frost was just about ready to shoot, when one of the four men feinted a thrust. As Frost made to counter, a second man, then a third man tackled him and hammered him to the ground. As the other two fell on top of him, Frost heard what he thought was the word, "Spy."

As they hauled him to his feet, Frost said, "Okay—no more Mr. nice guy." One of the four men apparently understanding just enough English to be perplexed relaxed his iron-fisted grip on Frost's left arm for a second. Frost lashed out at the man's instep with the heel of his combat boot. There was a cry of pain and Frost's left arm was suddenly free. Sweeping the arm around toward the throat of the man on his right, Frost smashed outward with his left foot and caught one of the men in front of him in the crotch, knocking the man back.

Frost's right hand was on the other man's throat by now and he ripped at the Adam's apple. The man made the predictable reaction and released his left hand from Frost's right arm and moved to protect his throat. Frost drew his right arm away, then straight-armed a karate "kiss" with the tips of his fingers right under the man's sternum, doubling him over.

But the fourth man was on Frost's back by then, his tree-trunk diameter arms locked on Frost's chest and pinning Frost's left arm. He tried elbowing the man—he couldn't quite reach him and Frost's legs were in no position for a kick. The big man was squeezing Frost hard and Frost was beginning to feel light headed. Realizing there were only seconds before he'd be unconscious, Frost snaked his right arm back as far as he could, hooked his fingers into his opponent's nose and started to rip.

There was a scream and the grip around Frost's chest relaxed. Frost crumpled down into the mud, his legs unable to support him. As he started to his feet, he slipped in the mud ducking fast as he sidestepped a combat-booted kick toward his head. The man's nose was bleeding badly and as he started toward Frost, this time a marine-style survival knife in his hand, Frost started for his pistol. As the man lunged and Frost brought his Browning up on target, both heard a voice, an American voice, speaking in what was apparently the native tongue. The big man coming at Frost stopped in mid-stride and Frost held his fire. Looking around cautiously, Frost saw Peter Curtis. The beard the young man had worn when they'd last met was shaved off, but the face was still unmistakable.

Frost started to put his Browning away as the big man with the knife stepped back, sheathing the blade and sitting down opposite Frost on the embankment, tactilely inspecting his nose where Frost had torn at it.

Frost saw Curtis gesture two of the four men with him to check the men Frost had taken on, now stirring in various conditions on the ground. "Same old troublemaker you always were, Hank. How's the eyepatch joke business going these days?"

"Isn't on the blink yet," Frost answered smiling, then with a shrug he picked himself off the ground, "How's the super-spy business?"

Curtis, coming over and shaking Frost's hand,

said, "Listen, I wish I could say it's a living—come on, I'll buy you some coffee." Snatching up his rifle, Frost followed Curtis back up the muddy trail.

Chapter Nine

All things considered, the coffee wasn't so bad, Frost thought—if you didn't mind getting glared at by four men who'd just tried to rip you to pieces while you drank it. Curtis had left Frost for a few minutes while he tended to some "business" he had called it. And, as Frost sat there with his second cup of the coffee and smoking a cigarette, he began a mental survey of the camp. He guessed it accommodated about sixty men—all of whom seemed reasonably well armed, but all Frost could see were small arms. If there were any artillery, any mortar equipment or armor, it was definitely held elsewhere, Frost decided. If this was all there was of the right wing rebel army, he thought, they wouldn't be of much help to him.

When Curtis returned and sat down, Frost said, "Pete, I'll get right to the point. I assume you know why I'm here—I want to kill Chapmann and get the money he stole from my old unit after he murdered them all. Can you help me?"

"Now why, Hank, would the CIA want to help murder somebody?"

"Ha—hell if I know."

"Yeah, well I did know why you're here—heard it through the grape vine, so to speak," and he gestured to the dense foliage on three sides of the camp. "My job here isn't to assassinate Marcus

148

Chapmann, Hank. But it won't disturb me if he just dies. I can't in all seriousness divert any of my men and equipment to help you carry out a vendetta. You can see what I got here."

"This it?" Frost asked, squinting through a cloud of his cigarette smoke.

"Not quite—but yeah, almost. This is a low budget picture, pal—no cast of thousands. Hell, the U.S. State Department officially is supporting the other side. We gotta be low key, covert—whatever the hell you want to call it. If the papers ever got hold of this, or the TV people, gees—there'd be a congressional investigation faster than you could say ouch."

"Oh, you're gonna love me, pal."

"Why," Curtis said.

"I got a girl reporter—tv reporter—down in the town."

"Well, good—she can just damned well stay there and you can go back there and hold her damned hand, man. A reporter?"

Frost shrugged, poured himself another cup of the coffee, and said, "You scratch my back, I'll scratch yours, pal. Those guys you got out there are big and everything, but it doesn't look like they know a hell of a lot. I want Chapmann, you want Chapmann out of the way so you can take over, right? Why don't we pool our resources?"

"Great—a one-eyed man with a shiny pistol and an assault rifle in the wrong caliber from what my men use is going to help me out. Now, I can just relax. How are you going to help us?"

"Well, that's a good question," Frost said, thoughtfully. Both men laughed.

"Well, there is just one thing—I don't know if you'd be too much help, but it would help us a hell of a lot. If we could get rid of the mercenaries, destroying the dictator's hold on the country, that would let us get things organized to fight the Communist terrorists.''

"Aww—just a little thing, huh?'' Frost said sarcastically.

"Well, not all that little. See, the National Bank of Nugumbwe is located right there in the capitol, and I've been thinking for a long time that if somehow or another the National Bank didn't have any money left—they use gold—then Chapmann couldn't pay his mercs—no supplies, no ammo—you know. Now if you could help us to knock off that bank, well, then I suppose you'd be getting what you want and we'd be getting what we want, right?''

Frost sighed heavily. Lighting another cigarette, he said, "That thing is probably so heavily guarded you couldn't spit at it without getting shot. It's in the heart of the old city, right, so we'd not only have to get in and out of the barbed wire stockade Chapmann put up but in and out of the old city walls, too, right? And I bet they're guarded.''

"Yeah, they're guarded,'' Curtis admitted.

"And then the bank probably has a wall around it. It does, I think I remember seeing it a few years ago.''

"Yeah, but not a very high wall, Hank,'' Curtis said. Suddenly, the two men were laughing so loudly that the rebel soldiers in the camp were starting to stare at them—two crazy Americans.

"They got the entire gold supply for the whole country of Nugumbwe in there,'' Curtis said, still chuckling.

Frost sobered up a moment, forced the smile off his face, then "You want to steal whatever we can, then blow the place up, right? What we can't carry away they won't be able to use. Then if you help me to kill Chapmann, I'll have my money, and my revenge and you'll have a bunch of leaderless mercenaries without money who'll get the hell out of Nugumbwe on the first ox cart, right?''

"That pretty much gets the spirit of the thing, Hank—yeah.''

The rest of that afternoon Frost and Curtis spent in planning. Early on, they determined that casing the bank would be next to impossible. It had long ago ceased to be a bank in any real sense of the word—it was the state treasury and only Chapmann, the dictator himself and selected public officials were allowed anywhere near it.

For a while then, they sat and chewed over old times during the Angolan Civil War, but suddenly Frost, who for a moment or so hadn't been paying attention at all to Curtis, said, "Hey, I got it. I know what we can do. Do they bother much with the government archives, I mean in terms of security—have they got a national archives to begin with?''

"Hell—let me think," Curtis said, ruminating a minute then saying, "Yeah—an old girl's school building, I think. Perfect place for you to break into. What are you thinking?''

Frost stood up, pacing the ground back and forth for a few moments, then turning to Curtis. "Why don't we take about a half dozen men or so, make it look like some kind of terrorist raid and get into the archives building, steal the plans to the bank and then just blow the place sky high, which will cover what we went there for?''

"One thing I wanted to ask, Hank. I wanted your help on one other matter—before I go along with you on this.''

"What do you mean," Frost said angrily, "before you go along with me—you're the one who wanted to rob the bank."

"None of this will have the effect we need fast enough unless one thing takes place—one other thing. I need the dictator, Dr. Kubinda, assassinated. I can't do it—if I got caught that would implicate the CIA and make big trouble for the U.S. But you, on the other hand, just a mercenary like Chapmann's people, disgruntled about Chapmann—just a vengeance slaying to kill the dictator. And like you said, my guys maybe are sincere and big, but they don't know a heck of a lot. If Dr. Kubinda is going to be tapped, it's got to be professionally done. I'll give you twenty-five thousand American for it—I can squeak that out of the budget."

All the humor of earlier in the day was gone now. Frost sat down, lit a cigarette and fell silent. After a while, Curtis said, "Look, Hank. What do you want from me? I'm trying to get rid of that two-bit thief before the whole country of Nugumbwe swings over to the Communists just as the lesser of two evils. Each day that turkey Kubinda stays alive and gets to rob the people blind and crush anyone who says boo about him, that's another step closer to the Communists being able to take over. My guys aren't too good at fighting yet, but they have a damned good intelligence net. Statistically, it looks like a two percent increase per day in the ranks of the Communist terrorists here should become the average in another few weeks—two percent per day, man! A month or six weeks from now, we're just gonna have to throw in the towel. And that'll be okay for me—I got somewhere else to go. But these poor guys and their families—they're gonna be dead. You hear about that slaughter Chapmann's men pulled at some village about eighty five miles from here the other day?"

"Yeah," Frost said, almost dejectedly. "Who the hell you think took out that tank and turned it against them?"

"You—You did that? Well then, God man, you know what I'm talking about! That's nothing compared to what the terrorists will do later."

Frost eyed Curtis warily, stubbed out his cigarette, then said, "Okay—make it twenty thousand to me and pump the other five back into your army—I'll kill Dr. Kubinda for you."

Chapter Ten

There was a way into the capitol city, Buwandi, that Frost had not imagined. The city had been originally built on the site of numerous other cities that had existed on the spot for more than two thousand years. At one time, Frost learned, a relatively advanced civilization had used the spot as its capitol and for some reason, perhaps from some remote contacts with the Romans—he couldn't accurately hazard a guess—the city had been built with a comparatively elaborate underground sewer system, which later centuries had ignored. Over the ages, much of the system had fallen into ruin, but according to Curtis's people a white missionary some thirty years earlier, who had rediscovered the ruins of the system, had mapped it out, and one of Curtis's men, who had been raised at the mission school the mapmaker had run, possessed the original—and presumably the only—copy of the map.

It sounded a little hokey to Frost, but since their only other choice was getting through the minefield surrounding the city, and if the operation were scrubbed for that night it could be tried by other means later, Frost decided the mysterious map was worth a gamble. Once they actually entered the sewer system, if in fact it really existed, they'd be easily enough able to determine if entry to the city that way was viable, he felt.

According to the map, the sewer system would lead them under the old walled city itself, up into a passage the missionary had carved out behind the altar of the church at the old mission school—that building some fifty yards away from the archives building and not far from the bank, either.

Late that afternoon, Curtis had sent out scouts to check the entrance area and see if the map were correct as far as that was concerned. By six that same evening, the four men Curtis had sent returned. Yes, they had found a large flat piece of masonry near the river, and underneath it there was a tunnel, but none of them had ventured to go inside. Frost couldn't blame them.

Fitting themselves with terrorist uniforms—simply more ragged camouflage fatigues and crusher hats, then substituting AK-47s for their own weapons, Frost, Curtis and the four men Curtis had selected were ready to move out by nine that evening. If everything went according to plan, and the scale of the map was anywhere close to being accurate—which Frost personally doubted—Curtis estimated they should reach the opening behind the altar in the mission church sometime around midnight. And in case the opening there was sealed, they'd brought along hammers and chisels. If it were sealed too well, even though they would be so close, they would be forced to abandon the project. The mission church was used on Sundays and for weekday services only occasionally, but it would still be too much to risk that noise coming from behind the altar would go totally unnoticed.

"This thing's starting to sound like a damned

thriller novel," Frost remarked to Curtis an hour or so before they left, the two men sitting together, while Frost took the time to field strip the AK-47 he would carry. Terrorists weren't much for keeping their weapons in top condition Frost knew. Though the AK was among the most efficient assault rifles in general use throughout the world, Frost wasn't about to take chances with a potential lemon.

The six men—Frost, Curtis and the four army volunteers—moved out single file through the darkness in a brisk but quiet commando walk. Chapmann used irregularly scheduled patrols at night and there was no telling if they might bump into one by accident. As they came near the river, their point man signaled trouble ahead and Frost and the others broke up and took up potential defensive positions along the track they had walked.

The point man remained up ahead and with no radios; there was no way to communicate with him and ascertain just what was wrong.

After about ten minutes of waiting, Frost edged over to Curtis—a half dozen yards behind him. "I'm going to check that point man," Frost whispered harshly. "We can't wait here forever while he clips his toenails."

"Hey, Hank, Kowbinte is a good man, if he's got us waiting here, there's a good reason. So hang on."

"Yeah—" Frost rasped. "And what if that good reason already killed him and is on its way to get us? Uh-uh. No, I'm checkin' it out—stay here. If I'm not back in ten minutes, get out of here."

"What, and leave you and Kowbinte—no way."

"You don't understand, Pete," Frost tried to explain, his voice low. "You went to a CIA school and they taught you all sorts of nifty shit—I've lived this

156

stuff. If neither one of us is back in ten minutes, it's gonna be because we're dead or captured—which for all practical purposes means the same thing around here anyway. See ya,'' and Frost got up into a crouch and started off into the brush.

As he moved ahead, slowly and silently, Frost could see nothing ahead that would have warranted a stop. Suddenly, he was almost on top of Kowbinte before he knew it. The huge black officer rose to his feet and clamped his hand over Frost's mouth, and as Frost started to react, took his hand away and held a finger to his lips in the universal symbol for silence. Frost could not speak Kowbinte's tongue and the native officer could not speak English. But through gestures, Frost understood he was to follow the man forward. Nodding, his AK-47 on full auto just in case, Frost soundlessly followed the larger man.

After about a minute, they were at the edge of the river bank. Kowbinte pointed twice—first across the stream to a clump of rocks and bushes. Kowbinte had been one of the men from the earlier expedition to find the tunnel entrance. Frost assumed that was it. Then Kowbinte had gestured toward a spot perhaps fifty yards upriver. There were tents pitched there, likely by Chapmann's people. Why there was a camp there was beyond Frost at the moment. He drew back into the bushes and sat there, thinking.

Then getting up on to his knees again and peering upriver Frost watched the little encampment intently for several minutes. Three tents, good sized ones, probably a squad, perhaps two squads of men—likely native soldiers under one or two of Chapmann's mercenaries. Though totally unrelated to the moment, Frost silently wondered if Chapmann were going to have these men killed too when at last he was through in Nugumbwe. Frost and his battalion had been the bulk of Chapmann's force, save for about thirty men who were almost always with Chapmann. Would these thirty men arrange the deaths of the rest of the mercs in Chapmann's current employ?

Frost forced his mind away from that and back to the problem at hand. If everybody in the assault team could swim, and everybody could be counted on for silence, they could cross the river more or less submerged, offering as little profile as possible above the water. Then they could get into the tunnel and pull the lid in after them. They would be able to go ahead with the operation then and to hell with the unexpected bivouac, Frost thought.

Frost signaled for Kowbinte to wait, then went back the way he'd come—reminding himself to tell Curtis later to commend Kowbinte for his foresight and his prompt action.

Once Frost reached Curtis, he called the men together around them. Quickly, remembering also to commend Kowbinte, Frost related what he had seen to Curtis, who in turn translated the bulk of Frost's remarks to the three Africans. "What's the word in their language for 'keep your fingers crossed'," Frost asked, and then ignoring any possible answer from Curtis signaled the men to move out.

In single file again, moving as slowly as they dared to preserve near-total silence, Frost, Curtis and the three men reached Kowbinte's position by the river bank. Curtis, gesturing rather than speaking, signaled that he would go first. Frost put his hand on the CIA man's arm, nodded a firm negative and signaled that he would go first, then pointed to Kowbinte as next and so on, Curtis last. Curtis shrugged and nodded his agreement.

Frost drew the small Gerber from under his fatigue blouse and the AK-47 held at a high port, skidded down the river bank, the knife in his teeth. He slid almost soundlessly into the water. Frost remembered he'd forgotten to ask about what lived in the water, but mentally shrugged off the thought. He kept the action of his weapon as much above water as possible, half swam, half crawled across the river, which at this point, he knew from the map, was at best four feet or so deep in most spots.

Frost reached the other side, crawled up on the embankment and got up toward the rocks covering the tunnel entrance. There was a leech on his hand. Covering the hand with his crusher hat, he took his lighter and touched it to the creature and it fell away.

"Goddamn bug," he muttered, then signaled across the river for Kowbinte to follow. Ten minutes later, Curtis came ashore and the six men, huddled together and oddly cold from the river swim despite the warm African night, set to removing the stone slab covering the entrance into the ancient sewer system. After a few minutes of struggling with the massive slab—granite? Frost supposed—as soundlessly as they could, Frost and Kowbinte at last pried the slab away. Frost felt a rush of cold, dank smelling air against his face. He could see nothing inside the entrance, but as he leaned into the darkness there, before entering, he could distinctly hear dripping sounds, like a hundred faucets all gone on the fritz at once.

"What do you think?" Curtis asked, whispering

close beside Frost's right ear.

Frost turned and looked at the CIA man, saying, "What do you mean, what do I think? It smells like a sewer and it's as dark as a sewer should be—oh, hell, it's just beautiful—hey, mister, when can we go in," he said mockingly. "What do I think? This time you can go first."

Curtis, followed by the three Africans aside from Kowbinte, entered the opening, then Frost and Kowbinte, moving the stone as close to the entrance as possible to still allow them to squeeze through, handed their assault rifles through the opening, pushed their way inside and in the darkness there, fumbled their way with the stone, pulling the slab behind them. Inside, all was absolute, total darkness, for there was no outside light, and using flashlights until the stone was in place would have been to reveal their position.

Wet, cold there in the cavern, Frost was the first man with a light on—the one out of terrorist character item besides his Browning and the Gerber knives that he'd brought along, lighting his way—a three D-cell medium head Kel-Lite. Soon, the others had their lights working as well, Curtis a GI issue angle head light, the others a collection of everything from good to bad—all that Curtis had been able to scrounge.

Flashing their lights inside the passage revealed little, but as they picked their way carefully by the light of their flashlights, after a few minutes of descent, they found themselves in the sewer system itself. "This was never used," Frost whispered.

Polished rock surfaces, water-stained in spots but quite clearly carefully assembled formed a high vaulted ceiling rising perhaps twenty feet overhead now, but dipping lower up ahead, Frost could see, to where it would be barely high enough to stand.

"My God," Curtis exclaimed, but the construction of the vault where they stood, the very rock itself echoed and amplified his words until they thundered back at them. One of the Africans, visibly, was gripped by fear, but good, sensible Kowbinte, Frost observed, was trying to calm the man, to explain to him. And now there was another danger for them, Frost realized. Each sound they made could be carried for hundreds of yards, perhaps amplifying like Curtis's words, and perhaps somehow alerting the enemy to their activities. It would be necessary not only to travel in almost total silence, but to guard each movement as well—one dropped flashlight, the overturning of a pile of rocks—Frost could barely imagine what sort of cacophony it would generate.

They moved onward, picking their way through puddles of ground water apparently seeping in from the river bed, water from above—condensed moisture—dripping down on them. Loose rocks barred their way and occasionally all but obscured the path, requiring the men to stop and move them aside. Frost realized the map was wrong. According to the diagrams drawn thirty years earlier by the mission priest, the route should have been virtually level once they dropped down from the entrance, but by Frost's rough calculations they were below ground level some three hundred to four hundred feet. And, there was no sign of the incline stopping.

Huddling so they could whisper to one another without catching the echo effect, Frost and Curtis conferred. Curtis didn't make their rate of descent as anywhere near that great. Frost, on the other hand, did. And so the six men kept moving. It was well along to eleven P.M. when they stopped again and before them there was a yawning chasm. Had it not been for the flashlights they carried, two of which were already dimming to the point of being nearly useless, all of them would have fallen into the pit.

Again, Frost called a conference, getting Curtis to do a running translation. "We've got no choice now," Frost said, waiting for the translation from Curtis. "If we just continue to go on, in another few hours these flashlights will be burned out." Again he waited. "And then we'll be stumbling around in the dark down here until we all get ourselves killed." Again, he waited while Curtis translated. "But we do have one chance to determine if this route will get us to our destination." As Frost waited while Curtis translated, the echoing effect like a thousand people whispering in a cathedral, he flicked off his own safariland Kel-Lite to save on the batteries.

"What do we do?" Curtis asked.

"One man goes on ahead for no more than a half hour, with two flashlights, the rest of us stay here, one flashlight on. That leaves three flashlights to get us out of here, and gives the man who goes ahead double the chance of getting back in one piece. If the man who goes ahead isn't back in two hours, we get the hell out of here. If, on the other hand, the man finds that we're going back up, that we're close to getting out of here, whatever, then fine. He comes back and we go on again with him, again with at least three working flashlights. That's the only way."

Curtis finished translating and the other men nodded in agreement. "All right, I'll go," Curtis said.

"What—you a born leader or something?" Frost cracked. "I'll go—I'm good at this. Back in my college days," he lied, "spelunking—cave exploration—was a big hobby with me. I've got a heck of a lot less chance of getting lost or getting myself in trouble."

Curtis looked at him, almost ghostly appearing in the light of the flash. "Bullshit."

Frost winked at Curtis. "Boy, you can say that again," and then added, "now who wants to loan me a flashlight."

As Frost held out his left hand, apparently no translation was necessary. Kowbinte handed over his light. Frost nodded and extended his hand to the man and they shook. Walking over to the chasm, for a moment Frost used both lights in an attempt to see across. Apparently, he assumed, the flooring here had fallen through during some kind of geologic upheaval. For, beyond the chasm, although he couldn't be sure, he thought he could detect solid footing once again. But, the distance across the inky black gulf before him was perhaps fifty yards. Although they'd brought heavy ropes for just such an eventuality, unless he tied several of them together, there would be no way to reach across the chasm. And, besides, there was no way to anchor the rope. Perhaps, he thought, all this brave talk about finding their way had been for nothing. But then, as he flashed the beams of light around the sides of the chasm, Frost could see that on his right, apparently not all the wall had given way. There was a ledge, as best as he could tell about six inches to a foot wide, running all the way around the side of the chasm and to the opposite side.

If he'd had mountain climbing pitons, he could have made the traverse with relative safety, but he didn't have such things. Tying a rope in a sling about his waist would have been useless, since if he were to fall, say twenty-five yards away, although the rope would keep him from falling down into the seemingly bottomless pit—his flashlight could not penetrate the shadows—he would impact against the chasm wall hard enough to die.

He took a large rock and dropped it into the pit. He listened and listened. There was no sound. "Wonderful," he grunted to himself. The leech bite was itching and before he got underway, he remembered to coat the wound with some antiseptic from his pack and to bandage it. Then, taking just one of the ropes and securing his gear as best as possible, he started out along the ledge, the others shining their one light which they would use after him to give him extra help in finding his footing. Frost had left his AK-47 behind with Curtis and the others, but aside from that had all his equipment. The flashlight he was using for the traverse was his own, and he had secured it to his wrist with a spare bootlace, winding the lace tightly against the junction of the flashlight head and body.

For the first five minutes or so—he estimated he was a quarter of the way around the ledge—the going was easy enough. Suddenly, though, as he put his right foot out, his face and body hugging the wall, he realized the ledge was gone. Frost drew his foot back and flashed his light ahead of him. There was a space of perhaps four and one-half feet, but no more than five feet it seemed where there was no ledge, just a drop. But on the other side of the empty space, the ledge continued intact.

Frost had two choices. Either turn around and go back, the entire mission being scrubbed, or attempt to step across the expanse, gambling that on the other side the ledge would be sufficiently strong to hold his weight. For Frost, there was really no decision to make. Edging as close as possible to where the ledge ended, flattening his body against the rock wall and outstretching his left arm as far as it would go, he raised his left foot high, extended his leg outward and stepped off.

His crotch felt as though he were splitting his body in half, and he leaned into his left leg harder—he had misjudged the distance, it was five feet or better. But he had a toe hold, then edging forward—for an instant he lost his balance but regained it—he got more of his left foot onto the ledge, then principally using his hands against the rock face as leverage, he pushed himself off and was on the other side.

In total darkness, save for the flashlight he held, Frost flattened his back against the rock wall and just stood there at the edge of the ledge for a moment, trying to catch his breath.

After a few moments, more cautiously this time, Frost went on. The ledge narrowed up ahead to little more than three inches in width, and in one spot when he put his foot down, a piece of the ledge crumbled away under his weight and he almost lost his balance and went over the edge. But he kept on. Snatching a glimpse at the black luminous dial of his watch, Frost noted he'd been traversing the ledge for almost twenty minutes.

Finally, up ahead, he thought he saw the edge of the rock floor, an end to the chasm. As he approached it, his heart sank a moment, for his light caught another void, but as he followed it with the light there was only a foot or so of emptiness and then there was at last the solid footing of the rock floor.

Once he reached it, he flashed his light three times to signal in the darkness to the men on the other side that he had made it across, hoping but not certain that they could even see it. After a few moments, bone tired from the traverse, Frost got himself to his feet and started walking. For another five minutes by his watch—the half hour would run from the time he had flashed the light that he was safely across—the stone floor continued at a downward angle, but then Frost noticed that it was starting to level. And, as he walked on, after another twenty minutes, he automatically forced himself to swallow hard to pop his ears. And then it suddenly dawned on him that he was going up. He walked more quickly now and knowing that he was risking being unable to reunite with his comrades, he still pressed on for another ten minutes. Just in front of him, his flash caught a lighter spot on the rock wall—a straight-lined square. He went over to it.

The thin line of cement almost chipped away with finger pressure. And beneath it, he was able to slip the edge of the Gerber boot knife in to perhaps an inch depth. On a chance, he killed his light, and his eye started to become accustomed to the total darkness he squinted along the crack in the stone. "Light," he said under his breath, and then repeated it as he sat for a moment, his back against the panel. In the darkness, Frost could feel his face creasing into a smile.

He checked his watch. He was already nearly overdue, his first half hour long elapsed. But if he hurried, he felt he could reach Curtis and the other men before they gave up on him. Being careful not to fall and break an ankle, Frost still moved along the uneven rock floor as quickly as he could, saving on the light now on the rare occasions when he stopped for breath. He'd packed the Kel-Lite with three fresh Duracells just prior to leaving the Curtis camp, and the light was still holding up well, but Frost had no desire to push his luck.

As he approached the chasm—it couldn't have been more than a hundred years ahead he reasoned—he checked the Omega on his wrist. By now, his friends should be gone. He quickened his pace but carefully shone the light close ahead of him to avoid running off the edge and accidentally falling into the pit.

When he reached the edge he shone the light, but could see no answering beacon from the total darkness on the other side. He dropped to his knees by the edge there in the total darkness and caught his breath. Suddenly, his hands were sweating and his stomach was starting to churn. It was an involuntary reaction, he knew, a reaction to being lost. He knew where he was, but he also knew that even after he made it back to the panel in the rock wall some forty minutes behind him, it would not be something he could move aside himself.

He tried the light again. Perhaps they were out there and there was no way they could answer his signal, he thought. He was starting to panic, he realized. Perhaps they were asleep. Having nothing to lose, Frost took his pistol and fired twice down into the darkness of the chasm.

As the echo began to die down, Frost saw a light, then another—soon there were four dim lights winking from the other side of the chasm, and he signaled three, then four flashes with his own light to identify himself and to say, "Come ahead."

The "mother hen" instinct anyone who has held a command function develops, told him that he should try to warn the others of the hazards of the ledge, but there was no way to do that. By the time he could reach that portion of the ledge, they'd be past it. To shout, with the echoing effect, would be meaningless. His pistol shots were still reverberating.

He'd smelled no gas, so he decided to risk it. He lit a cigarette while he waited.

Six cigarettes and four times as many anxious minutes later, he heard the first sounds of one of the men nearing him on the ledge, and Frost turned on his own light and saw that it was Curtis and helped him along the last few feet. Frost spoke to him, abandoning the need for quiet again, in his sudden desire to hear another human voice.

"Did everyone get across the break in the ledge?"

Curtis simply rubbed his hands across his face, then said, "Give me a cigarette, Hank—no, damn it all to hell. Kowbinte was trying to save the man behind him. Well, he saved him, but Kowbinte went over the edge himself. Didn't even scream."

Frost, by the light of his flashlight, caught the look of despair in Pete Curtis's face—and Frost knew the look because it was on his own face as well.

Chapter Eleven

"All right," Frost rasped, there in the darkness, "at the count of three—Curtis, go ahead, do it in their language." And, as Curtis reached what Frost assumed was the number three, Frost, Curtis and the three remaining men of the rebel right wing army drew aside the massive stone slab blocking the exit from the tunnel. And with the extra force that was needed, Frost once again felt the loss of the powerful and likable Kowbinte, the black officer who had gone to his death in the bottomless chasm behind them, while saving one of his men. They'd all waited a long time back there, even hitched one of the flashlights to a rope and run it down into the chasm. They had not quit the spot until no further possibility remained foolishly that the man could somehow have survived. And now, in total darkness, the stone slab leading—they hoped—behind the altar of the old mission church came the moment of truth. Taking his AK-47, Frost went through the opening first, the light of the church blinding him momentarily. When he was finally able to squint his right eye open, he realized that the intense light was really just moonlight through the church's clear, leaded windows. But, Frost and the others had just done the equivalent of walking on the dark side of the moon, for there was no light at all in the sewer system.

Frost reached a hand behind him into the passage and snapped his fingers once. After a few seconds, Curtis and the other men were through the opening and beside him, but Frost had to wait there with them for more than a minute before the last of the men's eyes had become accustomed to the light. While he waited, Frost assessed their new surroundings. The mission church was a long, narrow, flat-roofed structure, more similar to what one would expect to find in Old California, or perhaps New Mexico, than something just a few miles from the equator. And it was evident that the church was now little used for the roof had a gaping hole to the stars and some of the small-paned windows, on closer inspection, were broken.

The map, for all the earlier inaccuracies had been right, at least on the matter of the tunnel exit. They were indeed behind the main altar. Leaning over to Curtis, he whispered, "You and the others, try to get that stone back in place as quietly as you can—no way to tell when we might need to use this tunnel system again." Curtis nodded and then he and the three Africans set to shifting the stone back into position behind them.

That accomplished, Frost, Curtis and the other three men fanned out down the center and side aisles of the mission church and quickly crossed to the first entrance. Since the interior of the church was almost completely denuded of anything except some relatively inexpensive-appearing statuary, Frost assumed those front doors would be unlocked—and they were. Prying one of the wooden double doors apart a crack, Frost looked outside. The darkness still seemed terribly bright to him by comparison to the sewer system. He verified that they were inside the walls of the old city, and far down to his left, he recognized the huge ornate front of the National Bank building. And, down far to his right, there was a smaller edifice that matched the description he'd gotten of the two-story girls school which now served as the national archives of Nugumbwe.

There were no guards to be seen other than around the barbed wire fence topped walls surrounding the National Bank building. But in front of the church and apparently all the way down to the archives building, there was no one. Frost knew that what he saw was too good to be true—there would have to be roving motorized or more probably foot patrols—if for no other reason than to keep the standard dawn to dusk curfew in effect. As Frost prepared to slip through the doors, then down the steps at the front of the church, his mind drifted back a moment to Bess—a smile creased his face as he wondered absently how she was doing so far as a Moslem girl. Turning to the men behind him, Frost cocked his head in the direction of the street and then started through the doors.

When he reached the street, he moved quickly to the church's side wall and flattened himself against it. There in the shadows, all that could be seen was the deserted street, all that could be heard the faint murmurings of a radio playing some sort of familiar ballad Frost couldn't quite put his finger on, but the vocalist was singing the words in German. Her voice had a kind of faraway lilt to it, imparting a certain loneliness to the night as Frost, having been joined by Curtis and the other men, took off in a fast low run toward the shadows of the next building.

Unlike the older portions of most cities, here in Buwandi the buildings were not huddled together almost as if seeking companionship in one another. Just the opposite, the comparatively few buildings, though in most cases quite dilapidated, were spaced well apart with what could have been a pleasant greenway between them had someone bothered about it.

Each time Frost and the others dodged from the shadows of one building to the shadows of another, they moved that much closer to the moment of truth with the guards at the archives building. The plan was a simple one. In the back of Frost's pack,, and the packs of the other men, were enough plastic explosives to level a building twice the size of their target. Frost and Curtis, the best trained of the five commandoes, would take out the few guards surrounding the archives building. Those guards being black Africans, they would be replaced by Curtis's army men, then Frost and Curtis would penetrate the structure itself and get the plans to the bank building, set the charges and rejoin their comrades. And all went well as Frost and the others narrowed the gap along the deserted street to the archives building at its far end, another song played on the radio now, coming from a guard tower on the old city wall about two blocks distant from them. It was the same woman singer with the same warm, peaceful voice, and once again in German. Frost guessed that the program was some sort of satellite relay from a powerful West German radio station, and there were many of those.

As they reached the building closest to the archives, Frost signaled to the others to wait there, then he and Curtis cut back to the rear of the building and circled around it.

From the corner of the building walls—some sort of market, Frost guessed—there was a clear view of the two guards by the wrought iron gates. And, as they waited, they could see a third guard inside. According to Curtis's intelligence reports, there likely were other guards—the relief—inside the building, but there were only three men on duty outside.

Frost pulled Curtis back around the corner of the building, put his lips by Curtis's left ear and whispered as softly as he could, "I'm going after the inside man first, then as soon as I get him, I'll come through or over the gates and try for one of the outside guards—I want you to get the other one. Ever kill a man with a knife?"

Curtis just shook his head, his eyes fixed in a peculiar expression.

"Well," Frost whispered, "I don't think you're going to like it. Silence the man with your left hand over his mouth, the right hand driving the knife into the right kidney, low so it doesn't stick into the rib cage, then withdraw the knife as you bring the guy down—fall on him and push him forward or wrestle him back, whatever, then rake the knife ear to ear from the left side to the right and slightly downward." Frost eyed Curtis again. "Just like in the training films and the spy novels—you'll get the hang of it."

Then Frost slung his AK-47, diagonally, across his back, muzzle down so he could get the gun into action if needed. Putting the small Gerber MKI into his teeth and the large Gerber MKII in his right fist, like a dagger rather than a saber, he stood quietly for a moment, concentrating. He made his breathing slow and even, flexed his arms and shoulders, then his knees, then taking a deep breath as he scanned the guard posts, Frost took off in a low, dead run toward the wall surrounding the archives building. Just six feet in height, without barbed wire on top, it was almost too easy. He jumped and caught the flat top of the wall, pulled himself up and flattened himself there for an instant, then rolled down and landed on the inside perimeter of the wall in a low crouch.

Frost remained motionless for at least a minute, listening for even the slightest sound that would betray that his presence was even suspected. But there was none. He was within twelve feet of the sentry now.

Frost slipped the AK-47 from across his back and set it carefully on the ground beside him. Having encountered no resistance, he had not needed the smaller knife, so this he carefully set on the ground beside the rifle, not daring to risk the noise of replacing it in its sheath.

The larger of the two knives in his right fist, his fingerless black gloves against its catspaw handle surface, Frost moved forward in a low crouch. He could feel the camouflage stick making his face itch. Six feet now from the submachine gun armed sentry, Frost drew himself up to his full height and raced forward. Perhaps there was the telltale sound of gravel crunching under Frost's feet, perhaps just some sixth sense that alerted the man, but the sentry started to turn around. Already, it was too late for the man. Frost's left hand slapped hard over the sentry's mouth, Frost's right hand with the knife ramming deep into the man's right kidney, then snaking back in a sort of piston action. Then Frost's knife hand started for the sentry's throat, Frost's right knee pushing hard into the man's spine. At last, Frost's knife found the exposed, extended neck, and as Frost dragged the sentry down toward the ground, his knife drove deep into the left side of the sentry's throat, then ripped across it, the blade coming to rest against the right clavicle or collar bone.

Frost guided the dead sentry's body the rest of the way to the ground, then as he waited there for an instant, his body crouched and ready to spring with the knife again if needed, he listened again for any sound of alarm. There was nothing but the soft voice of the German girl on the distant radio. Frost moved soundlessly back toward the wall, retrieved his second knife and reslung his assault rifle across his back.

There were still the two remaining guards by the gate to be removed. Edging along the wall, keeping in its shadow, Frost reached the wrought iron grillwork of the gates and risked a glance toward the two guards outside. Curtis would be in position, Frost hoped, otherwise when he, Frost, went after one of the guards the other would either enter the fray or sound the alarm. In either case, Frost and his men would lose the element of surprise.

Beside Frost was a small stool, almost identical to the kind used on farms and known as milking stools. Frost moved the stool next to the wall, then stood on it and soundlessly pulled himself onto the top of the concrete wall. He moved in a crouch the few feet along its flat surface and toward its edge, the gates now below him. Frost snatched a glance outside of the compound, but Curtis was nowhere in sight. Silently, he hoped Curtis hadn't lost his nerve. Frost leaped down onto the nearer of the two guards, falling onto the man's shoulders and back and driving the man down to the ground beneath the weight of his own body, his right hand driving downward with the knife he held there and hammering it like a stake into the hollow of the guard's throat.

Frost looked up—still no Curtis. But the second guard was turning around. There was no time for anything fancy, Frost thought. Pushing himself to his feet, leaving his knife in the first sentry, Frost just continued the movement, going into a flying tackle toward the second guard's hips and dragging him down. Then he was on top of the sentry. Unable to reach his knife, Frost hammered his gloved fists into the guard's face and neck.

The man rammed his rifle butt up and toward Frost's groin, but missed, catching Frost in the thigh, the impact sufficient to jar Frost away from him and give the man room to get to his feet. Frost fell back, rolling away, then jumping to his feet. As the sentry raised his rifle to fire from the hip, Frost dove toward him again and smashed him back into the edge of the wall, winding both himself and his quarry. Frost fell back against the wrought iron gate, the gate swinging inward from the pressure of his body.

As the sentry started to regain his footing, Frost locked his hands onto the upper portion of the gate and drew his right leg up, propelling himself and the gate forward with his left leg.

Frost's right leg swung in a withering arc into the sentry's face, snapping the man's head back and knocking him down against the edge of the concrete wall. Frost fell to his feet in a crouch, then rising lashed out with his right foot, a savate kick into the sentry's groin. Then Frost wheeled, elbowed the man's rifle aside, and drove the heel of his right hand in a straight arm blow up into the sentry's nose, smashing it and driving the bone upward, ramming it piteously into the man's brain.

176

Forgetting the kill, Frost wheeled. The second sentry there on the outside of the gate was starting to move, Frost's knife still plunged almost sickeningly into his neck. He was groping for his assault rifle. Frost took two steps and kicked the rifle aside, then stomped his left foot down hard against the side of the man's head to kill him, then dropped to his knees over the man, drawing out his knife and snaking the sentry's head back and slitting his throat just to be sure. Frost let the head snap forward to the ground, wiping the blade of his knife on his victim's back to clean the blood away.

Frost's back ached badly—he had fallen hard on his rifle while fighting the other man. Drawing himself painfully to his feet, Frost finally saw Curtis, flattened against the outside of the wall.

Frost walked over to him. Curtis was just staring. "It's not like shooting a man, is it?" Curtis said, almost absently.

Closing his right eye, Frost bent his head a moment, then whispered. "No, it isn't. Can you still help me inside, should I let you?"

Curtis looked at Frost a moment, "Yes—I can do it. I just—I just got caught up in what you were doing; I'd never seen anything like that before up close. You were like a machine," the younger man said, his tone almost one of incredulity.

"I guess it isn't quite like the movies after all," Frost said, shaking his head, then awkwardly, he moved his rifle off his back and into an assault position. His back was starting to hurt when he breathed—perhaps, he thought, he'd damaged his spine.

Frost signaled for the three rebel army officers to move out of the shadows and he gestured toward the outside sentries. As they had prearranged, the bodies were pulled just inside the gate, then the body of the inside sentry Frost had also killed retrieved and placed beside them. The three native officers stripped off their own fatigue blouses and below them already wore the uniform of the loyalist soldiers, then trading headgear and weapons with the dead men, took up the posts as though nothing had happened.

Frost shot a glance at Curtis and Curtis nodded resolutely, then followed Frost, each man snatching up one of the field packs dropped by the native officers, Frost taking a second pack and, clumsily because of his injury, shouldering it. The five packs contents combined, Frost guessed, should make quite an impressive explosion.

Frost and Curtis moved quickly toward the building's front door, then seeing that Curtis was behind him and ready, they dropped the packs and Frost kicked in the front door.

There was a small night-light in the dingy, empty hall and Frost ran down the corridors to the end, kicking open each door along the way looking for the remaining guards, Curtis already starting toward the second floor. Frost made it that Curtis was halfway up the stairs when the shooting started. Curtis, Frost saw, was clambering over the railing, then jumped down to the stone floor, coming down hard, but going into a roll, his AK-47 opening up toward the top of the stairs as he hit. Frost flipped the selector on his own AK to full auto and fired up, from under the stairs, then punching a fresh magazine into place, Frost ran toward the side of the stairs, clambered onto them and started to climb the railing. Curtis, behind him, was on his feet, his AK to his shoulder, three-shot bursts aimed above toward the head of the stairs.

As Frost got over the railing, he opened fire again—two men at the top of the stairs, one already bleeding and on his knees but still firing, fell under Frost's fusilade. Taking the stairs two at a time, Frost reached the top and turned into the upstairs corridor, then opened up again at four men at the end of the hall.

Two of the men went down, one still firing, and as Frost's AK-47 went dry and he started for his Browning, gunfire opened up behind him and from the corner of his eye Frost could see Curtis, the CIA man's AK-47 held in an assault position, spraying the end of the corridor.

Frost reloaded, then pumped a three-shot burst into one of the men who was still moving.

Standing back to back in the hallway, the smell of gunfire still heavy on the stale night air, all was suddenly still.

As prearranged, the guards outside—the rebel army officers—would now be ready to move at a moment's notice. Frost grunted to Curtis, "Okay—we got 'em. Go down and get one of the guys to help with the packs and start setting the charges; I'll find the plans—hurry."

And, as Curtis started down the stairs, Frost called to him. "One thing—you're holy hell with a gun aren't you—so don't worry about the knife thing."

Curtis looked up at Frost, then said, "Somehow it's different."

"No—just seems that way," Frost remarked, then ran down to the end of the corridor. He could hear Curtis's footsteps on the stairs behind him. As Frost stepped over the bodies at the end of the hall, he began a room-to-room search for the archives room itself.

After three or four minutes of searching, Frost convinced himself the archives room was not on the second floor. He took the stairs down, two at a time despite the growing stiffness in his back, one of the black officers, carrying two packs of explosives, passing him on the stairs. Frost guessed they would have perhaps another five minutes before Chapmann's forces responded to the gunfire. Frost flipped the railing and bypassed the last six stairs, then shouted to Curtis, "Pete, let the guys finish setting the charges—they can do it, right? Help me find the plans."

He heard Curtis shouting something to the three men, then in a moment saw Curtis at the opposite end of the hall, going through the former schoolrooms as quickly as Frost was himself. Frost made it each of them had one more room to go, then he heard Curtis shouting—"Hank, come here—quick! I think I found it."

Frost turned in midstride and ran toward Curtis. Stepping inside the room, he saw an old, key-locked, fireproof safe. "Shit," Frost complained, touching his right hand to the lock. "You any good with locks?" he directed at Curtis.

"Yeah, if I've got a complete set of picks and some time. What do we do?"

"Blow the damned lock off—gimme a chunk of that C4 plastique." Curtis ran from the room and returned in less than a minute with a brick-sized portion of the claylike explosive. Taking his knife, Frost cut a piece the size of a pencil eraser and then pushed it into the keyhole. Taking a small length of fuse, Frost jammed it into the plastique and fumbled out his Zippo, lit the end and shouted, "Get the hell into the hallway," and both men ran for the classroom door. As Frost started through

180

behind Curtis the safe blew and Frost was hammered against the opposite wall. He slid down to his haunches, then shouted up to Curtis, "Go in there and start lookin'—I'm coming."

After a few seconds, he painfully got himself to his feet, his back so stiff now he could hardly breathe. But he jogged back into the smoke-filled room and joined Curtis at the safe, the door now hanging at an odd angle from one hinge. Curtis was fumbling documents from the boxes inside and hurtling them behind him to the floor and Frost elbowed his way beside Curtis and began to do the same. As they searched for the bank plans, one of the African officers ran into the room, said something excitedly to Curtis, then ran back outside. Curtis, said, "Told me the charges are all set, and that the man outside thinks he hears some heavy vehicles coming—better hurry."

"Gees," Frost cracked, "no kidding."

As Frost threw a box of documents to the floor beside him and Curtis started rifling a fresh box, Frost stopped, the documents in his hand suddenly getting his complete attention. "I got it—here, take a look," he rasped to Curtis.

The younger man snatched the plans from Frost's left hand and looked at them in detail a moment. "This is it—let's get out of here!"

"I hear you, man," Frost said, and his back hurting him now to the point where each movement was bringing a spasm of pain, Frost forced himself to run after the CIA man.

In the hallway, he could hear Curtis shouting something he couldn't understand—presumably the native equivalent of, "Let's get out of here on the double," because in a moment the two African officers inside the building with Frost and Curtis

181

joined them and they all ran from the hallway.

In the courtyard outside, Frost could see the one man on guard gesturing for them to hurry. As Frost turned to glance back toward the building, he saw one of the African officers leaning down to light the fuses for the explosive charges. Frost pushed the man away and gestured for him to go ahead. Bending down painfully, Frost took his Zippo in his hand and waited until the last of his team had reached the gate, then flicked the lighter and touched the blue-yellow flame to the fuse ends. He got to his feet and started to run.

As Frost reached the gate, Curtis and the others—stupidly he thought—still waiting for him, he realized it was too late to avoid a fight. There was an open top half track truck less than a half a block away, a searchlight aboard the vehicle going on and sweeping toward them.

Frost rasped to Curtis, "I'll fix that thing," then shouldered his AK-47 and loosed a three-round burst into the light, shattering it. Almost immediately, what sounded like a heavy machine gun mounted on the half-track opened up, chewing viciously into the concrete wall behind them. As Frost started to move, he glanced beside him and saw one of the African officers take it in the head and go reeling back against the wall.

Frost shouted, "Pete—tell 'em to concentrate their fire on that machine gun, I'll go for the front tires."

Like the others now, Frost dropped to one knee and shouldered his rifle and opened fire, the time on the fuse burning its way toward the explosives ticking away in his brain. If they didn't get out quickly, they'd be caught in the enormous explosion that was to come.

As the half-track slowly advanced, the volume of fire almost seeming to increase as it neared them, Frost could hear the sounds of bullets ricochetting off the vehicle's armor plate. Suddenly, Curtis was beside him, "One of these help?"

Frost looked down and in Curtis's hand there was a fragmentation grenade.

"Here, give me that," Frost said, smiling, then dropping his rifle beside him. He pulled the pin and waited, as the vehicle started for the final close, the gunfire about them unimaginably heavy. Frost hauled his arm back and threw the grenade. For a moment, there was nothing, just more gunfire. As Frost started to glance about him to see if Curtis had another grenade, spotted the other two African officers down for the last count, then he heard the explosion, and looked back. The half-track had become a ball of flame.

"Come on, Pete," Frost shouted, pulling himself to his feet. He snatched up his rifle and started in a dead run away from the archives building. He could hear Curtis, panting, almost on his heels.

Frost felt the explosion first and dove toward the dirt, his hands going to protect his ears and cover his head, the shockwave hurtling him forward. The ground was shaking beneath him, but as the initial shockwave passed, he rolled himself over—Curtis was already sitting up. The sky was almost as bright as day. There was a huge ball of flame where the archives building had stood—but it stood there no more. Frost glanced off to his right. The half-track was a smoldering ruin. In the distance, above the crackle of the flames, Frost could hear what sounded like an air raid siren—apparently some sort of general alarm.

Frost turned to Curtis, who moved over now and

crouched beside him. Curtis was saying, ". . . noticing it back there—hurt your back, didn't you?"

"Yeah—how could you tell?"

The younger man beside him broke out in a big grin, "I was a pre-med student once—just my diagnostic training. That's why I quit med school though—the same thing as the knife work back there. One of my professors told me that there are some people who just can't bring themselves to take a knife to human flesh. I'm one of them. That's when you hurt your back isn't it—when I finked out?"

"Why don't you just shut up and give an old man a hand," Frost said good-naturedly, starting to his feet.

Frost stopped for a minute, his motion frozen, then gradually got himself nearly erect. "We can't use that tunnel on the way back," Curtis said. "You'd never make it and I don't think the two flashlights we've got would last our way through it. You still want to try walking out dressed in Chapmann uniforms?"

Frost looked around him, leaning on Curtis for support now as they walked—Frost couldn't run. His breath was coming in heavy gasps. "No—you're right. Only chance get to—get to Benzahdi's house maybe. Maybe he can put us up. And damn it—I'm gonna need a doctor. My legs are starting to stiffen up."

The flames of the archives building fire still lighting the sky and the street, Frost and the CIA man hobbled off into the shadows.

Chapter Twelve

Chapmann men were everywhere. Already nearly two A.M., Frost and Curtis were forced to change their route toward the home of the Moslem merchant more than a half dozen times, several times lying in hiding for as much as a half hour before it was safe to move again. By the time Curtis left Frost standing in the shadows leaning against the wall opposite Benzahdi's armored back door, both men reeked of sweat and garbage, were covered with mud and Frost could barely walk.

After a moment or two, as Curtis made to hammer once again with his fist on Benzahdi's door, the door opened a crack on its chain, then closed again and opened wide. There was no light from inside. Frost watched as Curtis and whoever was behind the door—he guessed it to be Benzahdi—talked for a moment. Then, Curtis and Benzhadi, the latter wearing a silk brocade robe of some sort over pajamas, came across the alley and over to Frost. With one man under each arm for support, Frost helped drag himself across the alley and through the darkened doorway. They stood a moment, Frost leaning against a wall in the darkness, breathing hard, while Benzahdi behind him closed the door and from the sounds it made, locked and bolted, perhaps barred it. Benzahdi's hand passed in front of Frost's face and there was the sound of a pull chain in the darkness and suddenly the back room was lighted, a small bulb swaying from the low ceiling and making crazy patterned shadows on the wall and floor.

Benzahdi clapped his hands twice and the light from upstairs went on and Frost could hear the rustling sound of one of the chadar-clad women, in a moment seeing her standing by the base of the stairs. Benzahdi rasped something in Arabic and the woman vanished up the stairway. Curtis and Benzahdi, slowly, carefully, guided Frost up the stairs toward the living quarters and once through the doorway into the apartment helped Frost over to the largest of the settees and helped him to lie down.

Benzahdi was already marshaling the chadar-clad women to bring hot water to him. As one of the little black-clad ghosts whisked past him the woman stopped, looked down at Frost and despite the veil, their eyes met. The face dipped down to him. And though he couldn't see it, the voice was familiar, "Hank, darling—what happened to you?" And in a moment the veil was swept back and dropped onto the settee beside him and he saw her face—it was Bess.

"How you doin', kid?" Frost groaned, forcing a smile. "Just hurt my back a little—pinched a nerve maybe; should be fine when I rest a little."

He felt her hand against his cheek, bent his face toward it and touched it with his lips. Then Benzahdi was beside the settee. "This will hurt, Hank, badly perhaps. I want to look at your back."

"Let's roll over, pal," Curtis said with forced gentleness in his voice. Frost started to oblige but when he turned himself toward Bess, a sudden spasm of pain shot across his shoulder blades and he began to cough, then his face suddenly was cold and he could feel a sweat on his skin and the light in Benzahdi's ceiling started dancing and sparkling.

Frost opened his eyes. He turned his head, happy that he still could, and Bess was there beside him. "Hey, Frost," she said softly.

"What, you only call me Hank when you think I'm dying?"

"Then I hope I never call you Hank again," she whispered and bent over and kissed him lightly on the lips.

When Bess moved her face away, Frost tried—slowly—to move his feet and his hands, to see if the back injury had caused serious damage. There was pain and stiffness but everything responded. "Lie still," she said.

"Why?" Frost groaned, looking up at her.

"Because—that's all. Besides, you should be fine. Seems that Mr. Benzahdi—he's not the traditionalist he acts like, told me to call him "papa" while I was here, like his daughters do. But anyway, he was a kind of chiropractor when he was a young man, before he became a gems merchant. He thinks he straightened out your back. Curtis said he studied medicine a little—"

"Yeah, told me that too," Frost interrupted. "And a little knowledge is a dangerous thing."

"Bull," she said, almost petulantly. "Anyway, Curtis agrees with Benzahdi that you'll be okay in a few days, well enough to travel at least."

With less pain than he'd actually expected, Frost raised his left arm and glanced at his watch. It read eleven-thirty and the date was still the same as it had been when he passed out. He looked at the girl, and gestured with his wrist—"A.M. or P.M., Bess."

She looked at the watch she wore, then said, "P.M., Frost—you were out for quite a while."

Frost looked away from her when he heard a sound at the door, then saw Curtis standing framed in the small doorway. "Glad to see you're back among the living, Hank."

"You and me both," Frost said. "Gimme a cigarette," he said to Bess, then looked back at Curtis as the girl took a Camel, put it to her lips and used Frost's Zippo to light it. She inhaled, then put the cigarette between his lips.

Curtis said, "You're gonna be—"

"Nobody's going to be anything, my friend, unless we get out of this city. Have they started a house-to-house search yet?"

"About two hours ago," Curtis said. "But I've taken care of everything. But let me explain about your back."

"Okay—so explain," Frost said, looking around for an ashtray. When Bess held one out to him, he remarked, "I should leave you with Benzahdi for the next couple of weeks—I like the way your training's going." As she glared at him, he said, smiling, "Can't hit a sick man."

"Want to bet, Frost?" she retorted.

"That back," Curtis said, insistently. "You're gonna be okay—little stiff for a few days, but after this routine is over you need to see a doctor—not an ex-chiropractor and a dropout medical student. You've hurt it before, haven't you?"

"Well," Frost began, his face lining into a grin, "if you want the real story—"

"Hey, Frost," Bess said. "No jokes, not this time, huh?"

He looked at her, nodded silently, then said, "Yeah, when I was in Viet Nam. I was in a helicopter crash—just one other guy and I survived the thing. He lost a leg. I was lucky—just wrenched my back, spent ten days in the hospital, then was back on my feet."

"Well, I don't know what the army told you, but Benzahdi thinks you've got a disc that keeps working out, pinching a nerve. If you don't take care of it, it could leave you paralyzed someday—and soon."

Frost didn't say anything. Bess did. "Frost? Will you get it fixed? For me?"

He turned his head and tried to move, a spasm of pain shooting through his back. "Yeah, soon as I can," he said, gritting his teeth a minute against the pain.

"Change the subject," Curtis said, sitting down on the edge of the bed. "I think when we get out of town, the girl should come with us."

"I'll go along with that," Bess said.

"Just how are we going to get out of town?"

"Drive out—I've still got some people working here undercover—stole a Land Rover for me, we've still got the Chapmann uniforms. Well, actually they're stealing the Rover, going to take out the men using it and get us their papers—seems Mr. Benzahdi also has some talents as a forger—said he can put our pictures on the papers and make the documents believable enough to get us through."

"What," Frost asked, "and the girl too? Forget it—Chapmann doesn't have any girl mercs."

"No, I did some thinking on that too—one of Benzahdi's daughters can teach Bess a couple of Arabic phrases and a few phrases in the native tongue here—in fact, the girl already started. Gotta be careful, there. If Benzahdi did it himself, Bess might say something in a way only a man would say it. But anyway, Bess can walk out with the chadar on and nobody is going to frisk a Moslem woman or

189

look under the veil."

"That's a good plan," Frost said, sitting up in bed, wincing a bit as he moved his back. "But we can make it better, since it's going to be hard to photograph me with the eyepatch for the papers, or without the patch, chances are good we'll get stopped. Let's give Bess an SMG—she can sling it under the chadar. You said it yourself—no one frisks a Moslem woman unless he wants to start a war. That way, if something starts to go wrong, Bess can start laying down some fire and give us a chance to get to our weapons."

"Has anyone thought to ask Bess?" Bess said.

"No," Frost said pointedly, then smiled and squeezed her hand.

It was nearly twelve hours later when Frost and Curtis, resplendent in their camie fatigues with Chapmann insignia, walked through the back doorway of Mr. Benzahdi's gem shop and into the alley, Frost feeling almost normal again after twenty-four hours of bed rest, his back only paining him slightly when he bent over. But he was able to walk straight. They had no weapons except for their personal handguns—Frost the perennially carried Metalifed Browning High Power and Curtis a S&W Model 19 2½ .357 Magnum—and these hidden under their uniform blouses. Holstered at their belts were the Chapmann issued WWII vintage GI .45 Government Model automatics. Frost had checked both guns earlier, and unlike the excellent commercial MkIV series '70 .45s turned out by Colt, these guns were mere hodgepodges of parts, loose in fit and likely grossly inaccurate, and neither was Colt production. Although the .45s were loaded, both men planned to rely on their own weapons if a shootout started.

Bess, in full Moslem female regalia, had left a half

hour ahead of them, an UZI SMG under her chadar on a sling, two spare magazines for the weapon banded with heavy elastic to each leg. Watching her leave earlier, having kissed her good-bye before she put the veil in place, Frost had commented to her, "Be careful." She'd made one of her usual put-down remarks, then that had been that and she was gone. Frost disliked sending her out alone, armed with a two-year-old's vocabulary in the native tongue and a few Arabic phrases to use in a pinch.

The Land Rover was parked three blocks away and Frost and Curtis didn't leave the alleys until they were a block and a half from Benzahdi's establishment in order to avoid drawing attention to him. As Frost and Curtis worked their way through the streets, they saw Chapmann men everywhere. Unlike two days earlier when he had traveled in the city, Frost noticed that the Chapmann people were armed now with more than just handguns—M-3 Greaseguns in .45 adorned one out of every two shoulders. The house-to-house search was apparently still going on full tilt as well, for twice Frost and Curtis encountered heavily armed six-man patrols leaving or entering buildings. The idea of the search no longer bothered Frost—he and Curtis were gone from Benzahdi's place and represented no danger to the kindly merchant any longer, especially too since his "daughter" Bess was also gone. When Frost and Curtis finally reached the Rover, there was a black African sergeant standing beside it, casually smoking a cigarette. As Frost tensed and started to make his left hand drift toward the opening of his uniform blouse for his pistol, Curtis muttered, "Relax, Hank, he's one of our men—driving with us out of the city."

Frost glanced as casually as he could toward Curtis and nodded. As Frost and Curtis—both officers by their uniform insignia—approached, the sergeant snapped to and saluted. Frost and Curtis returned his salute and climbed into the Rover's back seat, Frost experiencing a twinge in his back as he did and having to stop for a moment before continuing to sit down.

Casually, the sergeant dropped his cigarette and stamped it out on the sidewalk and climbed behind the wheel, started the machine, waited until there was a break in traffic and moved away from the curb.

Frost lit a cigarette and checked his watch—he made it there were four or five minutes remaining until the vehicle would reach the main gate.

That morning, at breakfast, Frost and Curtis and Bess had talked. Bess had indicated that she intended to go on with her assignment for the story on the Nugumbwean Civil War—at least as best she could. One 35mm camera remained intact—had Frost brought it to Pete Curtis's camp?—and there were approximately four dozen rolls of film—all of it fast film, but she had said she could live with poor photo quality if necessary. Her proposal had been simple: she wanted Frost and Curtis to cooperate on a story about what was really going on inside Nugumbwe, the Chapmann police state and the wholesale slaughter of civilians and prisoners. She said she owed it to the producer, the cameraman, the soundman—the men who had died trying to help her get to Nugumbwe to get the story in the first place. She wanted to expose Chapmann, Dr. Kubinda's dictatorship. The valiant efforts of the rebel army under Curtis needed to be explained to the world, she had said. And, surprisingly to Frost, Pete Curtis had agreed, as long as his name and his agency were not mentioned.

"I don't want to give people the usual liberal routine that says terrorists are valiant people's revolutionaries, the routine that Dr. Kubinda is trying to hold the country together. I want to let the public in on the truth—that's all," she had said, looking appealingly to Frost to help her out with Curtis. All Frost had said was, "Just don't mention my name and I'll help—so long as it doesn't get in the way of the job, or us for that matter."

The cigarette burning Frost's fingertips jarred him back to the present and he tossed it down beside their Land Rover as it ground to a stop behind two half-tracks loaded with troops at the main gate.

In front of them, Frost could see orders being checked, identity papers of the officers and non-coms aboard the half-tracks being scrutinized. The guards were at the half-track just in front of them now and Frost whispered to Curtis, "We're not going to make it, Pete," then turned away and forced a bland smile onto his face. Benzahdi had played with the photo on Frost's identity papers, giving him a left eye instead of a patch and Frost now wore dark glasses to cover the fact that indeed he didn't have two eyes, contrary to the identity photo. But he realized, all someone had to do was ask him to remove his glasses for a better comparison with the photo and the game would likely be up. There was a realistic-looking bandage over his left eye where the patch had been and he'd even used makeup to color over the lines the eyepatch left on his face, lines not tanned as deeply as the rest of his skin. Frost had shaved away his mustache, but any sharp sentry would recognize him he felt, convinced that by now Chapmann knew he was still alive and working in the area and would be looking for him.

He looked over his left shoulder, awkwardly, because of course he still could only see with his right eye, but he saw a woman he thought was Bess—the chadar seemed a better quality and a little cleaner than the comparative few other veiled women in the square. She was near the gate and bending over to look at the wares of a street vendor. Frost hoped she could carry it off if she had to or at least could get out of the city and save herself.

Frost watched mechanically as the driver pulled the Land Rover forward to the guard post. Instead of the usual low number of guards, Frost could make out at least two dozen men, all armed with SMGs or FN-FAL assault rifles.

The guard doing the talking first checked the sergeant's papers. Frost watched as the driver handed them over, waited, lighting a cigarette, and then took the papers back. The guard took two steps closer to Frost, sitting on the side of the Land Rover closest. "Papers please," he said in heavily accented but reasonably correct-sounding English.

Frost smiled thinly and reached under his uniform blouse and produced them, then handed them over. The guard looked through the papers, glanced up at Frost's face when he came to the photo identity card, then looked at the orders Frost had and returned the papers. "Thank you sir, now," turning to Curtis, "may I see your papers, Lieutenant?"

"Certainly," Curtis said, then reached into his hip pocket, took out his wallet and pulled out the identity papers and orders. Frost almost smelled trouble as Curtis handed the papers past him—they were wet from perspiration. Frost's mind raced—would the ink have run, would—but then suddenly reality interrupted his thoughts. As the guard came to Curtis's identity card, the picture fell from the card to the ground. As the guard bent over, Frost heard him mumble in English, "This glue is wet . . ." Then the man, the papers in his hand, turned and shouted over his shoulder. In the native language, Frost could not understand. But, as Curtis started to extract the snub-nosed Model 19 revolver from under his uniform blouse, Frost got the message.

As the guard turned back toward Frost and Curtis, his sergeant running toward the Land Rover now with three or four armed men behind him, Curtis—his gun out first—stabbed the stubby muzzled .357 toward the guard's face and fired point-blank, less than six inches from the man's mouth. Frost turned his eye away, blood spattering onto his face and hands and clothes, his own Browning in his hand and firing at the second guard.

Curtis was already firing toward the Chapmann sergeant and his men, and their own driver had a revolver in his left hand, the Chapmann uniform .45 automatic in his right, firing. Frost heard himself shouting, "Drive, man—now."

There was still no response from Bess—Frost knew somehow she wouldn't have lost her nerve. Perhaps she was just holding back, he thought.

The Land Rover skidded to the left and Frost lost his balance—"The left front tire," the driver shouted in English. Then, as the Rover started up again, plowing past the Chapmann troops, Frost and Curtis still firing into their midst, there was a heavy thudding sound and the Rover stopped dead. "The radiator I think," their driver shouted.

Already, a fresh stick in the Browning High Power in his right fist, Frost was starting to step down from the Land Rover, Peter Curtis behind him. Curtis's gun was still while he rammed a Safariland Speed Loader against the ejector star in the cylinder and introduced six more rounds to the little K-frame revolver.

Chapmann troops were coming from all sides and Frost kept firing. As a man with an assault rifle stormed toward them, Frost extended his right arm and fired twice, catching the man in the chest. Then as Frost reached the ground, he turned to his left and fired twice from the hip, gut-shooting still another Chapmann man. Curtis, behind him still, was firing with the Smith revolver in his left hand and the .45 automatic from his belt in the other.

As a group of six more men—Frost didn't know where they all were coming from—raced toward the Rover, Frost now some six feet from the vehicle in a loping run, stopped in midstride and opened fire with his Browning. The 9mm was in his left hand, the borrowed .45 in his right. Bodies fell on all sides of them, like a slaughterhouse. The slow-motion death dance continued. As Frost emptied the borrowed .45 at two men coming toward him from over the hood of the abandoned Land Rover—catching one in midair like some sort of macabre clay target—out of the corner of his eye, he saw Curtis take a burst in his right side. Curtis dropped to one knee and, the right arm stiff at his side, kept on firing with the revolver in his left hand.

As Frost rammed his last fresh magazine into the well of the Browning, he heard the honking of an automobile horn—the first few bars of "Dixie"—and he turned. There was Bess, behind the wheel of a vintage Mustang convertible, the chadar gone, her straw blonde hair blowing across her face in lovely disarray, an UZI SMG chattering from her left hand braced against the top of the Mustang's door frame.

Frost looked back toward Curtis. The young CIA

man's six gun was empty. Frost fired twice as one of the Chapmann African troops started to crash a rifle butt toward Curtis's head. Then, bending over, Frost fired into the ever-growing crowd of attackers. He grabbed Curtis under his left arm, half walked, half dragged the young man toward Bess and the car, firing his Browning High Power pistol sometimes at point-blank range toward anything that moved.

Frost could hear Bess shouting, "Come on Frost—come on!"

To his left, Frost saw their driver coming and the man started helping Frost with Curtis. As one of the Chapmann men raced toward them and Frost made to fire, the driver beside him loosed a burst from an assault rifle— "Picked this up just a minute ago," the man shouted.

They reached the car, and Frost and the African driver beside him roughly pushed Curtis up and into the back seat, the African clambering over beside Curtis. Frost climbed across the Mustang's hood and over the windshield and into the front seat. Bess already had the car moving. One of the Chapmann troopers was hanging onto the driver's side door and Frost reached across in front of Bess and rammed the muzzle of his now empty Browning pistol hard against a man's nose. Even over the shouts and the roar of gunfire, Frost could hear the man scream as he died.

Frost glanced in front of them—a wall of Chapmann troops blocked their way to the gate. "Run 'em over," he shouted. Bess glanced toward him, shrugged and stomped down hard on the gas pedal. The wall of bodies fanned open in front of them and Frost could feel the car running over some of the men, the sensation like driving slowly across a series of railroad tracks, the car swaying up and down then up again. One of the white mercenaries sprang toward them, clinging to the hood of the Mustang as Bess accelerated past the last of the mob. Frost, his pistol empty, grabbed one of his knives and as the mercenary started to fumble a gun toward the windshield, Frost stood up, leaned over the windshield and hammered his knife blade into the man's back. The mercenary slipped away from the hood, screaming, falling under the wheels.

"Good thing they're trying to take us alive!" Frost shouted to Bess.

"You're crazy, Frost," she shouted back, the Mustang crashing through the candy-striped wooden barrier at the main gate and turning onto the main road leading from Buwandi. "You actually do this stuff for a living?" she shouted over the wind and engine noise, the gunfire behind them diminishing.

"Nice car," he shouted back. "Must belong to one of the officers." Frost looked down the road behind them. Already he could see several Land Rovers and at least one half-track in pursuit, he said, "Don't spare the horses, kid—we're still popular."

Bess glanced into the rearview mirror, then looking down at the dashboard shouted, "Hey, Frost, what the hell is that red toggle switch for?"

Frost followed her eyes down to the dashboard. "Get me—sure as hell is a red toggle switch though—try it."

The girl reached down with her right hand and flipped the switch. There was a roar from the engine and the Mustang lurched ahead, the girl's hands locking onto the steering wheel in a death grip.

She looked at Frost and he smiled. "Supercharger—wonder if he's got any other gadgets on this thing."

"Don't! Just don't touch anything—if this damned car goes any faster I won't be able to handle it, Frost."

Frost ignored her outburst, patting her hand on the gear shift lever, then turned around in the bucket seat and looked back to Curtis and the sergeant. "How is he?" Frost shouted.

The driver said, "Just some flesh wounds—if we can get him somewhere and do something about the bleeding, Mr. Curtis should be all right."

Frost nodded and turned back to Bess. "Where's that UZI?" he shouted. She reached down on the driver's side and hauled the SMG up and handed it across to him. It seemed like the car was flying now, past row upon row of low trees and scrub brush, the noise from the wind in the open car almost deafening. Frost checked the UZI, the magazine empty.

"You still got those spares?" he shouted.

"What?" she said.

"Never mind," he answered, then reached down to her right leg, pulled up the ankle length dress she wore, found the two spare magazines strapped to her right calf and removed them. As he leaned across her lap and got at the two magazines strapped to her left leg, he could hear her voice shouting, above him, "Frost, you'll do anything to cop a cheap feel won't you?"

He leaned back, ramming one of the fresh magazines into the UZI, then bent toward her ear, shouting so she could hear him. "Better damn well believe I will."

Frost glanced behind them again. The Rovers and the half-track weren't gaining on them, in fact the Mustang was beating them out nicely, but the road was rutted and bad and as he glanced toward Bess he could see she was having an increasingly difficult

199

time controlling the automobile.

Frost was balancing the odds on ditching the Mustang and escaping into the rain forest, its edge perhaps two hundred yards from the road. But as he looked ahead of them again, he dismissed the idea—two Land Rovers and another of the American-made four-man M-48 tanks, identical to the one they'd gone up against before, were coming down the road toward them.

"Stop the car!" Frost shouted and Bess jammed on the brakes and the car pulled left and skidded to a halt. "Move over," he ordered and jumped out of the passenger seat and ran around the front of the car, then getting behind the wheel, wrenched the car back into the middle of the road and started accelerating.

"What are you going to do?" the girl shouted.

"The only thing I can do," he hollered back. "Get this thing off the road and head for the rain forest, get as close as we can to tree cover and try to lose them on foot. Once we get where it's really dense, that tank will be useless."

"Hank!" The voice was tired-sounding. "Hank, listen." It was Pete Curtis.

"How you doing, my man." Frost shouted back to him. "Just hang in there."

"Hank, this car is solid enough—there's something we can try if you can do it. There's a bridge off an old road about a half mile ahead, nobody uses it any more. It was a narrow bridge. If you can get to it and get across, the tank won't be able to follow you."

"Okay, tell me when," Frost said, his mind already racing over what was available to them, trying to find a way not only to keep the tank from following but maybe blow the bridge entirely and keep everyone off their track.

"Now," Curtis shouted, weakly, and Frost wrenched the wheel into a skidding, hard right, double clutching and downshifting, then downshifting again to build up RPMs and going back up into third. Then, a second later, he upshifted into fourth. The road, a single rutted lane, was worse than the main road, and with each bump and chuckhole Frost thought certainly they'd break an axle. Suddenly, overhead, he heard the whine of a shell. "Duck!" Frost shouted, the 90mm from the M-48 tank behind them crashing a round not a dozen feet to their right, the projectile sending up a fireball buffeting the Mustang laterally and almost making Frost lose control. "My arm!" Bess was screaming and he glanced at her; her right sleeve was on fire. "Sergeant!" Frost shouted, and as he glanced from the road again, he saw the black sergeant reaching over the back seat, smothering the flames on the sleeve of Bess's dress with his hands.

Frost thought he heard the girl sobbing in pain beside him, but dismissed the thought since he could do nothing for her now beyond trying to get the car over the road and to the bridge, their one slim chance of escape. He dropped down into third, no longer able to take the road at top speed, kicked off the supercharger and then had to drop into second. Not doing even thirty-five now, but keeping to the lower gear for added torque, he could see the images of the tank, the half-track and the four Land Rovers growing in his rearview mirror. He saw the puff of smoke from the M-48's turret, heard the 90mm whine coming and upshifted, enough RPMs to shoot him ahead, hiking the Mustang to nearly 50 again, the shell impacting into the center of the road behind them.

In a few seconds, Frost had to drop back down to second, the road getting steeper.

It's just up ahead now," he could hear Curtis shouting to him. Then, "look—you can see it—there!" And the trestles from the small bridge were just visible on the horizon. Frost stamped down on the clutch, upshifted and shot ahead, another round from the 90mm gun crashing down just to their left.

Less than a half mile from the bridge, straining to see and cursing the fact that he had only one eye, Frost downshifted quickly, then downshifted again, wrenching the wheel sharply to the left and grinding to a halt just shy of the drainage ditch beside the road. "Look!" he shouted.

Bess, her crying somewhat abated, but still holding her arm, half stood on the passenger seat and looked over the windshield and past the front of the hood. The bridge was already down—one trestle was still standing, but the bridge itself had fallen away or been blown up. "Sit down," Frost commanded her, then hauled the car into reverse, backed away from the ditch, swung into first and wrenched the wheel around to the right and edged them toward the bridge. The distance across was perhaps twenty feet, the bridge having spanned a deep, narrow gorge. Below, Frost heard the sound of violently rushing water.

"All right—everybody hold onto something and pray." Frost wrenched the stick into reverse, backed away from the bridge into a short arc, the front of the car pointing back toward the advancing tank and the armada of Chapmann troop vehicles.

"What are you going to do?" Bess screamed.

"We can sit here," he said, wrenching the wheel around to his left and upping the box into second as

202

he tore down the road away from the bridge "and get killed or captured, or we can try to jump that gorge back there—none of those other vehicles can follow us if we do. If we don't make it," and he shot a glance at her and squeezed her thigh a moment, "you're one hell of a girl, Bess!" Then, going into a body-bending bootlegger turn, downshifting, then picking up RPMs as he straightened out and jumped it up into third—"Hold on!" Frost punched the horn button and the first few bars of Dixie played again. From behind him, he could hear Curtis, despite his wounds, shouting. Frost ground the box up into fourth and as they reached the edge, the Mustang swerving to avoid the bridge trestle, Frost flipped the red supercharger toggle switch. The car shot off the edge and he could hear Bess scream beside him and feel her digging her nails into his leg.

The rush of the wind, the momentary feeling akin to weightlessness, the quiet as the engine's roar seemed somehow more distant from them. And then, as Frost downshifted, the car impacted on the other side of the gorge, tilting up onto its right side. As Frost wrenched the wheel to the left and threw his body weight left, the car droppped, first onto the right wheels. But as he hit the gas pedal, it settled on all four wheels and shot ahead. Frost killed the whining supercharger, upshifted into fourth and bounced the Mustang back up onto the road. Frost glanced into the rearview mirror. One of the Land Rovers skidded to a halt at the edge of the gorge on the other side of the demolished bridge, nearly slipping over the side. Frost slapped Bess's thigh, shouting, "All right!" And Frost started laughing, so loudly he almost startled himself, then punched out Dixie again on the horn button.

Chapter Thirteen

"Anyone ever tell you they loved you, Frost?" Bess asked, strangely, quietly, as she lay in the darkness beside him.

"Yeah, my mother and father—separately though. I never saw them together after I was real little. Why?"

He could barely see the outline of her face in the darkness as she leaned up on one elbow beside him. "Well, someone's telling you now," she said, then kissed him lightly on the lips and rolled over again onto her back.

They were out of harm's way, at least temporarily, at a house Curtis sometimes used as a headquarters about a hundred miles away from Buwandi, up in the hills. Curtis, patched up and scheduled for a few days rest, had told them the place had once belonged to a gentleman white hunter who'd left the area during the 1950s, abandoning the house, furnishings and all. Most of the furnishings were long gone, and only half of the house still had a roof that actually kept the rain or the birds out, but it was better than an outdoor camp.

As Frost and Bess lay on their sleeping bags and blankets in the corner of what had once been the library and Frost reached out and touched her hand, he thought back to the events of the last eight hours. After making the jump across the gorge—he'd thought it was impossible but tried it anyway—they had finally been forced to abandon the battered Mustang and walk the rest of the way toward Curtis's camp. He'd asked Bess how she'd gotten the keys for the Mustang, but then looked down and seen there were none. Then he'd asked her where she'd learned to hot wire a car and she'd said, "None of your business." Halfway to the Curtis camp, Frost and the others had encountered a rebel army patrol, and with plenty of men now to shift the weight of carrying the wounded Curtis, they had reached the camp relatively quickly. Curtis had told Frost how to call in a helicopter and after another hour of waiting, an unmarked and battered Huey HU-1D of early Viet Nam vintage had shown up and evacuated them, dropping them less than a half mile from the headquarters where they now stayed. There were perhaps two dozen support personnel here, one of them a CIA man like Curtis, and there had been a doctor. Bess had insisted that after the man treated Curtis she would not have the burns on her arm looked to until Frost let the doctor examine his back injury. Out of desperation and exhaustion, Frost had agreed.

"We really don't know as much about the back as we'd like," the young black doctor had told Frost and Bess, after examining Frost, "but we're learning more all the time—millions, perhaps a billion or more humans all over the globe have one type or another of back trouble, some serious, some just occasionally annoying. You aren't as badly off as you were led to believe, Captain Frost. I don't think an operation to correct that disc would be necessary. A back brace for a month or so, and traction, the right sort of exercises and massage, then a small brace for another few months and just watching out for doing anything strenuous with it. You should be fine—might even get away without that small brace if you just avoid strenuous exertion for a few months.''

"How would lovemaking affect his back, Doctor," Bess had said, a wicked look in her eye.

The doctor had laughed and just shook his head. Frost said, "Tsk tsk—shameless hussy."

Her arm tended to, Frost and Bess had found where the liquor was kept and raided the supplied. And now, dinner behind them, initial planning for the assault on the National Bank to begin on the next day, they lay there quietly in the darkness.

"When will you get the back done, Frost?"

"After this is all over, probably."

"How old are you," she said.

"Old enough," he answered, still staring into the darkness at the ceiling, still holding her hand.

"I mean I want a straight answer—how old are you?"

"Thirty-four," he said.

"You keep doing what you're doing," she said quietly, "you'll never make forty."

"Things aren't usually this hazardous," Frost answered, getting up on his elbow and lighting a cigarette.

"Bullshit," she said, very quietly. "I told you I loved you a minute ago. Got anything to say about it?"

He stubbed out his cigarette, turned around and reached out and touched her face with his left hand, "Okay—I love you too, but I'm not saying anything else."

"I know, Frost" she said, her voice suddenly sounding terribly frail there in the darkness.

Frost drew her up to him, barely seeing her face in

the darkness surrounding them.

"What about the other people here?" she said.

"Let 'em eat their hearts out," Frost said, then bent his face toward her and touched his lips to hers, drawing her into his arms beside him and kissing her mouth hard, holding her tightly, her breath coming in short gasps against his face and chest.

"Oh, Frost," she whispered as his fingers touched her breasts.

"You like that?" he said, his hands caressing her, the nipples seeming to grow and harden beneath his finger tips. He didn't need words for an answer. Holding her close to him, with his left hand he began to rub the triangle of curly pubic hair at her crotch, then moved his fingers inside her, exploring her, searching out the spots that seemed to give her the greatest sensation. She buried her face against him, little moaning sounds coming from her now. She was moving under his hands, her body undulating beside him to some rhythm he was stimulating inside her. His fingers were wet from her and the strong, woman odor of her was unmistakable. He touched his lips to the nipple of her right breast and she arched her back and moved her right hand, a gesture of offering the breasts to him and he took it.

His mouth traveled downward, stopping to kiss her flesh along the way. And he touched his lips to the insides of her thighs a moment, then drawing her down beside him—their bodies beneath the blanket barely covering them from any prying eyes—he moved on top of her, felt the swelling of his penis as its tip kissed against her, felt her hand wrap around it and felt it swelling more.

Then he slid inside of her, the moisture and the suction it created making a loud sucking sound,

"Well, there goes our secret," he whispered in her ear.

Her only response was a beautifully purring, "Hmmm."

He could feel her thighs wrapping around his hips, her pelvis rising to press against him. He kissed her throat, then drew her mouth under his and crushed her lips beneath his own. At the back of his mind he was searching for the word—the contractions of her muscles that were now alternately squeezing and releasing his penis inside her, sending waves of sensation like electric shocks up his spine, sometimes almost hurting him when she squeezed too hard, giving him the vague sensation that somehow he was outside of his body and yet experiencing every centimeter of his skin as alive and feeling, every microsecond of time as an eternity. He buried his face against her neck and kissed her, then with his hands arched her back pushing her loins under him and pushing deeper inside her. Their bodies moved together, like one body rather than two, the pulsing of her muscles around his penis going faster and faster, the thrusting of his penis inside her faster. In the instant that it happened Frost felt almost a momentary paralysis as he wanted to drive himself deeper into her, as her body seemed to tug at him like a vortex in the ocean sucking down a drowning man. And then they sank downward, still locked in each other's arms, the movement of her muscles now sending tremors through him. And still she moaned lightly, softly against his ear, and after a few seconds, whispered, "Frost, oh I do so love you. Oh, Frost . . ."

And afterward, he kissed her lightly, wrapped her shoulders with his right arm and drew her head against his chest, her breasts, her still moist crotch, her burning warm thighs pressed hard against him. They slept, but before they did she whispered in Frost's ear, "You do all right, Frost—for a man with a bad back."

The next day, Frost and Bess saw little of one another—at breakfast they ate together, and once he bumped into her in the hallway. She was working with the doctor, Thaddeus Jacumbe, organizing medical supplies, making pre-prepared syringes, up-dating First Aid Kits. The assault would take place in a few days they all knew and then, despite what preparations they could make, medical supplies would be needed aplenty. Frost spent the day with the wounded Curtis in his room, along with three of the native officers and the other CIA man, Craine Holcomb, a veteran in the Company and a name Frost was familiar with, though they had never before worked together.

By dinner time, plans were relatively fixed and arrangements were made to use the few helicopters still available to them and in decent working order to bring in troops from the surrounding areas in preparation for the National Bank assault. Over half the helicopters available were more or less permanently grounded, since the administration in Washington supporting the dictator, Dr. Kubinda, would not sell helicopter replacement parts to the rebel right wing army and CIA was unable to get sufficient parts through clandestine sources.

After dinner that evening, Frost simply said to Bess, "Come on, I want to teach you something" and she followed him out behind the house in the twilight and down a slope toward the boundary with the forest.

Frost reached under the back of his uniform blouse and produced a four-inch revolver, broke open the cylinder and handed it to her. "What's this?" she said.

"Now don't be silly," Frost said, lighting up. "It's a gun, of course."

"But I mean what's it for—oh, why are you giving it to me?"

"Well, I don't know what's going to happen. Looks like you seem to handle a submachine gun or an assault rifle decently enough, but that time we stole the Land Rover to get into Buwandi and you were using my Browning—didn't look like you knew how to handle a hand gun."

"Well, you're right, I suppose," she said, thoughtfully. "My father taught me how to use a rifle years ago and how to use a shotgun, but he only owned a .22 target pistol and never showed me how to use it."

"Then I'll show you," Frost said.

"Don't I get one like yours?" she asked, faking a petulant tone in her voice and trying to look hurt.

"No—a lot of women and some men have troubles working the slide on an automatic—that's why a revolver. I scoured the arms cabinet and came up with a good one though—four-inch Colt Python .357 Magnum—its even nickel plated, see?"

And then Frost commenced to show her how to load and unload the gun, how to lower the hammer from full cock. When she asked about the adjustable rear sight, he said, "Don't worry about it—I'll fix it for you if you need it. Unless you want to go target shooting, it's fine as is—most people never change adjustable sights, anyway." And then he loaded it for her with some standard .38 Special 158-grain Round Nosed Lead rounds and let her try several cylinderfuls, then produced a box of .357 158-grain Semijacketed Soft Points and the recoil difference, though she said she felt she could handle it, surprised her.

"I've got some heavy canvas back up at the house—couldn't find a holster for this but figured you could sew something to carry it in—you do sew?"

"I even cook," she said, smiling. "Remember, Frost?"

He rubbed his stomach, forced a smile and said, "Yeah—how could I forget?" The flies weren't bad that high in the mountains and they sat outside at a rough wooden camp table while Frost showed her how to clean the revolver, how to remove the crane lock screw to free the cylinder from the frame, what end to start the patch from in the barrel. And as they talked, Frost started to tell her about himself, what made him tick.

"Yeah," he told her, almost defensively, "I like being a mercenary. But I don't know if you can really call it that anymore. I mean, there aren't always enough wars to fight in these days. Maybe that sounds stupid—sort of like Napoleon. Once he was supposed to have read a message and looked up at his advisers and said, "Good God, peace has broken out . . ."

Later, he looked at her sharply, lit a cigarette, then said, "No—I don't like war. It's the total surrender of common sense and reason, but sometimes it's the only answer, sometimes it's either fight or be killed or conquered. These people that I fight wars for—sometimes they aren't the world's best characters, sometimes they may really be just what the Communists call them—right wing dictators. But most of the times they aren't. But if you've gotta choose between a dictator and a Communist, you support the dictator. At least you can maybe reason

211

with him afterward, or pump money to him to get him to introduce a democracy, to teach his people to read—things like that. But if the Communists keep going, one of these days America is going to wake up and realize it's the only island of democracy left in the world—guys like me fight the wars the United States should be fighting, but liberal officials won't get involved with them. Like Khomeni in Iran. The CIA should have smoked that sucker before he ever got out of France—killed him stone cold dead. But nobody did, and he went back to Iran and look what happened."

"But how can you justify fighting a popular movement, even if it is Communist?"

He looked at her in the bare-bulb yellow light throwing a halo on the ground around them. "I don't necessarily support a man, or the reasons why he's fighting. But if he's fighting my enemy, the Communists, then I'll help him. Now maybe the next year I'll be back working for some democratic revolutionaries who really want to establish a Western style democracy, and then I'll be fighting my old employer. That's fine. But to me, and to most of the guys in my business—Chapmann and his crew are an exception, believe me—the money is only secondary and it's not that good usually. Somebody has to try to stop the Communists right now—in Latin America, in Africa, in Europe, in America—and right now, not tomorrow. Hell—I don't know if we'll ever have World War Three, I hope not. I don't want to see people die. But killing a Communist terrorist isn't killing, it's exterminating, just like shooting a hole in a garbage can. There's no more moral implication to it."

Then later, "Hell yes, it is simplistic. Communism is evil—period. Now fine, if we can get along with

Russia or mainland China and they keep their hands off us and stop trying to subvert the world, super—live and let live. But Russia in particular, and Cuba. Not the people, but the Communist bosses. I'd as soon shoot one as spit at one. Castro is working to turn Latin America Communist, and any fool except the fools in Washington can see that. And his revolutions have to be stopped—period.''

When she asked how he saw himself, he said, "I don't know. How does any man see himself? I guess you could probably read into me that I think I'm some sort of Crusader, and maybe I feel that way about myself. But if I'm some kind of crusading hero, then the world is in worse shape than I think it is.''

"Why?'' Frost answered Bess. "Think about me for a minute. I don't kill for any kind of kicks or thrill—guys like that are crazy. I don't like killing, but it doesn't really bother me to do it either. I can turn my conscience on and off like a faucet sometimes. Kill a Communist—that's stepping on a waterbug. But I'd never fight a pro-American, anti-Communist Government. Sometimes people say mercenaries who fight in Africa are racists. Bullshit! I'll kill a Communist whether he's black, white or any other color. Doesn't matter to me. I got into a fight in a bar with a Klansman once who was half drunk like I was and was yelling "nigger this'' and "nigger that'' all over the place and this poor black construction worker was down at the end of the bar just trying to enjoy a beer for himself. All the nice liberal white people were standing around the place just listening. I told the white guy with the big mouth to shut up and when he hauled off to slug me with a beer bottle I slammed his face into the top of

213

the bar and he almost choked to death on his teeth. You can't cubbyhole people. Most of the victims of the Communist terrorists are blacks or Indians—the Communists are the racists. Now, you want to know anything else or you want to go inside and make love after you get the gun oil off your hands?

She decided on the latter, Frost happily realized as she stopped talking and kissed him lightly on the lips. To hell with the oil on her hands, he thought.

"You're just like a knight, one of the knights in the Crusades," she whispered to him later that night in the darkness. "Maybe your armor is a little tarnished, but that's just what you are—a knight."

Frost laughed. "What's so funny," she asked.

"Bess . . . Bess . . .," he said, holding her close. "If I'm some kind of a knight, it's more like Don Quixote—trying to contain Communists and terrorists and fight wars everyone ignores on a shoestring budget makes tilting at windmills look like a cinch."

Chapter Fourteen

"No, dammit. All right—I love you. And you can't go. I'm not going to marry you, at least I don't think so because I don't want to marry anybody and I've got no right to tell you what to do and you're a liberated woman and all that other good shit—but you are not—repeat—not going. Got me?" Frost said, hurling his cigarette butt down to the ground and stomping it like a roach.

"But Pete Curtis thinks it's a good idea," Bess said.

"Yeah, well fine—let Pete Curtis send out his girl friend and keep his damned opinions to himself."

"You know, Frost—you swear a lot."

"I never did 'til I met you," he shouted. "Come on—let's see Curtis!" And Frost stamped off the paint-chipped, half-destroyed front porch and into the good side of the house—the part with the roof.

Curtis and the other CIA man, Craine Holcomb, were conferring in the kitchen when Frost, Bess close at his heels, found them. "Why the hell you tell Bess she could go on the raid?"

"What?" Craine said.

"No—Curtis. Why?"

"What?" Curtis said, visibly annoyed at the interruption, the young CIA man now virtually recovered from his wounds.

"I don't care if you're busy—why did you tell

Bess she could go along on the raid?"

"I figured," Curtis said, trying to catch Bess's eye, "that a photographic record of the thing wouldn't hurt, and it might help dramatize the cause of the rebel army."

"And it could also do a terrific job of getting her killed, too," Frost said angrily, lighting a cigarette.

"Listen—I got charge of release on all the pictures—we develop the film. I can't lose and those people need the public to be involved, to realize the cause they're fighting for is the right cause—the nobility, the sacrifice, the dignity of these—"

"Aw, shut up and can the hyperbole," Frost said disgustedly. "You're talking about a cause and I'm talking about a life—an important one."

"Hey, Frost," the quiet voice behind him said, her hand now on his arm. "I won't die—I promise. You're balling up your philosophy, Frost—I'm helping in the good fight, remember? I'm fighting the Communists, just like you are, because if Kubinda wins he and Chapmann will drive all the good guys to fight for the Communist terrorists and then the country will be lost—you told me you agreed with Curtis."

"But I don't agree with losing you." Frost stubbed out his cigarette, the tip of ash still smoking and left the room.

As he walked through the doorway, he heard Curtis saying, "If you'd told me Hank Frost would get so involved with someone—" But Frost closed the door behind him, at that moment the truth, the last thing he wanted to hear.

The next three days were spent rehearsing the operation that would take place that coming Saturday, and though Frost and Bess still slept together and ate together and spent as much time as possible together, Frost did not bring up the fact of her going along. The only lateral reference he made to it was the stepped-up training he gave her with the Python he'd found for her and the added training on how to operate an SMG—more effectively.

That Friday night, the entire force of 150 men assembled, the helicopters waiting at a nearby staging area, Frost, Bess, Curtis, Holcomb and the rebel army officers had dinner together. It would have been hard to call it a banquet, Frost thought—fancied up C-Rations and some fresh meat from a type of African deer found locally. That and a modest dip into the remainder of the liquor cabinet led to a final toast. By the light of a few bare bulbs, Curtis and the Rebel Army leader, General Wazibwe, who had joined them earlier that day, made a toast, "To victory and defeat—the victory of the forces of democracy in Nugumbwe and the defeat of the tyrant Kubinda and his evil butcher Chapmann."

Everyone drank the toast, Frost adding, "I'll shoot the first man who says 'Dark of the moon.' "

Frost and Bess made love again that night, neither of them falling asleep until well past two A.M., both the man and the woman who loved him thinking that perhaps this night might be their last. At six A.M., the usual reveille sounded—the officer of the day went around banging a wooden spoon against a cooking pot and shouting something in his native language that Frost was yet to understand.

Chapter Fifteen

Frost sat alone on the steps of the great, dilapidated white house, out of force of habit wearing gloves as he loaded the magazines for the Browning, checking the magazine springs after every three rounds or so, single loading the chamberred round for the first loading of the pistol itself, upping the capacity to fourteen rounds. He'd never had the followers of the Browning magazines ground down that fraction of an inch that would allow the packing of a fourteenth round in the magazine—double column magazines, although he liked the Browning, were really not that big a thing. A good man with a standard pistol like the Colt Government .45 or the superb little Detonics Stainless .45 could reload fast enough that the double column feature of the Browning, the Beretta 92S, the Smith Model 59, the MAB, were just convenience features, not really any sort of practical edge.

Frost carried the Browning because it was reliable and sure functioning. Though the 9mm, even the 115-grain jacketted hollow point, was far from the best pistol found in the world, you couldn't always find .45 ACP overseas. Unlike most mercs, Frost only carried one handgun—a great many favored a combination of a 9mm like the Browning and a .38 Special or .357 Magnum revolver. As Frost heard the insect like drone of the helicopters coming in for the job of ferrying the strike force to the Nugumb-wean capitol, he stood up, lit a Camel and inhaled the smoke deeply into his lungs. His Gerber fighting knives were sharp, his H-K 7.62mm assault rifle cleaned and loaded. In short, Hank Frost, the one-eyed mercenary captain, was as ready as he would ever be to stare death in the face and walk away or get carried out.

A moment later, he felt Bess beside him on the porch, wrapped his arm around her waist, offered her a drag on the cigarette and returned to watching the helicopters come in.

"It's almost pretty in a strange way, isn't it, Frost?"

"Yeah—in a very strange way. But, yeah, it is. You got that Python of yours ready?"

"Yes. Frost?"

"What, Bess," he said, turning around and locking his other arm around her waist. She reached up and took the cigarette from his lips, flipped the butt away and kissed him.

"What was that for?" he asked.

"For being Hank Frost, that's all. Okay?"

"Okay, kid," he said.

As he started to turn back to watch the landing field, she caught at his face with her fingertips and he turned back to her. "What?"

"I've never seen you without your patch—can I?"

"You won't want to," Frost said, and he raised the patch up for her to see. There was no eye, the lid was permanently closed. Instead of turning her face away in revulsion—there was a scar, of course—she reached up and standing on her tiptoes kissed him there.

He slipped the patch in place and held her close to

219

him. "You make it damned hard for somebody not to marry you."

"You don't have to now," she whispered, twisting the top button of his fatigue blouse in her fingers, then looking up at him. "And maybe it will take a long time, but one of these days—I guarantee it."

"You're buyin' trouble, kid—you know that." It was a statement, not a question.

"Uh-huh," she said, then put her face against his chest and let him hold her, both of them watching the helicopters land, ticking off the seconds, fearing the final separation of death.

There were ten choppers in all, three of which would carry the first strike force which Curtis and Frost jointly would command, the remaining seven carrying slightly more than two-thirds of the one hundred-fifty man force and under the command of Craine, the other CIA man, and General Wazibwe. The first three choppers would come down inside the walls of the bank enclosure, one at a time because of the lack of space, the other seven choppers landing outside once the interior of the bank enclosure was at least partially secured. Then they would attack. The choppers would carry out the bulk of the raid's survivors while trucks would carry out as much of the gold as could be loaded, then the bank would be blown—Curtis and Frost would see to that. No intermediate base was to be used, since each of the choppers would have double the fuel it needed for the round trip, and in the event a chopper were disabled on the return trip, there was little doubt the natural attrition of battle casualties would provide ample room for other of the choppers to pick up the stranded men aboard. Bess would be with the attack force outside the walls, with the rear

220

elements—Frost had arranged that with Curtis, and though she had wanted to go in with Frost, she hadn't voiced an objection. She'd told him, "If you feel better with me bringing up the rear, then fine—but don't you dare die on me." Laughing, kissing her, he'd promised he wouldn't.

Despite the early hour, they rode the Hueys with the side doors open because of the searing heat, Frost in one of the three lead choppers, Curtis in the second and the sergeant who had been the driver for their escape from Buwandi—in reality a colonel—commanding the third element.

The whirring of the rotors made talking difficult at best under normal circumstances and, since Frost knew none of the native language and the troopers with him knew nothing of English, conversation would have been impossible at any event. The pilots were likely CIA contract employees, fliers and not combatants, or perhaps sent in from some nearby Naval vessel or one of the U.S. Army bases in the Mediterranean. They wore no rank, carried no ID and had silenced .22 pistols slung in military-looking shoulder holsters strapped across their chests over their flak vests, .45 Government autos in hip holsters and one of the men Frost had noticed had a Walther PPK/S in a second shoulder rig under his flak jacket.

Of flak jackets there had not been enough to go around and so, since the troops could not wear them, Frost, Curtis and the African Colonel had elected not to wear any either. It was the sort of decision, Frost thought, that once you made you instantly regretted.

Frost had locked Bess into a flak jacket despite her protests that it was too heavy and told the man commanding her chopper that if she tried to take it off he should club her and if he—Frost—saw her with it off, he—Frost—would shoot the man dead.

Curtis was hoping for total surprise. Frost was more realistic, knowing full-well from the radar equipment he'd observed in and around Buwandi that they would be picked up fifty miles at least from the city and there would be a full-blown reception committee waiting for them. Had Curtis's rebel forces been stronger in the city itself, it would have been possible to start an uprising there to divert troops, but that could not be. Silently, Frost wondered why the Communist Terrorists had been so quiet—reports indicated practically zero activity. Almost bitterly, Frost realized the Communists were waiting for the Curtis attack and anticipating sufficiently heavy losses on both sides that they could just move in. There were probably right, he thought, though he hoped not.

The three lead helicopters with the first strike force quickly moved ahead of the slower-going main elements and, checking the black-faced Omega Seamaster 120 on his wrist, Frost estimated the first of the three lead choppers would be coming down inside the National Bank compound in under five minutes. He ran a last minute visual inspection of his men and their equipment—fourteen black African soldiers fighting to keep their homeland and rid themselves of a dictator. They weren't the most experienced men in the world. He'd learned that during the innumerable rehearsals for the operation, but they were fierce fighters and believed sufficiently in their cause to die for it. In some ways, Frost reflected, he couldn't ask for better men. Curtis had taught the men sufficient English phrases that they could respond to Frost's basic commands and Frost had mastered perhaps two dozen basic commands in their own language. That, sign language and a lot of luck, Frost judged, would either buy them a cup of coffee or win them a battle.

They were passing over the barbed wire ring around Buwandi now, and below Frost could make out a flurry of activity—armored half-tracks, a few tanks, almost countless Land Rovers. There was some sporadic gunfire aimed toward them already, but at the altitude they were holding, that was generally useless.

In less than a minute, Frost's chopper passed over the masonry wall of the old city and then the walled compound of the National Bank building was almost immediately below them. Frost eyed the pilot, who turned and gave him a weak thumbs up signal; Frost returned it forcefully and aimed his index finger toward the ground. Almost somberly, the pilot nodded and the helicopter started into a sweeping descent.

Frost glanced about to his comrades again. It had been difficult because pronouncing many of the names had been almost impossible to him at first, but in a manner of speaking he had finally mastered them all—the names of his fourteen men. Bokante, the sergeant; Untawi, the corporal leading fire team Alpha; Binka, the second corporal leading fire team Bravo; the young, short private who wanted to learn English, Junbiwati. The helicopter hovered for a moment a few feet above the ground and already Frost and his men were prepared to disembark. And then it was touch down.

Frost and Sergeant Bokante were the first two men through the wide-apart doors and onto the ground. Small arms fire was already heavy and Frost and the others fanned out in a semicircle at the base of the chopper and opened fire, then hauling themselves to their feet, took off in a dead run across the wide square and toward the cover of the service garage opposite the National Bank Building itself. One of Frost's men, Junbiwati, was already down, but Frost and the Bravo Fire Team Leader, Binka, snatched the boy up under his arms and dragged him with them. In the shelter of the stone walls as they set up their M-60s, the second of the first three helicopters landed, Curtis and his men doing the drill of fanning out for covering fire as the chopper went airborne again, then cutting across the square with the protective fire from Frost's element to cover them, heading for the far wall of the bank building itself. The heaviest of the fire was from the top of the wall, on the front of the bank building compound and on both flanks. At least a half dozen heavy machine guns that Frost could count were in operation. As the third chopper touched down, the last element of the strike force hit the ground.

The chopper lifted off. Frost signaled to Curtis and the African colonel and all three elements of commandoes converged for a frontal assault against the interior of the main wall and its machine gun positions.

Frost and his men, on Curtis's signal, split into two elements, fire support and maneuver. Sergeant Bokante took the fire support element, with six men, four using M16A1 assault rifles, the other two operating an M-60 link-belt fed machine gun, behind the cover of a Land Rover parked in the center of the square. Frost and five other men—the wounded soldier Junbiwati still under cover by the garage building—the Alpha fire maneuver element, cut a wide ace to the right and angled toward their objective, one of the three machine gun emplacements on the wall. Frost estimated two guns in each. Curtis and the colonel's commando squads were using similar maneuvers. The Huey gunships were having little effect, ground fire too heavy.

As Frost and the other two maneuver elements started toward their objectives, the support fire increasing in volume, Frost could barely make out the sound of the remaining seven helicopters coming in for the attack from outside the wall. But they were coming he knew.

As the maneuver elements raced through the hail of small arms fire to the wall, Frost wished for LAWS rockets, but at a prearranged signal, his men dropped, half keeping up sustained fire from their assault rifles, the others with a poor substitute for the LAWS—hand grenades. Then they were up and running again. For a minute, the machine gun nest was silent but as they got closer to the wall the gunners opened up again. Frost and his men—he'd lost two more—reached the base of the wall, and other than scattered small arms fire from other parts of the wall and inside the compound, there was momentary safety from the heavy fire above them. Frost knew that in a moment grenades would be popping down on them. Desperately, he wanted the outside assault force to launch its attack. As he heard the unmistakable sounds of the helicopters now, he signaled to Curtis and, from across the compound by one of the flanking walls, the CIA man started to talk into his radio.

Curtis signaled back to Frost and a minute later there was a huge explosion from outside the wall—missles from one of the helicopters. Frost alerted his men and they began laying out coils of ropelike plastique explosive by the base of the wall. From his vantage point, Frost could see that Curtis and the rebel army colonel were already having their men do the same. Then the coils were in place, strung against the base of the wall and up in layers almost to shoulder height, six coils in all. The last of the wires was in place and Frost sent his men twenty feet further down the wall's base, secured the wires to the pocket detonator he had and flipped the delay switch, the three C-cell batteries wired in series would, in 30 seconds, send their electric current back through the wires. Frost ran as fast as he could to join his men further down the wall. The plastique detonated behind him and Frost fell forward into the dirt, then rolled over. There was a hole in the base of the wall big enough for a truck to get through, and on the two flanking walls simultaneously there were identical explosions. Snatching the one M16 of the bunch fitted for firing 40mm grenades, Frost loaded the weapon, aimed toward the silent machine gun nest at the top of the wall and fired. The grenade hit, the high explosive round demolishing the sandbagged barricade surrounding the guns and crumbling the archlike upper section of the wall and bringing it crashing downward to the ground. Above the gunfire, Frost could hear the cheers of the rebel army men, dozens of them now pouring through from outside the wall to assist the first strike force in storming the bank itself.

Frost signaled to his men and they took off in a flat-out dead run across the square, their jungle-booted feet hammering hard against the dust, their assault rifles chattering at targets of opportunity along the way, the bulk of the attack force behind them now in a frontal assault against the defenders of the bank building itself. Frost signaled for the seventy-five or so commandoes to regroup on the bank steps, Curtis and the colonel's men laying down covering fire from the flanking walls.

Splitting the main body of the attack force into three elements behind him, Frost and his reinforced element charged up the stairs toward the massive metal doors of the bank. Halfway up the long, marble steps, they stopped on Frost's hand signal. Frost directed the rifleman with the grenade launcher attachment to go for the double doors. The man nodded, aimed and fired. The doors buckled inward in a puff of smoke and flame, the concussion of the explosion roaring back toward them and making the attackers shield their faces. But then Frost had them up again and, leading his men, they stormed their way into the bank, into a fusilade of small arms fire from the bank's defenders.

Frost had no way of telling what size force they were up against, but he estimated upwards of fifty men—apparently Chapmann's defense plan for the bank called for a last-ditch stand by the garrison inside the bank building itself and to hell with the grounds, Frost guessed.

And then the fighting began in earnest, close contact small arms fire, hand-to-hand fighting more reminiscent of two warring mobs than opposing armies. Frost led the five men remaining from the two teams of his original strike force down toward the vault room, one of the other attack elements now penetrating the bank building and joining with the force Frost had led, joining the close combat with the Chapmann troops. He could hear heavy weapons fire outside the bank itself, explosions. Glancing through one of the barred, shot out windows, he saw one of their Huey gunships go down as Chapmann fighters flew overhead and began strafing the ground outside with machinegun and rocket fire—and they were U.S. jets!

It was evidently a suicide force that was waiting for Frost and his five comrades halfway down the long stairs reaching to the underground vault level—a dozen men with submachine guns who had waited just a little too long to open fire. Frost and his commandoes were close in with them now and at point-blank range, the eighteen enemies exchanged automatic weapons fire. As the guns shot dry and the men closed the bayonets and fighting knives came out, pistols fired in full contact with their targets. A bayonet-wielding Chapmann soldier stormed toward Frost. Frost, his H-K assault rifle empty, brought the weapon into a guard position, stepped back and knocked away his opponent's first thrust. Again, Frost went into a guard position—he could not attack, his rifle without a bayonet. Again the Chapmann soldier lunged toward him, feinted and knocked Frost's weapon aside, then miscalculated and started a diagonal, cutting arc toward Frost's left shoulder. "Should have gone for a buttstroke, sucker," Frost rasped, bringing his weapon up, blocking the downward motion of his opponent's weapon, then snapping the butt of his own weapon hard into the Chapmann soldier's groin. "And," Frost said, "these things can work real great even without a bayonet on them." At that, Frost stepped inside his opponent's guard and smashed down in a vicious jab at his opponent's neck with the muzzle of his weapon, then stepping back Frost made a fast snapping horizontal butt stroke and caught his opponent in the jaw, sending the Chapmann soldier sprawling. As Frost wheeled to rejoin his men, two of the Chapmann soldiers charged toward him. Frost drew his Browning pistol and fired, catching the first man twice in the chest then rocking his pistol back down on line and at

228

almost point-blank range firing twice into the second man's face, blood spurting from it like juice from an over-ripe pear.

Two of Frost's men survived and none of the enemy. The survivors raced behind Frost down the stairs toward the vault, reloading their weapons on the run. Behind them—they turned—there were the sounds of running feet, shouts and, as Frost and his men positioned themselves to make a last-ditch defense, he could see Curtis and two dozen men. "Down here!" Frost shouted.

As Curtis stopped beside him, Frost said, "Look there—the vault itself is behind that steel grillwork—going to take two separate charges." Curtis and the last of Frost's men set to installing the charges while Frost took a dozen of the others and positioned them up along the stairwell as an advance guard against a Chapmann assault. "Fire in the hole!" Curtis shouted and everyone went down. In the confines of the vault room one story underground, the explosion was almost deafening. As soon as the smoke started to clear, Curtis and his demo men went back to set the charges to blow the vault itself. Again Curtis shouted, "Fire in the hole!" and again there was the anticipated explosion, only louder because of the greater amount of plastique it took to blow the vault door open. The concussion from the second explosion was so great that, as Frost looked around, he shouted, "Pete—watch out!" And an entire section of the vault room ceiling started to collapse.

Frost rushed to where Curtis had been, clearing away the rubble as best he could, other hands joining him then. Curtis was stunned and his left hand was covered with blood running down from under his sleeve, but as Frost and the others got him free,

Curtis managed to say, "I'll be all right—get to that vault. Hank, get the trucks coming through those holes in the wall out there." Frost nodded, snatched up Curtis's radio and as he pushed to talk, he froze. Some of the rebel troops were walking from the opened vault, their heads shaking in disbelief. Frost shoved the radio—unused—into his hip pocket and picked his way across the rubble and into the vault itself.

There were three cardboard boxes in the fifteen by fifteen-foot room, the gleaming steel shelves empty of gold. Frost reached inside each of the three boxes in turn—Nugumbwean paper money, still in bank wrappers. But there was no gold, not a single bar or coin. Frost lit a cigarette and picked his way back across the rubble and rejoined Pete Curtis.

He bent down to him, the noise of battle on the floor above them seeming to subside. "I know why Chapman and Dr. Kubinda had this place so well guarded, totally off limits. There's nothing here—three boxes of worthless paper and not an ounce of gold."

"What?" Curtis mumbled incredulously, then looking over his shoulder and starting to get up, "There should be over thirty million dollars in there." Frost, gently, pushed the wounded Curtis back to a sitting position.

"Chapmann and Kubinda must have cleaned the place out. I'd bet right now Chapmann is on his way out of the country and Kubinda may be with him. Let's get the hell out of here." Standing, gesturing to three of the rebel army force to help Curtis, Frost snatched up his assault rifle, rammed a fresh magazine up the well and signaled to the men, then shouted clumsily in their own language, the equivalent of "Move out."

Frost brought his force to a halt halfway up the stairs, armed men rushing down toward them, but Frost realized a second later that they were Rebel Army forces under the direction of the colonel who'd led the third element of the strike force.

Relieved at finding someone who spoke English, Frost said, "No gold—the vault was cleaned out. Signal the trucks. Unless we need some of them for evacuation, they can get out as best they can."

Slinging his assault rifle across his back, the colonel said, "We will need them—those fighter planes destroyed six of the choppers. Ground fire got two of the three fighters but not before it was too late. How many men here?" asked the colonel glancing back down the stairs. "We're the last elements then, I'll signal the evacuation. You might want to get your girl friend aboard the last chopper. Last I saw her, she was out there with an assault rifle helping hold back the counterattack against the building."

"Can you take my people?" Frost asked, then without waiting for an answer took the steps two at a time, reached the main floor and charged toward the blown open doors.

"What the hell are you doing?" Frost shouted as he saw her crouched beside the stairs firing an M-16 toward a small force of Chapmann soldiers some thirty yards distant. Pushing her down for added cover, he said. "You're a reporter—not a combatant!"

"What's the matter, Frost—I don't mean my being here, but there's something else?"

He looked at Bess, turned away a moment and said, "This was all for nothing—no gold, not an ounce. And Curtis is wounded. I lost two-thirds of my men and it looks like that is the general casualty pattern. We didn't just lose the battle—we lost the war."

"Look, Frost," Bess said, so quietly he could barely hear her over the gunfire. "Not if you assassinate Dr. Kubinda."

Frost looked back at her sharply. "Who told you that?" he demanded.

"Curtis let it slip before dinner last night. You can still win the war if you kill Dr. Kubinda—Chapmann probably cleared out, don't you think?"

"Yeah," Frost said, "I'm certain he has. All right, get on board that last helicopter while it can still get off the ground and get out of here—I'll meet you after I get Kubinda."

"Where?" she said, her voice betraying her anxiety.

"I don't know—stay with Craine at the base camp or wherever it moves to—I'll get in touch with you there."

"Am I going to see you again, Frost?"

He squeezed her hand, pushed her hair back from her face and kissed her lightly on the lips. Behind him, he could hear the Colonel shouting for them to get going. "Yeah," was all Frost said.

Grabbing her elbow, he half pushed her toward the waiting helicopter, firing his assault rifle inaccurately and one-handed for added covering fire. Frost snatched Bess up into his arms and set her aboard. Several more of the wounded were put aboard and the Colonel beside Frost signaled to the pilot to lift off.

Frost saw her hand in a gesture of farewell as the chopper raised from the ground, then turned to the Colonel crouched beside him. "Where was Curtis?"

"He wouldn't go with the wounded—I've already got him on one of the three trucks. Come on, I saved you a seat." The black officer smiled, clapped Frost on the shoulder and took off in a dead run toward the closest of the three two and one-half ton trucks, the canopies down, the backs of the trucks bristling with weapons. At a signal from the colonel, the remaining defenders on the ground hauled themselves aboard and the trucks started picking up speed toward the demolished front gates of the bank compound.

The two-and-one-half ton trucks roared ahead, past the walls of the old city, virtually every man aboard firing at the Chapmann soldiers, grenades tossed toward the abandoned sentry posts and toward any vehicle within range. From Frost's seat beside the driver in the first truck, he could see something looming up ahead of them as they careened through the streets of the capitol toward the barbed wire fence and beyond to freedom. "They're blocking the street with Land Rovers—up ahead there," he shouted, to both the driver and the colonel, Frost between them.

Then, turning to the driver, Frost shouted, "Ram 'em!" The driver looked at him a moment, uncomprehendingly. Frost turned to the colonel; the colonel said nothing, just staring fixedly at the barricade now just a block away. Then in the native language the colonel shouted something and the driver beside Frost hammered his foot down toward the floor and jumped the truck into a higher gear.

The barricade of Land Rovers was less than a hundred yards away now, and as they crashed toward it heavy machine gun fire opened up. The colonel, beside Frost there in the front seat of the lead truck, cried out in pain and slumped forward.

As Frost started to move him aside, he felt for a pulse at the man's neck—there was none. Sliding over the body, snatching up his own H-K, Frost slipped beside the passenger window and opened fire. From both sides of the truck and on top of the cab itself, Frost could hear the rest of the rebel army force doing the same. He looked to the street, drew his head inside and pulled his left arm up in front of his face to protect his eye as they rammed into and through the Rovers, their gunfire picking up again as Frost and the others shot down into the amassed Chapmann force on all sides of them.

He glanced back along the truck body to the third of the three deuce-and-a-halfs. One of the men there was tossing hand grenades into the junked Land Rovers they'd crashed past. As Frost turned around to look ahead of them he could hear the initial blasts of the fragmentation grenades, then the secondary explosions as the vehicles' fuel tanks caught and went up. Frost's trucks slowed for a curve, then started picking up speed again as the driver aimed it toward the main gates of the city. There was sporadic gunfire everywhere around them from scattered elements of the Nugumbwean army and the Chapmann Mercenary Corps. Frost turned and looked behind him, startled by a sudden explosion. The second of the three trucks apparently had been hit by a grenade, seemed almost to rise in midair for an instant and then crashed into the wall of a building after jumping the curb off the street. The third truck, behind it, tried going around it—apparently, Frost thought, its driver lost control. The truck rammed into the blazing rear end of the second truck and both vehicles exploded, a huge fireball, its sound almost deafening, rising behind them.

Frost turned to his driver, the man's face understandably paralyzed by fear. But the man kept driving. Desperately, Frost tried to remember if Curtis were in the lead truck with them, silently praying

234

that he was—the double explosion behind them could have left no survivors. And Frost felt for one of the few times in his life totally helpless—there was no way he could communicate beyond gestures with the driver. Neither of them spoke the other's language. If the man were to lose his nerve and stop, there would be no hope of Frost and the few survivors on the back of the truck fighting their way out of the city through the Chapmann forces.

Before them now Frost could see the main gates, perhaps two dozen Chapmann men in position around the area—fewer men actually than Frost had expected. Bitterly, Frost realized that by that same time tomorrow the Chapmann men would know their commander had cheated them and stolen all the gold from the treasury and that there would be no more paychecks, no more supplies, nothing. But now they were still ready to fight and die. Most of the men at the gate were mercenaries. Under other circumstances, they could have been his comrades, Frost realized. Pointing his H-K out the window of the truck, Frost shouted, "Cut them down," then started firing. The others behind him opened fire from the truck bed. As Frost's truck raced past then Chapmann men, Frost hurled a grenade, the another. He turned his face away.

The deuce-and-a-half crashed through the candy-striped wooden barriers and was on the raod heading out of the city. Frost made hand signals to the driver telling him to press on as fast as he could. Then leaving his H-K behind, Frost slipped through the opened window and climbed on top of the cab, then over the stakes into the back of the truck. As he dropped down, he was suddenly hit with a wave of remorse. Of the sixty or so men originally aboard, the trucks, there were twelve men unscathed remaining, three or four wounded, several dead. The other two trucks and the men aboard them were now just a memory. He tried making hand signals to convey something of what he was feeling, some sort of sense of comraderie to the men around him, but gave up, thinking it was impossible.

He leaned down to Curtis. The man's lips were bluish purple, his eyes glassy, his breathing shallow. Frost raised the blanket and looked where one of the African soldiers had torn away the sleeve Curtis's fatigue blouse. No one had removed the huge splinter from the collapsed ceiling, and it would have only served to hasten Curtis's death by increasing the bleeding. Most of the young CIA man's shoulder was gone.

Frost whispered, "Pete, can you hear me?" thinking that the young man could not.

But then Frost heard a sound from Curtis's lips and bent his head to listen. "Kill Dr. Kubinda—deal's a deal," and there was a rattling sound and Frost looked at the dark brown eyes. They would never look back. He thumbed the lids closed and pulled the blanket up over Curtis's face. Then, drawing the blanket away for a moment, Frost whispered. "Okay, Pete—a deal's a deal."

Chapter Sixteen

Everything had happened at once after Curtis died. Frost had found that the electronic detonator device in his backpack was still functional and as the pursuing Chapmann forces had followed them down the road out of Buwandi Frost activated the mines he had implanted along both sides of the road earlier that week. One half-track had gotten through and the combined fire of Frost and the remaining rebel army soldiers and a few well-placed hand grenades had finished that. Too late, the remaining Huey gunships of their force returned to help with the battle, having dropped their passengers back at the base camp. But they were only in time to take Frost and the precious few survivors, along with the recoverable bodies of their dead, back to camp.

It was evening by the time things were settled and Frost, having taken the commander's office for his own, decided it was time to quit. There was to be a midnight briefing with the general and other principals of the rebel army staff. Craine, the other CIA man, gave no contest to Frost assuming the command. Frost had told him, "It'll only be for twelve hours, then I'll be gone." That was at eight P.M. At nine, Frost fell asleep with his head on Bess's lap, instructing her before he closed his eyes to awaken him at ten to midnight.

As Frost concluded his debriefing in Curtis's old office back in the plantation house kitchen, he could hear the rotors of the Huey gunships warming up outside. Craine, the rebel army staff men and Bess were all present.

As he lit his forty-first Camel of the day, Frost glared at the persons around the table through the harsh bare bulb light overhead, saying, "Then two things remain. I'm leaving to assassinate Dr. Kubinda in Kinshasa then Craine here will have information about where I can find Chapman—I have a hunch Switzerland. I already have confirmed CIA approval for the hit on Kubinda and their promise of fingering Chapmann for me." When everyone except Bess and Craine looked uncomprehending, exhaustedly Frost said, "Locating him, pinpointing his movements. After he's dead, we can do whatever is possible to get back part of the Nugumbwean treasury. I don't know anything else to say. But if you guys are smart, you'll hit Buwandi with everything you've got about this time tomorrow—a night attack would be best, after the Chapmann people move out and before the communists move in. I think you'd have 'em then." Frost left the briefing abruptly, Bess running after him and stopping him on the front porch steps.

"I'm meeting you at the airport or wherever, after you get Kubinda—I'm going to stick with you."

Frost turned, touched his right hand to her face, said, "All right. I'd like that. You ever write obituaries just in case I need one?" She buried her face in his chest and he could hear her crying.

"I was just kidding," he said.

"I'm not crying because of that, but because it's almost over—and sometime too soon I'm going to lose you, aren't I?"

"If I knew how to answer that question we wouldn't have the problem, would we?" Frost said, kissing her, then snatching up his backpack with his clothes in it and running into the darkness toward the helicopter.

Chapter Seventeen

Dr. Kubinda sat between two submachine gun armed bodyguards, two more on the Cadillac's jumpseats in front of him and one more riding in the front seat beside the sixth member of his personal boydguard team, the driver. Frost knew that because he had seen them positioning themselves that way when they had entered the vehicle. Once the door had been closed, he could see nothing, the glass so heavily tinted that it was effectively only one way. The vehicle itself was heavily armored, customized at one of the Stateside custom limousine houses, able to withstand concentrated area hits from low-caliber supersonic projectiles at high cyclic rates. The man riding beside the driver controlled a sophisticated electronic monitoring system, able to detect radio signals directed toward the vehicle and able to emit multiple strong signals of its own, boosted through the power from heavy-duty batteries carried in the automobile trunk. That high level of sophistication was just what Frost was counting on—too great a reliance on gadgetry and not enough reliance on simple, good old-fashioned violence.

The technical information had been easy to get, as had been the equipment Frost had wanted, in both cases through a special covert-CIA case officer running a black (network) team that had wired Kubinda for a hit several months earlier, but had been unable to risk it because of his ties with the State Department.

With the death of Pete Curtis, Lawrence-like in his dedication to the people he fought with, and Frost to make the actual touch, the case officer had decided to go ahead. As he'd told Frost, "What they don't know in Washington won't hurt 'em, right?"

Frost took his eyes from the television monitor, the hidden camera having revealed all it could about the arrangment of Kubinda and his guards in the limousine. Lighting a cigarette, he looked out the window of the high rise and down into the street. Kinshasa had once been called Leopoldville in the days prior to Congo independence and struck Frost with the same European flare that it had when he had been there weeks earlier for a short time prior to entering Nugumbwe on his quest for Chapmann's blood.

"Wanna head on up to the roof, my man?" the CIA officer said to Frost.

"Yeah," Frost answered, nodding, then followed the carrot-haired cowboy-boot clad Texan into the dingy hallway and up the service stairs to the roof. One of the local contract employees was already up there waiting for them. Even before nine in the morning, the roof was steaming hot, the sun already high above them. Frost dropped to a crouch as he neared the roof line, the gravel surface sharp against the palms of his hands, the white suit he wore burning up at him with an unceasing glare each time his gaze drifted toward the sleeve of his coat or a trouser leg. Frost shoved the tails of his half-mast black knit tie inside his white shirt front and bent to peer through the spotting scope. In a moment he could see Kubinda's limousine, several blocks away still but homing in on their position almost as if the driver were on their side. It had taken three days for Kubinda to get out of Nugumbwe after Frost and Curtis had unlocked his dirty secret with Chapmann. He had spent three more days in Kinshasa, the private Mitsubishi jet having arrived that previous night, standing by at the airport to take

Kubinda to Spain according to the flight plan, but the Zurich according to the CIA informant at the Kinshasa airport. The guards with Kubinda had been his personal bodyguards for the three years the good doctor had been in power in Nugumbwe, the limousine they drove one of two identical cars, one now left behind in Buwandi, the other having been kept perpetually in Kinshasa for the doctor's frequent trips to his neighboring capitol.

Frost had studied candid photos of Kubinda for the last several days and try as he might had found nothing remarkable in the man's face. That he lived a soft life was evident from the heavy jowls and drooping eyelids, that he apparently enjoyed the cruelty he was noted for seemed somehow—indefinably—to show in Kubinda's eyes.

But that would all be over shortly, Frost thought. As he glanced through the spotting scope one more time, he whispered, "Okay—let 'em fly."

Frost, the CIA man and the contract employee unlimbered three identical radio controlled airplanes from black suitcases already open beside them on the rooftop, the controls for the planes housed inside the cases as well. Frost gave one last quick visual inspection to the "toys"—impact detonators were in place, as well as the wires for the radio controlled detonation. He checked the rudders and elevators, checked the radio controls for their movement. He glanced into the scope again. The limousine was coming down the block toward them now. Almost simultaneously, the three men launched the airplanes, having them take off across the flat roof, then arcing them out of the wind and by radio control bringing them into a ragged formation, their airspeed reading out digitally on the control boxes at over 120 MPH.

There was no need for the spotting scope now. The limousine was in plain sight. As the Texan took his RC model in for a dive toward the limousine, the black car swerved out of the way, almost hitting a street light post. Then the plane itself started behaving erraticaly. "It's working," the CIA man said. Frost and the contract employee homed in their planes as well. In his mind's eye, Frost could picture the man beside the driver in the limousine's front seat, trying frantically to jam multiple frequencies all at once with his jamming device, to distort the radio signals to the planes and keep them off target.

"Okay, you guys take over," Frost said, the Texan—who liked model airplanes as a hobby—taking over Frost's controls, running two of the three planes now.

Frost ran down the stairs from the roof into the first floor hall, ran to the elevator which they had jammed open and took the elevator straight down to the first floor, using an override switch they had installed to make the elevator an express.

At the first floor, Frost ran through the deserted lobby and out through the rear service entrance. In the alley, he spotted the dark blue sedan and the second contract employee. The man already had the trunk lid up and as Frost reached the vehicle and got inside, the man handed him the Bazooka, then ran to the driver's side and gunned the engine, the car peeling rubber for several feet behind them down the alley.

At the end of the alley by the street, Frost stepped out of his passenger doorway, checked the contact on his Bazooka and shouldered the 3.5-inch rocket launcher and waited. The chain saw like drone of the model airplanes was intense, and getting closer with second. The airplanes were only a device to channel Kubinda's limousine into the killing ground and from the corner of his eye Frost could see it coming, the airplanes buzzing toward it, then erratically falling away, correcting their flight pattern once they were out of range of the jamming device, then homing in again.

Frost stepped into the alley, placed his eye to the sight and as the limousine sped toward him, touched the trigger and made the electrical ocontact. There was a loud whooshing sound by his right ear, his shoulder was pushed back and over the sight Frost could see the high explosive round impacting into the grillwork of the Cadillac, collapsing the front end. As Frost threw the weapon down he started forward, the contract employee tossing him a riot shotgun as both men advanced to the burning car, its front end almost totally disintegrated. Frost wise-cracked, "Boy—these cars are solid, aren't they?"

The doors were still locked and even at point-blank range, Frost still could not see inside the vehicle. The contract man placed a thin strip of plastique inside the door frame and activated it with a small battery controlled detonator. As the door blew, both Frost and the other man turned away to protect their faces. Frost looked back and as the contract employee started spraying the car's rear seat with submachine gun fire—all the men were unconscious apparently, though some were stirring—Frost shouldered his riot shotgun and fired the .72 caliber slug load that was first up dead on Kubinda's slumped over head. As the body lurched under the impact, Frost worked the trombone pump and loosed the next round—a two and three-quarter-inch double O Buck load. It went all over the three men in the back seat, Kubinda in the center. As the control man sprayed the front seat, Frost emptied the remaining five rounds in the shotgun into the dead body of Kubinda until it was just an unrecognizable lump of tattered clothing and raw meat.

Frost tapped the contract man on the shoulder and both of them ran toward the waiting car. As they turned into the alley, the weapons left behind them in the limousine, Frost turned and shot a glance through the rear window. The model airplanes were homing in now, all three impacting on the limousine almost simultaneously, the explosives detonating and the limousine bursting into a ball of fire.

Frost lit a cigarette as the car rounded the corner at the opposite end of the alley and then turned into the main drag and pulled up at the front entrance of the high rise. The CIA man—the Texan—jumped into the front seat beside Frost. As the first contract employee, the man from the roof, piled into the back seat and slammed the door, the car sped away from the curb and into the mainstream of traffic. As the Texan, his face bright with a big grin took a cigarette from inside his jacket and Frost produced his Zippo to light it, the man drawled, "Well—we sure did that one right, didn't we?"

Frost, his face creasing with the smile-frown lines, whispered, "Be the job great or small, do it well or not at all."

Chapter Eighteen

Frost straightened his tie as he walked through the airport terminal, seeing Bess waiting for him. He felt stupid and knew he looked conspicuous wearing a white tropical suit in Zurich, since it was winter in Switzerland and the moment he set foot outside he'd be freezing. He walked straight toward Bess, knifing his way through the crowds of arriving and departing passengers, the loudspeaker system announcing flight information in French, German and English.

"I heard about your doctor's appointment, Frost," Bess said, as Frost took her in his arms and kissed her. He stepped back and looked at her.

"You clean up pretty good, kid," he said, smiling. She wore a belted suede coat with fur collar and cuffs and high heels. Since he couldn't see trouser legs, he assumed she was wearing a dress. "Open your coat for a minute," he said.

She looked at him strangely, then opened her coat, then almost as though she were oblivious to the crowds of people passing around them, turned as though she were modeling an outift in a fashion salon. She was wearing a dress, Frost observed—dark brown and close-fitting.

"You like?" she asked brightly.

"Yeah," he said, shrugging his shoulders, then taking her in his arms again and kissing her, said, "But I like what's inside it better—come on."

As they wrestled the heavy airport traffic, Bess handling the Mercedes diesel quite well, Frost filled her in on the details of Dr. Kubinda's assassination, omitting what she referred to as "some of the more graphic elements of the narrative."

"You know, Frost," Bess said, slamming on the brakes to avoid a small truck that had pulled out in front of her, "I think I'm becoming what I always called a CIA reporter—you know, the press people who work in the press but really have strong ties with CIA and feed them information or help them plant stories—things like that. I understand they have Colonel Chapmann all set up for you. Is it going to be just like your job on Dr. Kubinda?"

Frost lit a cigarette, fingered open the dashboard ashtray and leaned back against the headrest. "No. This is going to be more personal."

"And then what—I mean after you get your back taken care of?"

"Well," Frost said, "I guess you and I can spend some time together—if you want to?"

She looked at him and said nothing. He studied her face for a moment. She'd gotten her hair cut—after the butcher job that had happened to it she had needed it, he reflected. Now it barely touched the nape of her neck and had a much softer look to it. With earrings and makeup—he'd never seen her that way before—she looked like something out of the pages of a fashion magazine.

"Well?" She looked at him again.

"Keep your eyes on the road, huh," and as he said it she turned to look in front of them and cut the wheel sharply to avoid a Volkswagen that was cutting in on them.

Looking straight ahead, she said, "Frost, where is this going to take us?"

"What could I offer you?" he said, staring away from her, finding a bus of some kind in front of them in the next lane and trying to read the serial number on the back.

"I didn't ask that—I don't care about that. But we love each other, don't we?"

"Yeah," Frost said, his voice tight. "But you're not going to get saddled with a one-eyed man who can't get any kind of work that doesn't involve killing people. You'd make a lousy widow."

"I can worry about that if it happens," she said, her voice so soft he could barely hear it.

"Sure—and I could worry about it every time I had to take a chance. You know the guys who have the highest mortality rate in this business—well they're the guys with a wife and kids at home. So concerned about being cautious and getting back alive they do just the opposite, get themselves killed."

"I've read all that shit in fighter pilot psychological profiles, astronaut training—don't give me that."

Frost looked at her and their eyes met. "You got it right—I won't give you that. You want to keep this going the way it has been and see what happens, fine? I'd like that."

"You have to be so damned cool all the time, don't you? Like those eyepatch jokes you make. I'll stick with you and you know I will—I'll go away when you want me to and I'll come back again when you want that—and you'll want it, Frost. You'll want it. But someday you're going to have to stop playing cowboys and Indians with real bullets and try the real world."

"I tried it," Frost said. "What's the real world—someplace where people don't realize they were ever alive until they die? Where somebody commits some horrible crime and gets a slap on the wrist? Where you can't walk down the street after dark without worrying about some punk coming after your life for the two bits you've got left in your pocket after income tax? No, kid. If that's real, I'll take my 'cowboys and Indians' games any day of the week."

When they parted later that morning, Frost really had no idea whether she'd be waiting for him at the hotel room when he got back or not. He wanted her to be waiting, but wishing didn't make it so, he realized.

The plan to nail Chapmann had been in the works since he'd started work on getting Kubinda—that had been Frost's end of the deal with CIA, that and twenty thousand dollars. He took a taxicab to an address in the older part of the city, found three men whom he didn't recognize except by a code phrase and set to work. Two of the men were Company contract agents, the third was a technical specialist flown in from Langley, Virginia.

Frost would kill Chapmann at four o'clock, along with Chapmann's two bodyguards. By three P.M. Frost's hair had been temporarily dyed blond—it would wash out with ordinary shampoo, the Company specialist had told him. Using skillfully applied theatrical makeup, Frost's cheekbones were lowered, his chin made less prominent. He'd had to shave off his mustache again, then it was replaced with a brushy handlebar blond mustache to match his hair. Padding under his clothes and a specially tailored suit made him appear an inch or two shorter than he really was and added the look of another thirty pounds to his body, this to match the fattened face. Although he didn't like the idea of going without his Browning High Power and using a weapon he hadn't practised with, he accepted the specially modified .22 target automatic with the integral silencer.

The gun, plus two spare ten-round magazines, went into a specially built fiber shoulder holster, designed as a throw away. After the assassination and ditching the sanitized pistol, he could simply rip the shoulder rig from his body under his coat and toss it into a wastebasket and throw a match in after it. Instead of his own Gerber knife, Frost now had a long-bladed, single-edged heavy butcher knife, the blade a good eight inches long, almost an English Bowie pattern.

The hilt of the knife was strapped with heavy tape over padding just below his right elbow, the knife edge itself outrunning behind the upper portion of his arm. All this over his suitcoat. The raincoat they provided him had the upper portion of the right sleeve seamed together with hook and pile fasteners. By pulling on the epaulet on the top of the shoulder, he could rip the sleeve open, then after he ditched the knife find a quiet place and stick the two parts of the sleeve back together again.

The muscles of his right arm were already starting to feel stiff by the time Frost had donned the sunglasses to cover his left eye and entered the passenger side of the waiting Volkswagen's front seat.

As the little car pulled away from the curb, driven by one of the contract men, Frost checked the silenced .22 pistol again. The serial numbers had been filed off, but then to prevent acid etching from bringing out the numbers, the area where the numbers had been was drilled down perhaps a thirty-second of an inch. It was not one of the usual CIA/Special Forces pistols he'd used before, but a patch job welded together from two other vaguely recognizable pistols. Frost had been told it was tested to three-inch groups at ten yards, more than ample for the job at hand.

He used the base of the butt magazine catch release and checked the magazine again—the hollow point high speed rounds had a light film of plastic over the tips of the bullets themselves, inside this powdered ammonia.

He reholstered the gun and lit his last cigarette before the job.

He ran the details over in his mind—each day at four P.M. for the last five days Chapmann had left the Zurich Fiduciary Trust with a suitcase. Frost could guess at the contents. One of the bodyguards carried the suitcase, which observers noted seemed quite heavy. The other bodyguard always kept his hand in his right pocket—presumably on a pistol.

As the Volkswagen pulled up at the corner of the block, Frost got out awkwardly, keeping his right arm with the butcher knife stiff. He waved politely to his driver. The driver smiled cheerily and pulled away from the curb. Frost checked the borrowed watch on his wrist. It was three fifty-nine. As he started toward the long steps leading up to the bank building, he could see Chapmann and his two guards. Frost checked his watch. "Fool!" Chapmann was ignoring the cardinal rule of staying alive—never make regular movement patterns, break habits constantly.

In the back of his mind, Frost really hadn't expected Chapmann to be there. His palms were starting to sweat inside the skintight black leather gloves he wore. As he walked up the long low steps and for an instant saw Chapmann eye-to-eye, Frost had to fight himself not to leap at the man's throat.

Frost walked close to the bodyguard who kept his hand in his raincoat pocket. As Frost walked past him, going in the opposite direction, the hook and pile fasteners on his own raincoat's sleeve already separated, Frost bent his right arm, driving the elbow toward the bodyguard's right kidney, the butcher knife jabbing in up to the small round guard in front of the hilt. And just as quickly, Frost jerked his arm back and straightened it, the blade of the knife disappearing inside his raincoat. As he continued walking up the steps, his heels faintly clicking against the worn-smooth stone, his left hand drifted under his jacket. Because the guard he'd just knifed always walked on Chapmann's right, Frost had been forced to use his right arm for the knife and consequently forced to carry his pistol for a left-hand draw. His right arm still straight at his side, he shifted the pistol into his right hand from his left and halfway to the front doors of the bank turned around.

Behind him, the bodyguard he'd stabbed was sprawled across the steps. Chapmann and the second bodyguard, the suitcase still in his right hand, were staring about them. As Chapmann started to rise, Frost raised the pistol in his stiff right arm—there was no safety catch—and squeezed the trigger.

There was a loud primer noise but nothing else except the sound of the slide gliding back and forth out of and back into the battery, chambering a fresh round. His first round caught the bodyguard with the suitcase in the right side of the neck. Frost fired again, the second round catching the man in his gaping-open mouth. The guard crumpled.

Chapmann was reaching under his coat. As Frost moved down one step for a better shot, already the screams of passersby growing louder, he could see the profile of the highly engraved, ivory scrimshaw gripped Browning High Power. Frost's face creased into a smile—Chapmann would never get to use it, he thought. Frost fired once, then again, the first shot boring into Chapmann's right elbow, the second shot into his right knee. There was a scream of pain.

Frost pulled the sunglasses away from his face and walked down the low stone steps, Chapmann writhing in agony now less than a yard from him, the pistol out of reach.

Frost smiled, watching Chapmann's reaction and growing terror. Chapmann's china blue eyes were like little pinpoints of fear; there was blood running from the right corner of his mouth—apparently he'd hit his face when he had fallen. Both of Chapmann's hands, even the with one with the shot-through elbow, were clamped to his right knee.

"Does it hurt, Colonel?" Frost asked. Then gesturing with his left index finger to the exposed scar where his left eye should have been, Frost said, "Remember me, Chapmann?"

Chapmann started to crawl toward his gun. Frost let him go for it. As Colonel Marcus Chapmann reached his pistol and started to turn, pointing it toward Frost, Frost said, "One hundred and fifty of my friends—you killed them, left me for dead, but now you're the one." Frost fired once, then once more into Chapmann's chest and Chapmann fell back, head down along the steps.

Frost walked down the steps and dropped to one knee beside him. Methodically, Frost pulled Chapmann's head forward, pushed the muzzle of his silenced pistol to Chapmann's exposed neck, against the spinal column. Then Frost fired his pistol twice.

Frost stood up, the crowd of spectators surrounding him now. Taking the low steps four at a time, he reached the suitcase, hefted it in his left hand and pushed his way through. The men and women were eyeing the muzzle of his silenced pistol nervously and parting like waves before him.

At the bottom of the steps, there was a trash can and Frost flipped the pistol into it.

Chapter Nineteen

"I don't think I like you better as a blond, Frost."

Frost set the suitcase down by the door, then slammed the door behind him and put on the chain. He'd opened the suitcase when he'd ditched the butcher knife in a booth in a hotel washroom—there were fifty, one-pound bricks of gold, more than $950,000 dollars, "call it a million bucks" he thought.

Frost pulled off his sunglasses and put his eyepatch in place. Although he still had to wash the dye out of his hair, the theatrical makeup was already gone, along with the fake mustache.

"I'm rich—at least for a day or so."

"What are you going to wind up with, Frost?" Bess asked, sitting on the chair by the hotel room's combination desk and dresser, brushing her hair. She wore nothing but an ivory white, lace-trimmed slip.

"Twenty thousand for getting Kubinda, and since this is a little light on what Chapmann owed my people, I'll probably get about six or seven thousand bucks out of this."

She stood up and lit his cigarette for him, then sat down on the edge of the bed.

"How much did you spend in order to get into the Congo and over into Nugumbwe—total?"

Frost eyed her a moment, then stripped off his jacket and placed his Browning High Power on the desk-dresser beside her hair brush. "Total? About five thousand, give or take."

"So you're twenty-two thousand ahead, before the cost for getting your back fixed."

Frost stubbed out his cigarette. Then said, "Shut up and lay down on your own back."

As he stripped away the rest of his clothes, then naked, lay down beside her, he stared at the ceiling for a moment.

"Frost?" he heard Bess say.

"Thanks for waiting, kid," Frost whispered, his words barely audible. He rolled over onto his side and took the girl into his arms, his right hand sliding up under her slip and bunching it up at her hips. She wore nothing under it. He caught the hair at the nape of her neck in his left hand, pulled her head back and kissed her slightly parted lips almost savagely.

As he slid between her thighs, the warmth there almost burning his skin, he could hear her whispering, her lips pressed against his left ear. Over and over, she was just saying his name.

READ THESE ZEBRA BEST SELLERS

THE BIG NEEDLE (512, $2.25)
by Ken Follett
Innocent people were being terrorized, homes were being destroyed—and all too often—because the most powerful organization in the world was thirsting for one man's blood. By the author of *The Eye of the Needle.*

NEW YORK ONE (556, $2.25)
by Lawrence Levine
Buried deep within the tunnels of Grand Central Station lies the most powerful money center of the world. Only a handful of people knows it exists—and one of them wants it destroyed!

ERUPTION (614, $2.75)
by Paul Patchick
For fifty years the volcano lay dorment, smoldering, bubbling, building. Now there was no stopping it from becoming the most destructive eruption ever to hit the western hemisphere—or anywhere else in the entire world!

DONAHUE! (570, $2.25)
by Jason Bonderoff
The intimate and revealing biography of Americas #1 daytime TV host—his life, his loves, and the issues and answers behind the Donahue legend.